WHEN TIGERS ARE HUNTING:
THE COMPLETE ADVENTURES OF CORDIE,
SOLDIER OF FORTUNE, VOLUME 1

WHEN TIGERS ARE HUNTING

THE COMPLETE ADVENTURES OF CORDIE, SOLDIER OF FORTUNE, VOLUME 1

W. WIRT

ALTUS PRESS
2015

© 2015 Steeger Properties, LLC, under license to Altus Press • First Edition—2015

EDITED AND DESIGNED BY
Matthew Moring

PUBLISHING HISTORY
"He's a Good Little Guy at That" originally appeared in the May 1928 issue of *Frontier Stories* (Vol. 8, No. 2).

"The Major Wanted Him Alive" originally appeared in the June 1928 issue of *Frontier Stories* (Vol. 8, No. 3).

"According to My Size and Disposition" originally appeared in the October 1928 issue of *Frontier Stories* (Vol. 9, No. 1).

"Private Property" originally appeared in the October 10, 1928 issue of *Short Stories* (Vol. 125, No. 1).

"The Jewel in the Lotus" originally appeared in the November 10, 1928 issue of *Short Stories* (Vol. 125, No. 3).

"When Tigers Are Hunting" originally appeared in the November 1928 issue of *Frontier Stories* (Vol. 9, No. 2).

"That Fish Thing" originally appeared in the January 1929 issue of *Frontier Stories* (Vol. 9, No. 4).

"Right Smack at You!" originally appeared in the April 1929 issue of *Frontier Stories* (Vol. 10, No. 1).

"About the Author" originally appeared in the September 8, 1928 issue of *Argosy* magazine (Vol. 197, No. 5). Copyright © 1928 by The Frank A. Munsey Company. Copyright renewed © 1955 and assigned to Steeger Properties, LLC. All rights reserved.

THANKS TO
Richard Hall, Chis Kalb & Gerd Pircher

ISBN
978-1-61827-188-4

Visit *altuspress.com* for more books like this.
Printed in the United States of America.

TABLE OF CONTENTS

HE'S A GOOD LITTLE GUY AT THAT

A fortune in temple jewels in their grasp, but hemmed in by a fanatical mob of blood-thirsty Malays, Red Dolan and his fellow-adventurers grinned, kidded one another— and pitched into one whale of a scrap!

THE HIGH PRIEST crouched in the temple balcony, his evil, bestial old face working with passion, his eyes like those of a king cobra.

The young chief beside him stirred uneasily, his curved shining sword advancing a little, like the tongue of a snake. How long were the white men below to profane the temple? Did not the priest see that they were trying to hurl the Snake God from his throne? Even he might not be able to curb the many demons that would come to avenge the god. What was the old fellow waiting for? He had ordered that they be taken alive. Some day he, the young chief, would lead his people instead of his father and this priest and then....

The priest turned his head and looked at him. The young chief tried to return the cold, deadly glare of the small beady black eyes that seemed to be drawing the breath and heart from his body. Finally the priest turned back to watch the white men and the young chief drew a long quivering breath.

He lay motionless now, his chin on the blade of his sword, his body in the bright red and yellow sarong as still as that of the priest, and waited.

There, now the god had been overturned, his men would not stand much more before they attacked. Couldn't the priest hear the quick breathing?

He felt the priest touch him and turned to see him slowly

wiggling back toward the opening to the hill. He followed reluctantly.

THE LITTLE TEMPLE, built on a gentle slope, the towering Gunong range above it, the green of the mangroves and the darker greens and browns of the jungle and swamp behind it, was a thing of beauty.

The white men inside did not look at the exquisite carving and dainty inlaid fretwork of mother-of-pearl. To them it was simply a place that held what they had fought their way through the jungle from the west coast to get.

"Come on, Dolan, give us a hand," one demanded. "What are you doing—lookin' at that image of your great grandpa?"

"Boy, ain't he a lovely piece of cheese?" Dolan marvelled. "I—"

"Where do you think you are, you redheaded Mick?" demanded Grigsby. "Come on, help shove this baby over. The stuff may be under any one of 'em and we got to work fast."

"He'll come to when one of those Malay krises get kissing his short-ribs," grunted Putney, as he shoved on the big idol with Cordie. "Come on, you redheaded ape, put your beef to this. Let's get it over. This place don't look good to me."

"You and me both," agreed Grigsby. "It's too blame quiet. Come on now—altogether—yo—he—yo—he—over she goes!" and the four men heaved and lifted at the heavy ironwood Snake God.

"Look!" shouted Dolan, a minute later, staring down at the hollow base. "Look—it's them! Look at 'em!" and he knelt and began to paw over the hundreds of loose gems.

"Steady does it," warned Grigsby. "We can look them over later. It's the T'ient-sung stuff all right. Get back to your gun, Jimmie. Put them in the sack, Red, and let's be getting out of here. These Malays will be raising— Heads up!"

The roar of his Colt's .45 came with the warning. The four men came together, Jimmie Cordie and Red Dolan at the machine-gun, Grigsby and Putney at their back, the sack, half filled with the priceless gems, at their feet.

The native whose movement had attracted Grigsby fell from the balcony to the floor. From the balcony, the dark corners, from behind the idols, came a swift, silent rush of swordsmen. Most of them were armed with the long curved chenangkas, the blade of the fighting Malay.

If the attack was swift and deadly, the defense was not less so. The white men made no attempt to get at the Winchester .30-30s slung on their backs, but met it with their Colts. It was the fire of veterans, cold, hard, accurate and merciless. For ten years these men had fought together in the far flung places, and before that in France. The Browning poured a stream of steel jacketed bullets into the dark corners and swept the balcony clear of crouching figures.

It lasted less than two minutes. Then the attack ceased; there was none left to attack. Thirty of the best fighting men of the tribe lay dead or wounded on the floor.

"Ain't that somepin," said Red Dolan, "Did ye see me cold-cook that big guy from the top of that doflicker over there? Boy, he was all spread out to drop on me,"

"Go on, Irish," said Putney; "you was shootin' with your eyes shut. I—"

"In front!" shouted Cordie, swinging the machine-gun around to face the door. "Gimme room accordin' to my size and disposition."

THIS time the rush was led by an old chief, the hilt of his chenangkas gold-encrusted. Grigsby shot him as he came through the door, his sword slithering along the floor almost to their feet as he pitched headlong. They were bunched more this time and the bullets couldn't miss. Cordie literally shot a lane as wide as the doorway through them. The few that were left were killed by the other three.

"All right," said Grigsby; "I guess that does it. Get the rest of the stuff in the sack and let's go."

"Let's go is good," said Dolan, who had gone to the door.

"There's about a million of 'em rallyin' around the old flag. Boy, I can see 'em comin' from all sides."

"Yeah," said Cordie, "come on and give me a hand with this piece of junk and don't talk so much. You must think you're a passenger on board this ship. Take your time, you guys, and get 'em all. Me and Red will play with the neighbors' children."

"Lay off any more shooting," commanded Grigsby, "Unless there is a rush. Wait till we have to make a break."

"Which same will be pretty blame quick," called back Cordie, "if you aim on going anywhere, old-timer. They're ganging up all around."

"My gosh," said Putney when he and Grigsby came to the door, "I should say they were. That lad in Penang that told us there was only a few of them sure didn't know how to count. What now, Gineril?"

"Only thing I can see to do is to head west," Grigsby offered. "It'll be a case of shoot our way through, at that."

"Ain't that somepin'," demanded Red Dolan, looking down on the hundreds of natives. "Wait till I get me a couple of Mills out," and he shifted his knapsack around.

They were all in heavy marching order, as they were on the west front, with the exception of the tin hats.

"I hope if you get hit it'll be in front, you son-of-a-gun," said Cordie. "Packing a dozen of those things loose around with you that way."

"Whaddaye mean, loose? I got 'em packed in here, ain't I? What are ye crabbin' for? I bought 'em off that Tommy with my own jack, didn't I? I'm carryin' them, ain't—"

"Yeah—and if you get hit we all go to hell. Get away from me with—"

"Can it, you two," interrupted Grigsby. "We better be highballing it away from here. Start her off, Jim. Wait a minute. What's going on over at that shack by the creek?"

"High gazoozalum's house," grinned Cordie. "Looks like G.H.Q. to me. See the old bird with the rubber snake—no, by gosh, it's a live one! How'd you like to have that baby huggin' you, Red? What's he doing with it? Look, he's kissing it! It's about two fifty or sixty—bet five dollars I can knock that snake out of his hands from here."

"I got yer," said Red, promptly. "Go ahead and do it."

"No; hold her a minute," said Grigsby. "Look, he's letting them touch it. He's getting them all het up to come and scrag us. That's the high priest's house, I'll bet. Maybeso he's got something in there we can grab off and swap 'em for a clear road."

"Let's go and get it then," said Putney.

"All right, we'll take their G.H.Q. and see what makes the wheels go around. Take the sack, Putt. Shoot us a road, Jimmie. Go easy on those Mills, Red. We might need 'em worse, later."

THERE is no better fighting man in the world than the Malay, but against that sleet of lead they went down in groups, the heavy machine-gun bullets going through two or three of them at a time. They attacked without hesitation, their swords and krises eager to drink the blood of the white men who had dared to invade the temple of the Snake God.

At the first burst of fire from the machine-gun the priest disappeared. The young chief jumped to the ground and charged straight at the gun. He went down with several others as Cordie swept the gun around. As he fell the natives charged from all sides. Cordie fired four more rounds and the gun jammed. He rose and drew his Colt's. In spite of the falling brown bodies all around them, the Malays came on. It was like leaves being blown into a fire, consumed always, yet more and more coming.

Red Dolan stepped forward and threw one of the Mills bombs into the thickest group, then turned and threw another to the rear. The explosion blew several of the Malays to pieces and stopped the attack. They all knew what guns were, but these white men had profaned the temple and as yet the Snake God had not struck them dead, and now this calling of fire and the tearing to pieces from a little round thing like an orange! It was too much even for them, and they turned and ran.

"Get to the house," commanded Grigsby. "Never mind the gun, Cordie, if she's jammed."

"No more shells anyway," said Cordie, cheerfully. "At least I don't have to pack the darn thing."

The way was practically undisputed. Here and there a native, amok, rushed at them, his naked sword or kris gleaming, only to be shot down and killed as coldly as would a mad dog.

The big snake was still on the platform where it had been dropped by the priest. As they came up it coiled, ready to strike.

"My gosh," said Red, "it's a hamadryad. Ain't that a nice little buddy to have around?"

"He'll be nicer in a minute," said Cordie. "Nice snake—want to go an' see the Snake God? You do? All right then, hop along," and a forty-five bullet tore the head of the snake to pieces.

"Get in; they'll be getting fussy again in a minute."

The house was made of bamboo and rattan, set on piles, on the bank of a little muddy stream. There was one big room and several smaller ones leading off from it, with ten or twelve foot platforms front and rear. Two ladders were still in place in front.

"Looks like a big hunk of nothin'," said Red, as they entered. "These birds don't go much on furniture, do they?"

"What did you expect to see, you baboon? The bridal suite at the Carlton?"

"Why not?" demanded Red. "If I was the head push of this outfit and had all them dancin'—"

He stopped and listened intently, as did the rest. From one of the smaller rooms came the unmistakable crying of a child. Not a loud cry—just a whimper of pain and despair.

"What the hell?" snarled Red, locating the room.

He took one long stride and crashed in the flimsy door with a brawny shoulder. Out again in a minute, carrying a little girl about twelve. She was bound at her ankles and wrists and a gag had been placed in her mouth. All she had on was a little white cotton slip which was torn and discolored. Her skin was milk white, her blue eyes wet with tears, and her hair golden.

Red was holding her tight with one arm, trying to untie the gag.

"There, acushla," he was crooning. "Never mind at all. Sure 'tis old Red Dolan has got ye safe. Turn a little, alanna, so's I can reach this bad old rope. Now—be still a minute, darlin'. Nothin' can hurt ye any more. Stop cryin' for Red now. There— 'tis off you at last. Now for the rest. Come on, Misther Dumb, gimme a hand at these cords. Cut them. The black curse of Crum'ell on whoever tied her up this way."

The little girl buried her head in the hollow of Dolan's neck; her little arms went around his neck, and she clung to him with all her strength.

"Oh, please don't let the big snake have me! I'm afraid! Oh, please, don't let them! Don't let them!"

"Nothin' will have you," said Dolan. "Sure it's all right yez are," and the big Irishman began petting her and kissing the top of her blonde head, his own blue eyes, that had been as cold and wintery as the blue sheen of ice during the fighting, as misty as her own. "See, machree, here's plenty of good men to guard ye. Stop cryin' now, darlin', and let old Red fix the pretty little feet an' hands where the cord drew tight."

SHE LIFTED her head for the first time and looked at the big men, who were all smiling at her. Her tear-stained little face lighted up and she smiled in return. It was a tremulous little smile, but a smile just the same.

"I—I'm not afraid anymore," she said. "I—will you take me back to my daddy?"

"You bet we will, honey," answered Grigsby; "right away, soon as we have whipped some of these bad men that were going to hurt you."

She nodded gravely. "That bad man that took me from Wong ought to be whipped, too."

"We'll 'tend to him, alanna," said Red. "Here, eat this piece of nice chocolate I been savin' for you. I wonder now where—"

"We better be getting up our umbrellas," Putney announced from the doorway. "From the looks of things out there I think it's going to rain in a minute."

"Tend to your own knittin'," said Red, who was pawing over his knapsack. "Now where the h— heavens did I put that salve; I dunno. Sure it's a whole box I had—a new box, never opened. Did ye take that salve now, Cordie, ye baboon?"

"It's under your left hand," grinned Cordie. "You're blind in one eye, you north of Ireland chimpanzee."

"It is not—yes, it is. Sure now, darlin', I'll stop the hurt for ye an' then we'll go an' find daddy; leave it to old Red Dolan."

"My gosh," said Cordie, from one of the windows. "The whole darn Malay Peninsula is out there, I bet you. Look at the old bird with another snake! I thought I knocked him off the Christmas tree."

"He's giving them a regular colonel's bawling out for not getting us before we got to his bungaloo," said Grigsby, unslinging his Winchester. "I've only got about thirty cartridges left for my gat. Count up, you birds, and let's see where we're at."

"Fifty Colt's and four boxes of thirty-thirties," announced Cordie.

"Same here, as far as the thirty-thirtys go and—holy smoke, I only got twenty-three Colt's, not counting what I got in her," said Putney.

"Well, I got six boxes of thirty-thirtys and a few loose in my pocket that I emptied out when I put it away. How you hooked up, Red?"

"Don't bother me," answered Red, from the corner, where he was gently wrapping torn clean white handkerchiefs around the girl's ankles and wrists. "Go and attind to the war an' leave me in peace. Must I fight a lot of coons for ye lily-livered young ladies when I have more important things to do?"

"We got ten Mills left, anyway," said Cordie. "Better lay 'em out, Red, if you want to see Cork again."

"I think," said Putney softly, "that, for the peace of nations in general and ours in particular, I will," and his cheek went down against the stock of his Winchester, "remove from the scene—" a whip-like report—"the head push." And the high priest fell forward on his face, a .30-30 steel-jacketed bullet in his brain, the snake dropping from his nerveless hands.

"Not so bad," said Cordie. "That's shooting, old kid. Look at 'em mill around like a swarm of hornets."

"Bees, dumbbell," said Putney. "Bees swarm, not hornets—an' you a Boston Tech man."

"You'll think it's a combination swarming in another minute or two," answered Cordie. "How about the rear, George?"

"Twelve foot from the platform to the mud. Not much chance of 'em coming up the stream at the minute. The push is coming in front. They're going to mop up this time, no foolin'. There's that young assistant chief or what not. I thought I got him before."

"I know I knocked him over," said Cordie. "He's got a bandage around his head. I must have creased him. This is—"

"Get busy," Grigsby said, his Winchester spitting lead before the words were out of his mouth.

THE PRIEST'S house was built on a gentle slope about fifty yards above a little ditch that crossed directly in front; then the ground again rose through the clearing to the jungle. The rainy season had just started, and already the ground between the slopes was a mixture of slime and mud and unclean things washed in from the jungle.

The Malays charged straight through it in a front of twenty feet, four or-five deep. Several of them carried ladders.

"My gosh!" gasped Cordie, as he knelt to reload for the fourth time. "These birds are sure hard to—"

"Get outta the way," said Dolan, pushing by him, a Mills in either hand. "I gotta attend to it meself, I see. Go an' get me some more of these oranges."

"Get to the rear, Putt," commanded Grigsby. "Let 'em have it, Red."

When the Malays saw Red Dolan they bunched together for a moment. They recognized his red head and the little demon that burned and tore in his hands; then they came on.

Dolan threw two, reached back and Cordie handed him two more. He threw those, and the Malays wavered. As he posed to throw two more they broke and ran.

"Ain't that somepin," Dolan demanded. "Now how about my pack—"

A shot from inside. Putney's shout of, "Got you—you—" A despairing cry of, "Red! Red!" A sobbing cough and a fall.

Dolan wheeled and literally threw himself back in the room, followed by Grigsby and Cordie, who halted in the doorway so as to take care of any frontal attack that might still come. They were just in time to see the naked brown arm of a Malay disappear through a hole in the back wall, holding the girl. The bodies of two Malays were sprawled out on the floor, and across them lay Putney, a kris through his shoulder, his face and head covered with blood.

Dolan's hard, bronzed face was gray and his lips waxy. He whispered, "Oh, Mary Mother," and jumped the bodies in front of the hole.

The whole back of the house seemed to crash in, and the Malays poured into the room from the back platform. They had gained the cover under the house from the stream and, when Putney went down, had used their ladders.

Dolan emptied his Colt's, threw it in the face of the nearest, stooped and picked up one of the curved swords. He was stark staring crazy with desire to cut his way through to the girl, wherever she was. That cry of "Red! Red!" had made him two hundred pounds of living steel. As he bent over to pick up the sword a Malay swung his sword up with a grin of triumph—to go down with a forty-five bullet between the eyes from Cordie, in the doorway.

"Give 'em hell, Red!" he called, his voice the same amused kidding drawl as ever. "Make 'em like it. Heads down, George; keep out of my line."

He shot twice more, then stopped. He couldn't shoot now. Grigsby had dropped his empty Colt's and, following Dolan's example, picked up a sword. Cordie had shot two Malays from in front of him as he did so.

The two big men, looming up against the slighter, shorter Malays, cleared the room and platform like two gorillas would clear a tree of monkeys. Grigsby got a kris in the left arm; Dolan was untouched.

"Steady, Red—steady," Grigsby began when the last two natives went down. "Easy does it, old-timer. Come on, Red; it's over. Red! Snap out of it!"

"Easy hell!" Dolan snarled, his eyes getting a little sense in them as Grigsby's slow, penetrating voice took effect on his fight-fogged brain. "Which way did they take her? Come on, you guys."

He started for the platform, the bloody sword in his hand.

"Hold 'er, Red!" shouted Cordie. "You'll only get cut up. Wait—"

Dolan stopped and whirled around. He looked at them, his eyes slits of frozen blue.

"You heard her callin' me? Are ye comin' wid me, ye two? Come or stay; I'm goin!" and he turned again.

"Stay with Putt, George," said Cordie, calmly; "I think he's coming to. I'll go with you, you wild Irishman."

Red grunted like a buffalo and started for the platform, Cordie behind him. He had stopped and scooped up four of the Mills bombs.

Grigsby, kneeling at Putney's side, started to call a warning when the rain came.

IT SHUT everything out like a blanket over a light. Not like the hard rains of the north, but in one solid sheet of water. There was no wind, just the emptying of the clouds.

Dolan and Cordie were driven back into the room, almost strangled. Nothing that drew breath could live in it without shelter.

"Break out that first-aid stuff, Jimmie," Grigsby commanded. "I'm going to draw this kris out. I don't think it got the lung at all. These head cuts aren't bad. Come on—snap into it. Get that iodine ready, Dolan. Keep quiet, you fool; they can't do anything to her in this rain. They're as bad off as we are."

"The poor darlin', wid her little feet all bruised, callin' for me—an' me out enjoyin' meself instead of bein' there to watch her." Red's voice was rising into the high keening pitch. "May the good saints—"

"Holy Moses!" gasped Putney, sitting up, struggling under Grigsby's hold. "What the hell's coming off? Quit that or I'll—"

"Plenty! Plenty!" said Grigsby. "What are you trying to do, give him a bath? Lie still, Putt. You got a kris through your shoulder and I'm doping it for you. Bandage it, Cordie, and his head, too. You're all right, Archibald, old settler. Come on, Red; stop that damn yowling and pull this hooker out of my arm. Do your praying in church. Hurry up—that's the boy—pull! Pull steady, you big Mick; don't wiggle it—*madre de Dios*—come on with the iodine, monkey face. What are you laughing at? Try and get one of the babies pulled out of—plenty! I got a good mind to jam some down your throat, you're so damn generous with it."

"I am the doctor, Mister," said Cordie, firmly, "and know how much to pour. Hold out your arm again, you big stiff."

"It's holdin' up a little," said Red. "I'm goin'."

"Wait a minute," said Grigsby. "Soon as this kidder gets my arm bandaged we'll all go. How about it, Putt? Can you cut the buck?"

"Yeah, boy," said Putney, staggering to his feet. "That nap I had rested me up, to say nothing of Jimmie Cordie's doctoring putting the jazz into me."

"All right. We'll get down in front, circle around back of that bunch of shacks, crash one, make whoever's there tell us where they took the girl, then go and get her. The next time you get you a girl friend, you big red-headed piece of tripe, stay with her. Let's go."

"I'll take me little plaything along," said Red, picking up the sword. " 'Tis a neat thing to have in a scramble."

"Pack some of those Mills, Cordie. I'll do your shooting for you," Grigsby said.

They felt their way along through the rain and mist, almost blindly. Not a living thing got in their way. Grigsby was easing the way for Putney, who staggered now and then in spite of his efforts to hold himself taut.

Cordie, who was leading, bumped face first into a wall and they felt along it until they came to a door. One shove of Dolan's shoulder and they were in.

Two Malays lay on the floor, their sarongs around their heads. Grigsby jerked them to their feet, one in each hand.

"The little one?" he demanded in Spanish. "Where is she?"

The Malays took one look at Red Dolan, and any thought of resistance went out of them. The knees of one gave way and he would have fallen if Grigsby had not held him up. The other knew what Grigsby meant and pointed with one hand, babbling something in his terror.

"Take your friend with us," suggested Cordie. "He knows."

They went through the rain and mist, down past the priest's

house again, then alongside the little stream, now almost a torrent.

Putney suddenly pitched forward, rose, fell again, then staggered to his feet. "I guess here's where I pass out of the picture," he laughed. "My head hurts like hell and I can hardly see. Go on, you birds; I'll be all right."

"Hold them bombs," said Red to Cordie. "Like hell ye pass out. Come here to me, ye omadhaun." He lifted the one hundred and eighty pounds of Putney, one arm under the armpit, the other under the crotch, and slung him on his back. "Get goin'," he commanded. "Sure I'll carry little Rollo, the Sunday school scholar. 'Get goin' an' leave me to me knittin'," he says. Wiggle over on the side of me remainin' bombs, ye big stiff, or I'll upend ye in the mud."

The Malay stopped and pointed to a house set back on the crest of a little knoll.

"Keep him with us," said Cordie, "until we see if he's been steering us right."

"Get around to the back, Cordie," Grigsby directed. "Put Putt down, Red. All set? Let's go!"

THE MALAY had told the truth. In the house, lying on a mat rug, was the girl, with two old women sitting beside her. When Red and Grigsby came hurtling through the door, Red was first. One of the old women gave a yell of terror, ran to a square cut opening in the rear wall and dived through it. The other groveled on the ground at their feet.

"I knew you'd come and get me, Red," sobbed the little girl in Dolan's arms.

A scream of agony came from below, where the woman had jumped, and a rustling and hissing could be plainly heard. Grigsby went to the opening and looked down.

"My gosh, she jumped square into 'em," he exclaimed.

"There now, alanna," Red was crooning, holding the little girl tightly in his arms. " 'Tis old Red's fault. Sure an' it's not again I'll be leavin' ye until yer daddy has you safe in his arms, darlin'."

Cordie came in, half carrying, half dragging Putney, who was conscious again.

"Couldn't get to the back, George," he reported. "It drops off into a big den of snakes. What did you do—throw the old lady in?"

"What! Me? Throw a woman into—I got a good mind to knock your block off, and I will when we—"

"You and who else of the Grigsbys?" demanded Cordie, who was the smallest by far of the four. But what he didn't have in size he made up in nerve. "I just wanted to know. I saw her come sailing out of that hole right after you and the ring-tailed monkey from Cork went in."

"All right, shrimp, give this guy a start and let him go, and this old lady with him," Grigsby directed the disposal of the Malays.

"The rain has stopped," announced Cordie from the doorway, after carrying out instructions. "We better be seeing where we're at. They can't sneak up on us from behind this time. Boy, that's an awful looking hole; bet there's a million snakes there."

"There, acushla," Red said. "Now 'tis all right ye are, an' in me arms ye'll stay this time. Where's the bombs, Jimmie? Get the rest from the knapsack. Six I ought to have in all."

"You have. What are you going to do—hold her in one hand and throw 'em with the other?"

"Since when have you been tellin' me how to do? Wid me one hand I can do better than you wid—"

"Tell it to the Queen of Bavaria," interrupted Grigsby. "Let's see how we stack up. Any further light repartee between you two kidders can wait. I got twelve cartridges and what I got in the gat. How about you, Red?"

"I have the sword and nawthin' else, except an outrageous thirst on me—"

"You have me, Red," spoke up the little girl from his arms.

"Sure now, 'tis not the time ye give me to finish, darlin'. I was goin' to say that as long as I have ye in me arms that nawthin' else matters at all. And that reminds me, ye lads, in case now it comes to the finals wid me, ye understand, I'll be askin' that one of ye will attend to what I mean. Have I the word? 'Tis best that way instead of the—"

"Any one of us will attend to it, Red," said Grigsby, gently, "especially after seeing that pit back there. How are you, Putt?"

"Not so bad. I got forty or fifty cartridges and a heck of a thirst, like Red. My head feels better. This hole in my shoulder is not so good."

"Hand me the iodine, nurse," said Cordie. "I'll—"

"You do, you grinning baboon, and I'll take you apart as bad as I am. Once is enough of your doctoring."

"Them's harsh words, Nell," grinned Cordie, going to the door. "Someone better be doing a little look-see around here. They won't let us alone long, that's a cinch. I likewise got a thirst like a camel's. You haven't got anything on your hip, have you, George?"

"Why," said the little girl, "there's something to drink in that jug over there. The bad old women were drinking out of it all the time."

"What!" shouted Red and Cordie at the same time.

RED, being nearest, got it first. He raised the jug and sniffed. "Aguardiente," he pronounced, "and new—at that." He brought the jug to Putney. "Here, Putt—hop to it. Darlin'," to the girl, "you saved old Red's life."

"Not so bad," said Cordie, when it came his turn, as he put the jug down. "Not—so—bad."

"Give it to me," Red commanded. "There is no use in half a blanket."

"Better go easy on that stuff," warned Grigsby. "After nothing to eat since morning that's dynamite to fool with."

"It is so," said Red, taking another drink just the same.

"My daddy says it's bad to drink," said the little girl.

"It is," answered Red, promptly, "an' 'tis not often we do it, darlin'. Who might your daddy be, an' where were ye when the bad men got ye, do ye know, now?"

"Why, of course, I know. My daddy's name is Wyeth, and he's a judge. I'm Betty Wyeth, and my daddy's boat is at Gunong Jera. I made Wong row me over to the other shore when my daddy was away, and the bad men jumped out of the bushes and carried me away. They gave me to these bad men. My daddy'll be awfully angry with me."

"No he won't, darlin'," said Red. "He'll be so glad to see you that he'll hug you tight, like this."

"Well, no use of standing around talking. The next rush'll cook us sure. Let's get started," said Grigsby.

"Come on then," said Red. "Is this a conference of staff officers or somepin? Let's get started. I'll take me good sword here and cut me way through fifty miles wid herself in me arms."

"Listen to the red-headed terror of Cork sounding off," scoffed Cordie from the door. "That's the boy, Red. I'm wid ye and for ye. You and me, Red—we whipped the whole German army, didn't we? Whadda we care for a few coons and fifty miles. Man, howdy, here comes three or four feet of water down the pike. Look at her come!"

"Back water from somewhere," said Grigsby, going to the door. "See—she's slowing down. That dinky stream is a regular river. Holy mackinnaw! Look at that proa floating down—not there, dumbbell, over by the big log."

"Yeah, I see her," Cordie nodded. "Say, if we could get that baby we could go away from here."

"Yeah, boy. Go and get her."

"Who—me?" from Cordie. "Boy, that water is full of snakes and things, I bet."

"What do you care? Think of the fun you're having. Come on; show me something. It's getting away. I'd go but my arm's too stiff."

"Aw, for Pete's sake," said Cordie, but he half waded, half swam to the proa and brought it up to the house. "Look, paddles and everything. Call the guests, me lud, the carriage awaits."

"Look behind you, Jeems, me lad," answered Grigsby, grimly. "There's more than the carriage awaits, old kid."

WITHIN one hundred yards was a flotilla of proas, manned by at least two hundred Malays. In the first, a small one holding two sub-chiefs and himself, was the young chief. The water had stopped flowing, and it was deep enough for the proas in all but the high places.

"My gosh, I should say so!" Cordie exclaimed, wide-eyed. "Call out the navy; the army's retired. Let's tie this warship up and get under cover. Red will have to sink some of the enemy before we can sail out of the harbor."

"Well, we got a boat," Grigsby announced when they entered.

"Yeah? Snappy work. Let's go," said Red.

"And we got a few enemy cruisers to sink, also. I counted twelve of 'em."

Red went to the door.

"Aw—not so bad," he decided. "You guys do the rowin', an' I'll torpedo 'em."

"If it was us alone," said Grigsby, who had gone to the door with him, "we could take a chance and try it. With the kid, though, not so good, Red. I'd hate to think of her going under in that muck."

"You and me both," and Red swore softly. "We could stand the gaff all right, but with her—I dunno, George. We got to protect her."

"Here they come! No, it's the little chief—here he comes by himself. Well, I'll be darned, look at the white flag. He's stopping; he wants someone to come out to him. Untie that proa, Red. I'll go out and see what's on his mind. I can handle one of those things with one hand."

"Like hell. Wait till I get a couple of bombs an' I'll go along as bodyguard."

"If you did, you ape, he'd turn and run. It's you they're afraid of. Hey, Jimmie! Come out and go and talk to your friend. You can savvy more Spanish."

"Here it is," said Cordie, ten minutes later. "This bird is the son of the old chief that we knocked off in the temple. He says he's glad of it: that his pa and the priest were doing him dirt all the time, keeping him down. He jumped out on them once and served a hitch in a native regiment in India for the British. He says he's top cutter now and that the water is high enough in the creek back of the priest's house to go all the way to the Kelantan. He'll give us a clear road, provided we leave the jewels, the machine-gun that he don't know is jammed, all the bombs that Red has left, a Colt's forty-five and some cartridges. He figures if he can get all of that junk he'll be cock of the walk around here. He knows what the Mills are and is not afraid of them. Then he wants one more thing. He wants the girl left to square the Snake God."

"What did ye tell him?" asked Red, softly, the little girl's arms clinging frantically around his neck.

"Well, you damned good-for-nothing mutt!" swore Cordie viciously. "You red-headed ass! I told him the same as you'd tell him, you damned ape. I'd break you in two for a cent."

"Aw, now, Jimmie, darlin'," coaxed the big Irishman; "sure ye know I wasn't meanin' any such thing. It's nervous I am on account of herself, here."

"All right, Red," said Cordie, "I'm kind of fussed up myself, I guess, but you get my nanny, you flannel mouthed Mick."

"When you two get all done," said Grigsby, "we'll get back to the main line. Anything else, Jimmie?"

"No, except he said he'd wait ten minutes before attacking and that this time they'd go through in spite of hell and high water, or words to that effect."

"We could cut our way through," said Putney, from the corner where he was sitting propped up against the wall, "but with her along I—"

"Do ye value them stones against wan scratch on her little—" began Red, hotly.

"Throw something at that lunatic for me. Jimmie. Listen, idiot, why not let me finish? I was going to say that we'd swap the jewels and the rest of the junk for her."

"We'll try something first," said Grigsby. "Jimmie, you tell him that we'll leave the jewels on the priest's platform, the gun also. That we go in the clear with the girl, and that he and a couple of his men go with us until we are. When we are, we will give him the Colt's and the bombs. Tell him to ease his navy over so they can see the back of the house and see if the red-headed man with the demons isn't ready to blow the snake den to hell. If he isn't satisfied with that, tell him to cut his wolf loose and come and get us—if he is man enough. Red, go out and hang over the pit with a couple of bombs ready to throw. Make faces at them."

"Leave it to me," said Cordie. "Do your stuff, Red."

The young chief knew that the destruction of the snakes would complete the terror already installed in the minds of his followers; that the sight of the big red-headed man at the den would settle any question of not agreeing to any terms; and he wanted the Colt's and the bombs as he had never wanted anything in his life. He could restore the jewels and find plenty of sacrifices.

The little fleet eased over where they could see back of the house. There was the big red-headed man, brandishing his arms, one of the little demons in each hand, howling like a lost soul. One good look and the proas backed water, several disappearing in the flooded jungle. The young chief with two men came boldly up to the platform a moment or so later. He had served under British officers in India and knew these men were of the class that kept their word.

A DAY later, Red pulled the smaller proa, that had been towed behind the larger one, up alongside.

"All right, me bucko. Here is the four bombs for ye," he said.

"Whin ye throw them, pull the little pin out, here. Wid ye thumb and finger, this way, an' count wan—two—three—an' leave it go. Throw wid a stiff arm, like this. Here's the Colt's, an' here's twenty shells for it. Go on now, beat it for home while the goin's good for the likes of ye."

"And a fair exchange it is," said Cordie, tickling Miss Betty Wyeth, who giggled. "What's a few stones against a beauty like Betty?"

" 'Tis my girl friend, she is," said Red, firmly, "an' I want none of ye to try an' flirt wid her."

The four men, who had given up a million dollars in jewels so as not to submit a little girl to the hazards of war, grinned cheerfully at her.

"Wait a minute," said Grigsby to the young chief. "Here—take this to go with the Colt's," and he handed him his belt and holster. "You're a game little cock, at that. See—shove the gun in deep and keep the flap buckled down when you don't want to use it right quick."

The Malay took the belt and holster, his eyes shining, his dark, intelligent face glowing with delight. He snapped an order to one of his men, who reached down in a food sack and produced the canvas sack.

"My gosh! It's them!" Red shouted. "Now what—"

"Shut up," commanded Grigsby. "Translate, Jimmie."

"We have shot square," began Jimmie. "He is a real chief now, himself—he doesn't care for the blood that has been shed—all Malays rather die in battle—he can get plenty of men now that he has the gun and the bombs—Grigsby gave him the belt of a warrior. He's going about three hundred words a minute and my limit is fifty. The jewels of the pirate did him no good on account of the priest—we helped him a lot by scragging the old boys for him—they stole the jewels themselves. He thanks us for not scattering the snakes. Red is a mighty swordsman, and he loves him like hell and all—hopes Red will come and live with him—they could clean up on all the rest of the tribes—and—it would be all right if he put half the jewels back under the Snake God; these birds with him wouldn't dare tell—we are all fighting men and have helped him a lot and— What the hell is *tener palabra?* Oh, yeah—we are *caballeros* who keep our word and—*quisiera*—I should—he should like to— Holy smackers! He says that half the jewels are ours!"

"Ain't that somepin," said Red, little Miss Wyeth snuggled down in his arms. "Tell him we'll take 'em, Jimmie. He's a good little guy, at that."

II

THE MAJOR WANTED
HIM ALIVE

Federal agents and deputy U.S. marshals had
gone down before their guns; the Texas Rangers
and the border patrol were powerless to curb
their lawless activities—yet for Jimmy Cordie
and Red Dolan tackling this murderous gang of
border desperadoes was all in the day's work.

MAJOR SCOTT, CHIEF of the special intelligence unit, did not look up from the report he was reading as his door opened. His usually ruddy old face, with the close cropped white mustache, was white and drawn.

"Beat it," he said curtly. "I don't care what it is; I'm busy."

"If the major pleases," began the deeply bronzed, well set up young man about thirty, with a grin, "I——"

"He don't please—what! God bless my soul!" and the major rose, his face beaming now. "Why, you young scoundrel, I gave orders to have you shot long ago. Jimmy, my boy, I'm glad to see you. Sit down and—and—by the nine red gods! Who saw you come in here?"

"Why, no one," Jimmy Cordie answered, lightly. "As I was coming down the hall a beautiful red-headed lady came galloping out and ducked in an office across the way marked private, general council or something. The door to the anteroom was open so I came right in. I opened this door on general principles."

"Go to the Willard, room 657—here's the key—and wait for me. Snap into it. Get out of here without being seen if you can."

"The last time I accepted an invitation like that from you I woke up in France and everything. I came in to say—"

The major sat down.

"Why, of course, Jimmy," he said, gently, "I shouldn't have asked you. I looked up and saw you and it seemed as if you'd been sent in answer to my prayers. Sit down and tell me what you have been doing. Someone said that you were in the Malay peninsula."

Cordie looked at the major for a moment. Now the face that had lighted up on seeing him was again drawn with worry.

"Room 657, Willard," he said, saluted and was gone.

There was no one in the office or the hallway as he went through, his handkerchief to his eyes as if removing something in them. It covered his face but was not necessary; there was no one to see.

RED DOLAN had taken a steaming hot bath and, dressed in light blue silk pajamas, was sprawled out on a couch that actually sagged under the weight of his two hundred and twenty pounds of bone and muscle. He was alternately reading the sports sheet and admiring the pajamas.

"How come you back so soon?" he demanded, as Jimmy Cordie came in. "Hey, Jimmy, I'm goin' to get me two more suits of these here pajamas to wear. Some class, ain't they?"

"The next thing you'll get to wear is a wooden overcoat, you big ape. We're going to the border tonight."

"Who's goin' to the border?" Red demanded, in astonishment. "You're goofy, boy. Not me—I ain't commenced to spend my jack yet."

"You heard me. We leave for Arizona at six-thirty."

"You can, but not me. How come you crazy that way, Jimmy?"

"I'm not crazy. We're going down as specially appointed Federal agents, with big guns and everything," Cordie enlightened him.

"What! Me—and you—Federal agents? Now I know you're goofy."

"Goofy hell. I just signed up for both of us."

"You what? Sure now, the black curse of Shielygh be on ye, Jimmy Cordie, for doin' such a thing—an' us wid the jack we got off the jewels the little Malay give us not half spent yet. To

the border—an' as Government cops? Double shame on ye if ye do be tellin' me the truth. Here I am wid me silk paj—"

"Tell the rest of it to the Queen of Bavaria. Listen, you red-headed baboon, are you going with me and get killed like a man, or are you going to stay up here and loll around in silk pajamas? Answer me yes or no and no more wah-wahing."

"Sure, I'm goin' wid ye, Jimmy, ye pup," answered Dolan promptly, "an' bad luck to ye for even askin' the question. What the hell was ye doin' playin' around where there was a chance of—"

"Well, I went over to see Major Scott and—"

" 'Tis enough! Go no farther. An' to think ye didn't have sense enough to keep away from that old hellion that ran us all over France an' the divil and all. Did ye not get enough M.I. over there widout—Jimmy, how's the old lad lookin'? Did he ask after me, I dunno?"

"He did. He said for you to remember you had nine million years K.P. coming to you if he caught you. Well, here's the dope, Red. He told me to go over to the Willard and he'd meet me. I did, and he did. There's a bunch down there that's running dope and Chinks and what not over the border between Nogales and Yuma."

"Ain't that close figurin'? Between Nogales and Yuma. Why don't ye say between the Atlantic and the Pacific? 'Tis all of two hundred miles from Nogales to Yuma, ye poor—"

"Will you keep that trap of yours closed long enough to let me finish?"

"She's closed, Jimmy."

"All right, now listen. This gang maintains headquarters on this side at an old ranch in the foothills of the Santa Rita Mountains about thirty miles from Nogales. They have a Mex headquarters at Sonoyta, which, dumbbell, is halfway between Nogales and Yuma on the Mexican side of the border. Is that plain? Well, there's been three Federal agents killed down there in the last year, and a couple of U.S. deputy marshals. There is a hell of a leak somewhere. No sooner does a man go down there than he gets knocked off. The Rangers and the border patrol are after these birds, too, but can't catch 'em with the goods on, the major says. He sent down two of his best men after they found Frank McGhee sitting in his car with half his head blown off on the Santa Rita trail. They all got theirs one by one. One bird they found in his room at the hotel with a knife through his heart, and he hadn't been off the train a day. The major was trying to dope out how to send an absolutely unknown man that no one would know about but himself when I—"

"Ain't that somepin'," said Red. "An' now we go down to get ours—an' me wid silk—"

"You said that before. Well, there it is. Where the leak comes in, the major doesn't know; it might be in his own office. That's what's worrying the old boy. They knocked the last one off from a car that came by him as he was going into a cigar store the day after he arrived at Nogales. It may be in the district attorney's office down there, or in the United States marshal's. These birds are figured on as having run over a million dollars' worth of stuff this year. They're organized, boy. The Rangers can damn' near stop anything, but they can't put their fingers on this outfit when they are doing their stuff. No sooner does a Federal man land than he gets knocked off the Christmas tree. They seem to even know the color of his hair."

"Ain't that nice," said Red, reflectively rubbing his own brick red head. "Do we get measured for them wooden overcoats up here before we go, Jimmy?"

"They keep 'em in stock," answered Cordie, with a grin.

"Yeah? Well—I ain't been killed for a long time now. I wish we had George and Putt along. The four of us could—"

"Maybe so they'll hear about it and come and cover us," said Cordie, with another grin.

"Ain't that a relief. Why the hell didn't ye say they was—"

"Open the door, Red; there's the corn licker I ordered on the way up."

ONE of the group of men on the veranda of the ranch-house between two of the foothills of the Santa Rita range in Arizona pushed back from the table, which was covered with bottles and glasses and dirty playing cards. He walked to the rail and stood, loosening the collar of his soft silk shirt.

"Of all the good-fer-nothin' countries God ever made, this is the worst," he snarled. "Look at that damn' blisterin' sun! You can see the heat comin' up from the ground."

"Wadda you care?" sneered a stockily built young Slav sitting with his chair tilted against the wall. "You're gettin' the jack, ain't you? Why don't you go back to New York if—"

"Listen, you," the man wheeled on the speaker, "I don't need any jaw out of you, either. Sure, I'm gettin' mine—as you're gettin' yours—an' I'll go back to New York when I get good an' ready. Any time you think you can ride me, feller, you start in an'—"

"Yeah? So that's the way you feel about it?" and the young Slav's chair came down to the floor. "Well, big boy, I don't like the way your face was pushed on you an'—"

He started to rise.

A slim man with dead-white face looked up from riffling a deck of cards. There was a scar running from the left corner of his mouth to the top of his ear. His face was cold and hard, and his eyes looked as it they were filmed over.

"That's plenty from you two," he said softly. "Take your hand off your gat, Lewis. Don't do any reaching, Stan—"

They both obeyed him instantly, the Slav's hand remaining half way to his back pocket, Lewis's coming out from under his left armpit.

"I've decided that we might as well have that jack," the white-faced man went on, taking no further notice of them. "It'll take four men and the driver."

"An' there's two hundred grand in the safe," said one of the men sitting opposite him. "It'll be a pipe, Tony. Go in shootin' and—"

"I ain't worried about the shootin' part," white-faced Tony dismissed the interruption. "It's only that we're doin' so well with the snow and the chandoo and the yellow bellies that I didn't want to mix things up. And that reminds me, there's something I want to say to you moll-buzzers, and that's—"

A girl came around the corner of the ranch-house with a pail and started for the well on the right.

"Wait a minute, girlie," Tony called, rising. "I want to see you for—"

"Aw, tend to business," objected one of the men. "You always got to chase a kite—"

Scarface Tony Mareno struck him across the mouth with a blackjack. The blow was as swift and deadly as the strike of a snake. The man fell backward, chair and all.

"I been waiting for that gay-cat to shoot off his mouth," he said, swinging his jack back and forth by the loop. "Any of the rest of you lush-touchers got anything to say about my going? No—just like that, hey?"

He went to the well, still swinging the jack idly in his hand.

"That kid you got out here with you," he said to the girl, who shrank back a little against the well frame. "Where'd old Mag get her?"

"Why, she came up from Douglas, Tony. She isn't a—she's

just visiting one of the girls. She don't know that this is a—she's going back down tomorrow."

"Yeah? You see that she's in my room right after supper. You go and tell her that she's my girl friend. You go fix her up for me or I'll beat your head off."

The girl went white beneath the pitiful little showing of rouge and powder on her haggard face.

"I'll—I'll tell her," she stammered.

"Yeah? See that you do, sister, if you want to keep healthy."

Tony turned and walked back to the veranda. On the way he stopped and took a little round box from his pocket and deliberately and slowly sniffed a pinch of the white powder.

"My God!" whispered one of the men. "He's on the habit. There'll be hell popping around here."

TONY stood on the top step, where he could see all of the eight men on the veranda. The man he had blackjacked lay on the floor moaning, his hand to his bloody mouth.

"There's something I want to tell you rats before we go to this plant, and that's this," he addressed them; "there's a beefer got in this mob somewhere. I got word that Ferdinand was knocked off by the Government cops in Sasabe. He only pulled out to meet a shipment night before last, an' they were there, waiting for him. I just as soon make cold meat outta any of you pigs as not; remember that. If I get to thinking that one of you even looks like an elbow I'll—"

"Who the hell do you think you are?" suddenly shouted a big, beefy man, who had been drinking whisky and brandy steadily. The silk shirt covering the upper part of his fat body was wringing wet and clinging to him. The heat and the alcohol had made him insane with rage. "You dirty little monkey-faced wop. Who made you top cutter? That lad you jacked is my buddy. You didn't give him a chance, you scar-faced buzzard."

Tony stood and stared at him, his face impassive, his eyes contracted to mere pinpoints. Two of the men, in line between them, swiftly and silently pushed their chairs back. Even the man on the floor shrank closer to the wall and was still.

"Go on!" the big man roared. "Let's see you strut your stuff, you damn' Tommy-buster. I know you got a rod in the pit—so've I. Reach for it!"

As he spoke he stood up and his hand flashed to his hip pocket so fast that the eye could hardly follow—but it was not fast enough. Tony straightened out his right arm as if pointing at the man. An automatic slid into his hand from his shirt sleeve and he fired twice before the big man's gun had more than half left the pocket.

"My God!" said Lewis, as the big beefy body crashed over the table. "Didn't that poor fool know that Tony's gat was on a spring under his—"

"An' that's that," said Tony softly. "Anyone else want to know who's top cutter? That makes two—I just as soon make it three as not. No? Take that hand-painted shoestring out and plant it. I'm going to take a little walk and—"

He did not finish his sentence but, after lighting a cigarette without another look at the men on the veranda, he walked around to the rear of the ranch-house. Sitting on the ground just outside the kitchen door was a man with a greasy, dirty cook's apron on over a nondescript lot of clothes that seemed much too large for him, busily engaged in scouring pans. He looked as dirty and greasy himself as the apron and had a three or four days' growth of beard.

He looked up as Tony came by.

"Did someone get caught trying to make his elegant, Cap n," he inquired with a silly grin. "I heard the shot out here."

"Yeah?" and Tony looked at him in disgust, then suddenly more intently. "Who the hell are you?" he snarled.

"Me?" answered the man, shrinking back against the wall and dropping the pan. "I'm McCarty's cousin, Capt'n. I been here two weeks now helpin' the cook. I make the skyblue and the weenie and everything and—"

"What the hell kind of a flying jib are you? Who's McCarty?"

"Why—now you're foolin' with me, Capt'n," the pot-scourer said with a giggle, "pretendin' you don't know who McCarty is—"

"Stand up, you louse!" snarled Tony. "I just croaked a man for getting funny with me. I just as soon beef you as not. I asked you who McCarty was?"

THE MAN scrambled hurriedly to his feet and cowered against the wall, his right arm raised as if to ward off a blow.

"I didn't mean nothin', Capt'n," he whimpered. "I'm a right guy. Please don't go an' use no wood on me, now. He's the homesteader over in the valley. I been sick, Capt'n, and on the turf, and I got to him after I—he said that he wasn't goin' to have no guy like me eatin' on him, and he gets me this job helpin' the cook."

"You been in stir?"

"Yessir, Capt'n. I done a finif at the Stout House down in Florence, an' a hell of a place it is. Them screws use the wood all the time on a guy. I got—"

"Stir crazy," sneered Tony. "What did you get dropped for?"

"I was gunnin' for a peter man and them dicks—"

"Yeah? Well, you better stick close around the kitchen, Oofty Goofty, or some of these bad men will give you the wood."

"Yessir, Capt'n, I'll do what you say."

"Yeah? Some day I'll let you take a guy for a ride for me. Then you'll be a regular gorilla."

"They'd burn me, Capt'n." The man shrank back. "I ain't no killer."

Tony's eyes became dull, and the film began to creep over them.

"I might as well beef you right now," he snarled. "What the hell good are you, a stir-crazy con and—"

"Capt'n, if you do," the man said, earnestly, "there won't be any chuck tonight; the cook's sick."

That struck Tony's drug crazed brain as funny, and his mood changed.

"Yeah? I'll let you live then until after supper," he chuckled and strolled along. One of the men had come to the well for a drink and Tony called to him, "Tell Stan to come around for a minute."

The hard-faced young Slav joined him, and they walked over to the shade of one of the barns.

"In a little while," Tony told him, "drop around and take a look at that woody bird in the kitchen."

"Who, the nut that's helpin' Sam?"

"Yeah—I know that English Mag is right, and I ain't afraid of any of her kites squawkin'. They don't know anything anyway. There isn't anyone comes here but us any more. Sam's been with her for a long time—ever since he got out of Copper John. This bird tells a pretty tight story, but since he came Ferdinand was knocked off and—"

"Hell, Tony, you don't mean that you think he's an office man? We didn't get no line about anyone else since—"

"I ain't thinking anything, feller. You and me have been in this business long enough to know that you got to watch all ends. It's just being careless about things like the back side of the hangouts that's landed many a good mob in stir for track thirteen and a washout or salt creek. No," and Tony snapped his half burnt cigarette away, "it may be that old Sam is getting lazy and this guy is right, but—take him for a ride tomorrow."

"All right, Tony, I will," the Slav assented. "We been gettin' pretty heavy on these—"

"Yeah? An' you don't like it, is that it?"

"Aw, Tony—you and me have been buddies for a long time. What do you want to—?"

"I'm not taking a chance with anyone," said Tony, walking off. "You take that nut out tomorrow and slip a sparkler under his chin."

The young Slav stood and watched him go toward the front.

"The snow has got him," he said aloud. "He ain't no good any more. I got a good mind to—"

He didn't finish his sentence.

THE GIRL Tony had spoken to hurried up the stairs to one of the back rooms.

"Get up, Sally," she said, shaking a young girl roughly by the shoulder. "Get up, quick! You got to get out of here. Tony is after you. Get awake! Hurry up!"

"I'm afraid, Marie." The girl began to cry. "I wish I never had come up to this place to see Helen. All these men around here drinking all the time and—"

"Listen," said the other, in quiet desperation, "if you want to keep on being a good girl you get dressed and beat it out the back way. Tony'll beat me up for this, but I don't give a damn about me any more. What you come here for without knowing what kind of a place it was, is beyond me."

"I wanted to surprise Helen," the girl whimpered. "She wrote me she had a swell job as housekeeper and—"

"Hurry up, I tell you, while he's out in front. He's on the habit and is worse than a rattler."

"Where can I go?" Sally whimpered again. "I'm afraid of snakes out there in the desert, and there's no place to hide. I—"

"There's a worse snake right here, you little fool. Get over in the foothills and hide. I'll go with you as far as I dare. Maybe we can reach that homesteader that brings stuff over for Sam. Though what the hell he could do against Tony is—Come on; we'll sneak down the back way and—"

"Gee, you ain't lamming, are you?" demanded the pot-scourer, as the girls came through the kitchen. "Mrs. Mag will raise hell, no foolin'."

"Which way does the homesteader live?" demanded Marie.

"You couldn't make it there tonight before dark. You'd get lost, sure's shootin'."

"We're playing hide and go seek, and we must find a place to hide, quick," Marie humored him.

"Go hide in the big barn then; lots of places there," he joined in enthusiastically. "Can I play after I get the work done?"

"Next time." The girl drew a long breath. "Listen—I don't know—you only been here a little while, and I know that you're—"

"A little goofy," supplied the man, with a grin. "I got that way in stir—prison, you know. Pretty angels come and talk to me and everything. I—"

"Oh, my God!" the girl panted. "Listen—this is a good girl— you know, a real good girl, and a bad man wants to hurt her. If I hide her away from him you won't tell, will you? He'd hurt her awfully?"

"No, I won't tell, honest Injun. You go and hide her in the barn. I won't tell, cross my heart and hope to die."

"I don't know your name," said the girl, "but I got a hunch that you won't and I—"

"No, I won't tell," he assured again. "I ain't scared of no man, I ain't," he crowed, valiantly. "Better get goin'. In the mornin' I'll bring you some chuck while they're sleepin', and then you run for the homesteader. It's over that way, see—" and he went to the door with the girls and pointed the way.

IT WAS after supper and quite dark when Tony came into the kitchen, his evil, dead looking face set as a mask. His eyes were glittering with rage. He walked up to the man who was standing by the stove, swaying a little as if he were walking on eggs.

"How'd you leave things in Washington?" he asked, softly.

"Washington, Capt'n? I ain't been in—"

"Quit stallin', feller," Tony snarled. "You're good, all right, but I'm a little better, see. You got the patter and that nitwit stuff down fine. I been talking to old Sam. You slipped in two things, you damn' flattie. Homesteaders don't bribe cooks to get a job for their cousins; they ain't got the jack. I just noticed the other, and that is that no stir crazy con that's flunkeyin' around a kitchen has got white, even, teeth. Come clean, feller, and I may just let the boys bump you off easy with a gat. Who else is down here with you?"

"You got me wrong, Capt'n," said the man, earnestly. "I ain't no—"

"Listen," snarled Tony, "I'm going to give you one chance more to come clean. First, where are they?"

"My pretty angels, Capt'n? They don't come until night."

Tony stepped back a foot, his voice silky, "The girl they call Marie and the little girl that was visiting here. Tell—"

"Sally? Ain't she a go-getter, Capt'n?"

"You think you can kid me?" Tony yelled. "You damn rat? I'll teach you something before I—"

The drug with which his brain was burning made him feel superior in strength to any man; he felt that he could do as he pleased without opposition. His left hand shot out and seized the man's right wrist and began to force the hand down on the red-hot stove.

The wrist turned without seeming effort in his grip and the hand slid half way up to his elbow and closed with a grip of steel. A second more, and Tony's left hand rested on the stove. He screamed like an animal and tried to raise his right arm, but the body of the kitchen-helper was close to him, the left arm around him, holding him as in the grip of a boa constrictor.

It was only for a split second that his hand was held to the stove. The man released him, stepped back six inches and his right fist crashed to the point of Tony's jaw. The killer went down and out. Already there was the sound of running feet and calling back and forth from the front. The man blew out the lamp on the table and ran noiselessly out the door, just as the kitchen filled with men. He started for the foothills, then stopped.

"My gosh, I forgot about the hide-and-seekers," he muttered, and turned toward the big old feed barn, used in the days when the ranch was a real ranch, not a honkatonk and a hangout for crooks. "This is no place any more for Old Man Cordie's son Jimmy," he told himself, as he gained its cover. "As a Federal agent I'm a fine advertisement for tooth powder," and he grinned, cheerfully.

There was an old flight of stairs leading to the loft at the right of the big open sliding doors that hung half off the rails, and he went up softly. The doors where the hay was formerly swung in were open also, and he eased over to them and listened to the commotion in the kitchen. The moon had come up and it was fairly light outside.

In a few minutes he could hear Tony's hysterical screams and commands to find him and bring him in so that he, Tony, could burn him to death.

Several men ran out of the kitchen and began hunting around the outhouses. Tony came to the doorway, his hand and wrist bandaged, yelling instructions in a high pitched voice that had a peculiar whinny in it.

"Find those two frails, too!" he yelled. "I'll beat the heads off of them after I burn that dick. Get in the big barn, some of you. I'll—"

A BIG powerful roadster came around the house and stopped half way to the barn.

"Hey, Tony," one of the three men called, as they jumped out, "hell's poppin' down below!"

"What?" yelled Tony, running to the car, as did most of the men in sight. "What?"

"The boys are bringing what's left of the stuff up here," informed the man who had been driving. "We come across all right, an' on the way to Arivaca we run into two revenue cars. I was pilotin' an' got back in time to turn the boys. Then we got started for Calabasas, and damn' if there wasn't some of them damn' border patrol that almost cut us off! We dodged 'em and come around by Tubac, an' there was the Rangers. They shot hell outa one car an' got the Kid an' Angelo an' Mac. Only way that was open was up here. The boys'll be here in a minute; they was right behind us at the creek."

The burn, the knockout and the drug he had sniffed when he came to had made Tony literally insane.

"I don't give a damn!" he yelled. "I don't give a damn who comes up here. Get the hell outta here and find those frails and that buzzard for me or I'll do some killing right now. I'm going to burn that sneak to death."

"There wasn't no car tailin' us, Tony," one of the men tried to soothe him. "We shook 'em off way below. The boys got a pretty heavy load in the car that came through. All that hop from Li Wong came over. Ferdinand won't tell 'em nothin'. We're all jake."

"I don't give a damn what came over!" Mareno stormed. "Go and help find—"

"Here comes a car now," said Stan, the Slav, who had been watching Tony's every move. "That's the—yeah, it's the big Cat, all right. Better hear what the dope is, Tony. To me it looks like a knockoff."

"I'll attend to that. You go and find that damn' dick for me. I don't give a damn what happens; I'm goin' to get him first. He burnt me, the—"

Another car, a touring car with four men, pulled up, and Tony walked over to it.

The Slav muttered an oath, then hesitated a minute.

"If I thought I had a chance and the rest would stick—" he muttered half aloud.

Then he turned and walked toward the barn, where Lewis had already gone.

Jimmy Cordie heard a muffled scream and the sound of a scuffle somewhere below and to the rear. He ran down the stairs and in the dim light located it as coming from one of a row of box stalls almost at the back of the barn.

The girl, Marie, was struggling in the arms of Lewis. The other lay huddled in a corner.

"Help me hold this damn' wildcat; she's a fighting fool," Lewis called, when Cordie came in, thinking he was one of the gang.

"Most women are when they get started," answered Cordie, laughing.

Lewis let go the girl and whirled around, to look directly into the muzzle of a Colt's forty-five revolver, taken from under Jimmy Cordie's left armpit.

"What the hell!" Lewis gasped.

"Put 'em up, you!" Cordie snapped. "Reach for the sky. You're done."

Two things probably contributed to what happened. First, Lewis only saw in front of him the half-witted helper of old Sam—although Tony had said he was a Government cop. Second, the soft, easy kidding tone and the grin. His brain didn't comprehend the language in time to save him.

"You crazy ass," he sneered. "Gimme that gat!"

With that he jumped forward—to meet a soft-nosed forty-five bullet between the eyes that hurled him back in a corner of the stall dead before he hit the floor.

"Oh!" wailed the girl. "You killed him and—and—are you a dick, mister?"

"Yessum, with a badge and everything," Cordie assured her. "Be good girls now and get over in that corner. There'll be doings around here in a minute. I feel—"

"Lewis?" a man called. "Who shot? Are you all right, Bill?" Then a pause, and from the doorway, "Lewis? Where the hell are you? Hey, Tony! Somethin' wrong here!"

Cordie and the girls could hear Tony's high-pitched whine of response, "Yeah? Come on, you gorillas! Here's where I do a little burning myself."

"Ain't it the truth?" said Jimmy Cordie, with a grin. "If I get you lined up with my sights, old kid, you'll go somewhere and burn, I bet you."

"Oh, they'll kill you," sobbed the visiting girl.

"I'm going to do the killing," corrected Jimmy Cordie, firmly. "Snuggle down in the corner, children, and give the old man room according to his size and disposition."

RED DOLAN sat in the one room of the homesteader's shack tucked away between two of the foothills. With him were Major Scott and two big, deeply tanned men about thirty-five.

"Sure, it was Jimmy's plan altogether. We come down to Langhorne lookin' for a ranch, an' we buys a little flivver an' drifts down alongside the Santa Cruz River. Man, we was offered all the ranches in the country, but it was damn' particular we was. Finally we finds this wan, and the man was so glad to sell he threw in a cow that was just comin' fresh. Jimmie had me go over to the snakes' nest wid milk to sell, which I did widout any trouble."

"You must have been a fine looking milkman," said Putney.

"I was," answered Red, firmly; "a regular wan. Was I not born on a farm, ye poor fish, up in the north of—"

"You was born in a tree, you ring-tailed monkey," interrupted Grigsby. "Get on with it. I don't like the idea of Jimmy being over in that bunch of copperheads."

"Get on wid it! And me leavin' me silk pajamas an' the life of swellness an' peace to come down to this corner of hell where—"

"How did you get Jimmy in there?" Grigsby demanded.

" 'Twas his idea. On the way down he wahwahs on the fact that they was all hooked up to guard in front, wid their spies an' informers an' all. They was lookin' for attack that way, an' the thing for us to do was to take 'em in the rear. I told the owld cook that I had a cousin that I wanted to get rid of an' I'd pay him ten a week to take 'im off my—"

"You bribed the cook?" interrupted Grigsby. "Not so good— by a damn' sight. You boneheaded fool, if that cook ever lets that out, Jimmy's cooked. Why the hell didn't you send over a note saying you wanted to put a Federal agent in there?"

"It's stuck for two weeks," said Red, loftily. " 'Twas what we thought best and—let's go an' get Jimmy outta there."

"You and Jimmy did well, Red," said the major. "It was the word that Ferdinand was to meet a load and where, that Jimmy passed for you to relay to me, that broke the chain for them. We got him, and he told us all about it. He was Tony Mareno's pay-off man and with him from the start. We got 'em, Red— thanks to you and Jimmy."

"An' he that big—an' squawkin'?" Dolan marveled.

"Well," said the major, grimly, "he may have been persuaded a little by two old Apache Indians from the reservation that happened to be around the Ranger camp when the boys brought him in. They wanted to ride to Nogales, and the deputy marshals left with them and the prisoner, who was very hard-boiled indeed. I've read somewhere," went on the old major, who had lost three of his "boys," "that when those old Apaches really extend themselves they can make a stone image tell the real name of its grandmother. On the way to Nogales Ferdinand decided to talk a lot, and he did. They brought him back for me to hear it, and he repeated all he had said and a lot more, the two old bucks sitting cross-legged at his side. The roundup has started, Red."

"Did he tell where the leak was, Major?"

"He did—and my private secretary, who came from Nogales years ago, is being held for the Federal in Washington with a charge of murder against him."

"Ain't that somepin'," said Red. "How'd you birds get in?"

"We'll tell you on the way. Let's get to Jimmy," answered Grigsby.

"I'd like to have Tony Mareno alive," said Major Scott; "he's the one that killed Frank McGhee."

"If he's around there wid Jimmy Cordie," said Red, reaching into a suitcase and producing a holstered Colt's and belt, "an' he starts anythin', the chances are ag'in' ye, Major, darlin'. For the love of all the good saints, look at me silk pajamas—all wrinkled an' dusty. May the devil fly away wid Jimmy Cordie for gittin' me in this—"

"Sing us the rest on the way, Red," said Putney. "What right has a flannel-mouthed mick from the north of Ireland to have silk pajamas?"

"Plenty," said Red, firmly. "Ye cross between a polecat an' a gibboon."

A MAN lay on the barn floor, dead; another outside the window of the box stall, with half his head blown off. Jimmy Cordie, crouching in the corner that commanded both the window and the door, ejected the empty shells and reached into the pocket of the much too big pants, pushed his hand further down, and withdrew it—empty

"Not so good," he said. "Most decidedly not so good; they wore a hole through when I crawled along under the house to the front that last time, I bet you. Well, three is a darn' sight better than none."

"What did you say, mister?" came a small voice from the other corner. "Do you think someone will come and—"

"I said, children, that the old man has been darn' careless in where he kept the reserve ammunition. Sure, someone will come and get us. In another minute a red-headed comet is going to come busting over the hill, four bells and a jingle. Don't—"

Two shots came from the darkness, and Cordie slipped forward on his face.

"Got him!" yelled someone. "Hey, Tony? Here's another dick to add to the collection."

"Bring him out here!" shouted Tony.

"I hope to hell the damn' sneakin' spy isn't dead. I want to—"

Cordie shot twice at the figures that loomed up in the doorway. They fell half way across into the stall.

"Tony!" he called, mockingly. "Oh, Tony, I've added two more to my own collection. Teach these tinkers not to believe all they see, you poor wop."

"What the hell is—my God!" Tony screamed. "He got Stan and Mike!" He went stark staring mad for a moment. "Burn it down!" he yelled. "Burn the rat with it! Burn it!"

"That's right," called Cordie. "Stand way back, Tony, so you won't get hurt, you yellow mission stiff. Why don't you come in and get me, you mongrel?"

The taunt steadied Tony for a moment.

"Wait with that burning stuff," he said, calmly. "Three of you go around back and break a way in. You two get over on the side and throw lead through that window. I'm going in and get this buzzard like he asks for!"

He slunk into the barn like a weasel would slink under a chickencoop and edged his way along the row of stalls to where the box stalls commenced. There was a patch of moonlight slanting across the floor about half way, and he stopped as he came to it.

"Here I am, you yeller sneak; come on out where I can see you!" he yelled.

"Where your whole army can see me, you mean," jeered Jimmy Cordie. "Send them back, and I'll come out."

"I knew you wouldn't," Tony yelled. "You—"

A burst of shots from the rear, the shouts of men in front, another volley of shots, the whiplash crack of the gangsters' automatics mingling with the heavy *pow—pow—pow* of the Colt's forty-fives in the hands of the U.S. deputy marshals, who had the death of two of their comrades to avenge. There was no asking or giving of quarter; the automatics cracked until the men shooting them went down.

Tony paid no attention; his drug-crazed brain held only one thought: to kill this dick who had flouted and burned him.

"Come out!" he yelled. "Come out and fight, you—"

"I'm coming, Tony," answered Cordie. "Get something in your hand, old-timer; I'm coming in the smoke."

Cordie's figure became outlined in the moonlight, and Tony fired twice. Cordie laughed and shot him through the heart.

Tony's first shot had drawn a thin line of blood on Cordie's head, just above the ear; his second had missed.

"Not so bad, old kid," Cordie said, looking down on what had been Scarface Tony Mareno, gang leader, "for a snowbird."

"Jimmie! Jimmy Cordie! Where the hell are ye?" Red Dolan came running into the barn, with Grigsby and Putney close behind him. "Did ye kill him, ye bloodthirsty shrimp?" he demanded, reproachfully. "An' the major wanted him alive. Did he hit you now, Jimmy, darlin'?"

"Creased me. Gee, I'm glad to see you birds."

"Let this be a lesson to ye," said Red, severely; "next time keep away from these owld service devils and save—"

"—me silk pajamas from getting all crushed," finished Grigsby for him.

"Ain't that somepin'," said Jimmy Cordie, grinning at Red.

III

ACCORDING TO MY SIZE
AND DISPOSITION

Here is another of those splendid yarns about Red Dolan, Jimmie Cordie and their hard-hitting buddies. And as usual, they tangle into some of the finest redhot fighting that you ever heard of— and this time a bit more than they figured on!

UP THE HILL charged the Chinese mob, led by the lieutenant of Kuan Chung.

It was met by the spanging .30-.30 Winchesters of the three white men, who had shot their way through the lieutenant's force when he had tried to seize them to the top of one of the gently sloping foothills. Back of them was the towering mountain; in front, the long slope to the woods.

It was a swift, silent charge, the swords and lances flickering in the hot sun. One or two of the officers had rifles, some of the men old trade guns, but the majority were armed with the weapons their ancestors had fought with, the long curved swords and lances.

If the charge was swift, the defense was equally so. The three big men were all veterans, all marksmen and all with chilled steel nerves. They shot to kill—and did with every bullet.

Before the charge had come a hundred feet the ground was dotted with fallen men. Kuan Chung's lieutenant fell in the first ten yards, a bullet in his heart. The rest came grimly on, scattering out, trying to avoid the death that came sleeting down on them.

"My gosh!" said Red Dolan, the largest of the three white men, as he reloaded. "These babies sure can eat lead. This is the—"

"Less talk and more shootin'. We got to stop 'em, boy—" said

Grigsby, beginning to shove shells in his own magazine as Red
raised his Winchester.

The steady "*pow-pow-pow!*" of the Winchesters, the falling
of a man at every report, broke the nerve of the Chinese, and
they turned and ran down the hill or sought cover where they
could find it.

"Ain't that somepin'?" demanded Red. "It was about time. I
only got about two rounds left."

"Use your Colt, you big ape," said Putney. "Then go and get
you one of those curved babies out there. I wish to hell, George,
that the next time you sign on to get a concession for that damn
English syndicate they'd pick out some other place besides
Hainan!"

"Yeah—an' the black curse of Crum'el be on ye, too, George
Grigsby," said Red Dolan, "for pullin' me away from me play—
an' me wid money not yet spent. Sure we should have waited
for Jimmie Cordie. If Jimmie was here now wid a machine gun
we'd slap these birds outta the way an' go on wid our knittin'!"

"Make it two curses," answered Grigsby, cheerfully. "You
better be gettin' your trigger finger oiled up, old settler. I'm down
to twenty shells myself. It'll be old man Colt, the next time."

"Ain't that somepin'?" mocked Putney, grinning at Red and
poking him in the ribs with the butt of his rifle. "How about
that, Red, old-timer?"

"Quit, ye divil. Have I not enough on me mind now wid

gettin' killed widout ye— Here they come! Give 'em hell an' make 'em like it!"

Once again the three rifles crashed out their song of death, but this time the Chinese came steadily on. Putney emptied his Winchester and drew his Colt forty-five, the heavy revolver rising and falling with the regularity of clock work.

Red Dolan was still using his Winchester, his blue eyes frosty and cold. Grigsby lay flat on the ground between them, shooting as calmly and coolly as if on the target range. They had fought side by side in the French Foreign Legion and then in the A.E.F., and for ten years after in the places where might still made right and the flash of sword and the whine of bullet decided supremacy.

One of the Chinese stopped, knelt and fired. Putney whirled around, sank to his knees, fired twice and fell.

Red Dolan snarled like an animal, dropped his Winchester, drew his Colt, shouted, "Come on, Grig, ye son of a sea cook! Show me something!" and started straight down the hill, his revolver roaring defiance and vengeance. Grigsby laughed, rose, dropped his rifle, drew his Colt, and started after Red. "I'll show you, you crazy ape!" he yelled.

The sight of the two big white men, heavy blued-steel revolvers spitting death, coming down on them, each man thinking he was the objective of the charge, was too much for the Chinese and they broke and ran a second time. The man who had shot Putney lay dead, a bullet in his heart from Red Dolan's forty-five.

Grigsby halted as they broke. "Red!" he shouted, "Red! Hold 'er! Back to the top! Red—you damn fool—come back! We got no chance down there. Hold 'er, Red!"

Red halted.

"I can lick all them—" he began.

"Yeah, I know. Let's get back. Come on, Red!"

"Whin I get one of these long babies," answered Red, picking up one of the swords, "I bet you—"

"Write a letter about it. Come on, Putt may be only wounded."

THEY went back up the hill to the little top. Putney lay where he had fallen, one side of his face apparently curtained in blood. Red knelt and gently lifted him up to his knee. As he did so, Putney stirred, then opened his eyes and shook his head as if to clear his vision. He blinked once or twice, looked up at Red and then at Grigsby.

"Where's the lovely blonde nurse that ought to be holding my hand and saying 'take this'?" he asked.

"Be content with the red-headed, homely one you've got," answered Grigsby, grimly, as he rose. "You damn near scared us to death, you big cheese!"

"I suppose it was my fault? I remember singing away and cracking down on a bird, then the next thing I know is that this red-headed baboon has me in his arms."

"Creased him," said Red, "and knocked him for a goal. Gimme that canteen, George, and I'll fix this delicate young lady up. He's— What the hell! Heads up—on the left!"

The two men faced a vicious charge around the side of a big rock, to the left and behind them. There was a rush of a dozen or more Chinese. Red emptied his Colt gun, threw it in the face of the closest man, stooped and picked up the curved sword. A lean, gray old swordsman sprang in to meet him, his sword darting in like a streak of blue light. It was a hard fast thrust— but it was met by a harder parry. Red stepped in and the iron hilt of his sword crashed between the eyes of his foe, and the Chinaman went down like a poled ox.

Grigsby's Colt was empty, and he was facing two men, the only ones left on their feet.

"Gimmie one!" shouted Red, heaving up the big longsword.

Grigsby's gun-butt came down on the head of one of them as he stepped inside of the wild swing of the swordsman, just as Red almost cut the other one in two.

"Ain't that somepin'?" demanded Red, looking down at the

body. "I'm goin' to keep one of these babies. I wish Jimmie was here, now. Bad luck to the scut for not bein' where he—"

"That bird almost got you," said Putney from where he sat, holding his head with both hands. "Don't you know how to parry a carte point, yet?"

"I did," defended Red, stoutly, "I parried it, me bucko—Hey! Look down the hill. Here comes an owld billy goat wid long gray whiskers and a million Chinks behind him. Look at 'em spreadin' out. Ain't that somepin'? And me wid six shells left in me pocket. 'Tis well I have me sword!"

"You should say 'me good sword,' you red-headed ape!" jeered Putney, staggering to his feet. "By gosh, I guess all Hainan has come to the funeral!"

A crashing and crumpling on the steep side of the wall behind them came from the brush and tangled second growth and the two men whirled to meet it.

Out of the thickest part, sliding the last twenty feet, came four Chinese, each with a square wooden box frantically clutched to his belly; right after them came a white man carrying part of a Colt machine gun the same way; after him, another with the rest of the gun.

"Jimmie!" yelled Red. "Jimmie, ye monkey faced scut! How the hell—"

"Gimmie room—" said the first white man, scrambling to his feet, "according to my size and disposition! Out of the way of a good man, you chimpanzee. Me and the Bean have arrived!"

"My God!" said Putney, weakly, "what do you know about—"

"Come on!" commanded Cordie. "Set this gun up. Come on Percival, kiss George after a while. Chase those Chinks down the hill, Red. Open me a box, Putt."

"Ain't that somepin'?" asked Red, as he started the last of the bearers down the hill. "How come—?"

"Never mind how come—tighten down on that screw. Come on, Algernon, put that belt on. Back away, gents, and watch your Uncle Jimmie play with the neighbor's children!"

" 'Tis time some wan played wid them," said Red. "They run us ragged. Here they come—mop up, Jimmie, darlin'."

THE CHARGE up the hill was made this time with more men than either time before, but did not last as long. Jimmie Cordie literally swept it out of existence—as a charge—with the machine gun. The Bean, whose name was John Cabot Winthrop, squatted down beside him and fed the gun, as he had done in France, ten years ago.

"Ain't that pretty?" asked Red, admiringly. "Knock off that baby over there on the left. The wan wid the nanny goat whiskers!"

"Are you tied?" demanded Jimmie Cordie, not looking up, "Do your own knocking off!"

What was left of the charge wavered, broke and ran, this time not stopping at the woods below.

"See!" said Jimmie Cordie. "Me and the bean-eater here can run the Chinese army anytime—can't we, Codfish?"

"We can," answered Winthrop, gravely, "and now, allow me to suggest, Mr. Good-shooter, that we go away from here before they get angry and come back and run us."

"That's a good idea," said Cordie with a grin, standing up. "Although I need no suggestions from buck privates. George, how come you birds jazzing off here without the old man along?"

"We hunted for you all over Hong Kong, you shrimp, and all we could get was 'No see—no see—clome aglain—maybeso see—'"

"My gosh," said Jimmie Cordie. "That was it, I bet you. I was holed up in old Yen Yuan's gardens, with dancing girls and everything and left word that I was not to be disturbed."

"What?" yelled Red. "The owld divil! 'Tis me he looked square in the eye and swore that he hadn't seen you for a month. Where do we go from here, George?"

"Well, I hate to go back without seeing Tsai Wo. I sent word ahead that I was coming to talk about a concession, but after getting jumped by his outfit, darned if I know. I thought Tsai Wo was the top man around here."

"**WHICH** shows that you ought to have waited for me," said Jimmie Cordie. "I could have told you that all Hainan is up and that your boy friend Tsai Wo is fighting Kuan Chung to see who is going to be cock of the walk. That was some of the Kuan Chung gang you were playing with. They probably thought you were reinforcements going to Tsai Wo."

"Listen to old man Cordie's son, Jimmie," scoffed Putney. "Who wised you up on Chinese politics, James?"

"Old Yen Yuan," answered Cordie with a grin. "He's high gazook in the T'aip'ings and—"

"Ye bloody highbinder," said Red. "What the hell are ye doin'—"

"Never mind, ape. He told me where you birds were heading for and where the launch was and all about it. What that bird don't get reported to him about any doings in this neck of the woods just naturally ain't—that's all."

"If you will allow me," said Winthrop, firmly, "I really must suggest that we get away from here as quickly as possible."

"We will not allow you," said Jimmie Cordie. "Since when have volunteers been allowed to suggest to regulars?"

"An' not only that," said Red, severely, "ye poor bean-eatin' piece of tripe from Bosting, since when had a machine-gun squadman the likes of ye the right to do any worrying wid officers around?"

"Listen, you damn idiots," interrupted Grigsby. "Cut the bushwah out for a minute. The bean-eating kid is right, we can't stay here. Either we go through to where Tsai Wo is, or shoot our way back to the launch."

"Why hurry?" demanded Cordie, lazily. "We will get all the fight we want, anyway or either way. Why not stay here until they settle it among themselves. Only thing is I don't want to see Percival here get killed until he's had some fun. Let's—"

"Never mind about me," said Winthrop, with a grin. "It's fun enough getting with you birds once more. I just as soon be killed here as anywhere else."

"Well, what to do?" asked Grigsby. "Personally, I say to go through to Tsai Wo, wherever he is."

"Whatever Jimmie says, suits me," said Red Dolan. "Though how the—"

"All right—we'll go through," said Grigsby. "Who's going to pack those ammunition boxes? How many .30-.30 shells you two got? I see you've got about a hundred Colt forty-fives."

"I got two boxes not opened, and what I got in her. How many you got, Beany?"

"I put four boxes in my pockets and some loose ones, about a hundred and twenty, I think."

"Good enough, split 'em up between us. Who's going to carry the boxes?"

"Not Beany or me," said Jimmie Cordie, firmly. "They weigh a hundred apiece. We brought 'em here. Load 'em on Red, he's the biggest."

"You brought 'em!" yelled Red. "Ye mean that ye had Chinks to carry 'em and where ye got them, I dunno. Put them on Red, he says, sure—"

"Hold 'er," said Cordie. "That gives General Cordie an idea. We caught those four birds and by gosh we can catch some more—can't we, Bean? Sit tight in the shade, gentlemen, and me and my friend from the codfish center will go and round up some more. Come on, old-timer. Leave your rifle here, we may have to do some running."

"It is very probable we will," said Winthrop, getting up from the box he had been sitting on. "But rather than carry one of those darn things, I'll do some."

"My gosh," said Red Dolan, after Jimmie Cordie and Winthrop had disappeared around the big boulder to the right. "That divil will go anywhere and get anything. Where the hell did he pick up Beany now, I dunno?"

"You've asked and answered your own question," said Grigsby, grinning at the big Irishman.

AROUND the boulder, an hour later, came a little procession. First four Chinese, in nondescript rag-tag uniforms, then Jimmie Cordie and Winthrop, forty-fives in their hands.

"We got them," announced Jimmie with a grin. "These gents insist they are tired of fighting for Kuan Chung and want to enlist in our S.O.S. department." He waved to the four boxes with his Colt, and the four Chinese, with an air of resignation, each hoisted one to his shoulder. "I also found out where Tsai Wo is," said Cordie.

"Yeah? Now, how the hell could ye do that and ye not talkin' Chink talk?" demanded Red.

"Me? You're goofy, boy. I'm a Chinese scholar and what I don't know, the Duke of Massachusetts does. Watch me closely!" He poked the muzzle of his Colt in the ribs of one of the Chinese, who shrank back and almost dropped the box. "Tsai Wo?" questioned Jimmie, sternly.

"Wenchau," the Chinaman quavered.

"Which way?" demanded Jimmie, waving his left arm around.

The Chinaman pointed to the right with his free hand.

"See?" asked Jimmie. "Want me to ask him something else?"

"That's plenty to demonstrate your ability," said Grigsby. "We'll hit it about night and make a play to get in to Tsai Wo."

One of the Chinese seemed to be trying to arrive at a decision; he opened his mouth, then closed it, nodded his head once or twice, then opened his mouth again.

"Me top slide boy, Hong Klong club," he announced. "Know Wenchau likee dlamn. We go—" and he pointed to Jimmie, "—he no shootee?"

"Yeah?" said Grigsby. "Top side boy at the Hong Kong club, were you? All right, you take us to Wenchau and Tsai Wo and this man no shootee."

"Velly good, Claptain," said the Chinaman, cheerfully. "No shootee fliends?"

"No, no shootee friends either. Get going," assured Grigsby.

JUST as dawn was breaking, Tsai Wo sat in the audience chamber of his palace, his officers and bodyguard about him. He had spent the night strengthening the defenses of his city against Kuan Chung whom he knew would attack at dawn.

In front of him stood Grigsby and the rest, the four Chinese behind them with the boxes and machine gun. They now considered themselves part of the outfit and looked at the assembled followers of Tsai Wo with insolent eyes. Were they not the bearers for the white men who killed and laughed and were not afraid?

"I am told," said Tsai Wo, in perfect, precise English, "that you came to the south gate of my city and demanded audience. What is it you want?"

"The Clougher syndicate of England sent me," answered Grigsby. "To talk to you about a concession to work the gold fields of Hainan."

Tsai Wo smiled grimly.

"You come at an opportune time to talk about concessions when I am fighting for my life against odds. I know your syndicate. I was for five years the secretary of the embassy in London. Yet," he paused and looked at the five white men and the machine gun, at their equipment and at their calm confident faces, "you are all men who have seen much military service?"

"Yes, we were with the American forces in the last war," answered Grigsby. He did not think it worth while to mention the fact that they had been in the Legion before that, and had been fighting ever since.

"I see you have a machine gun. My men tell me that Kuan Chung has one also. You come for a concession to work the gold fields? Help me with Kuan Chung, and the concession is yours—if we win!"

"We'll be very glad to help you," said Grigsby, "and—"

Jimmie Cordie stepped up beside him.

"Yen Yuan asked me to say to you, 'The faults of a Prince are like the darkening of the sun or moon. The fault is seen of all and when he breaks free—all men admire.'"

Tsai Wo's eyes widened and one or two of the officers behind him stirred, and sucked in their breath. He rose from his chair. "If you will honor my insignificant self," he said, "and assist me in killing the tiger at my door, all that I have is yours to command."

"Ain't that somepin'?" demanded Red in a stage whisper to Putney, "now where does the little divil get that stuff?"

"Pipe down!" answered Putney, "I want to hear."

TOPPING the roof of the palace, muzzle between two of the stones of the coping, commanding the south gate and the square in front, was a machine gun manned by Jimmie Cordie and Winthrop. Putney, Grigsby and Red Dolan were at the corners, their Winchesters taking care of any snipers on the roofs below.

Inside the walls, on three sides, the fight boiled and eddied. Kuan Chung's men had taken the northern gate before noon and now his men were in the city on three sides, fighting their way slowly towards the palace and the southern gate, met at every yard by the swordsmen and guns of Tsai Wo.

It was hard, desperate fighting, with no quarter. Tsai Wo had asked them to keep the south gate and square clear that he might not be taken in the rear, and was himself in the thick of the fight. Twice bodies of Kuan Chung's men had broken through the defense of the southern gate, only to be picked up and annihilated by the fire of the machine gun. From side streets leading into the square, his troops had charged time and again, trying to get possession of the square and palace, but the deadly little gun barred their way.

"Tsai Wo better be mopping up darn soon," announced Jimmie Cordie, during a lull. "This baby is going out of commission pretty soon. She darn near jammed on me the last round."

"They got him on three sides now," answered Grigsby. "Knock that bird off that roof to the left, Putt, he's getting the range!"

"Ain't that somepin'?" asked Red. "If that guy don't win, what becomes of us?"

"Depends on the life you've led," said Winthrop. "Gimme a pill, one of you guys."

"Listen to that language from the Bean," jeered Putney. "He's reverted to type all right."

"And that reminds me," said Red, tossing a package of cigarettes over to Winthrop. "How come you buttin' in on our party, ye piece of brown bread widout butter?"

"Butt in is good," said Jimmie Cordie, cleaning the gun, lovingly. "The Boston Bean here cried himself in. I was down by the dock waiting for one of Yen Yuan's launches that he'd loaned me to come and rescue you birds, when a cutter came along from a yacht almost as big as a liner that was in the harbor. Who's sitting in the stern, all dressed up in a blue coat and white pants and everything, but the gent you see now sitting beside me with the dirty hands and face. He sees me on the dock, lets out a wild yell of joy, knocks eight of the cutter crew into the water, jumps overboard, swims to the dock and—"

"Why the hell," said Red Dolan, "you don't try tellin' the truth once in a while I dunno."

"Well," answered Jimmie, "I may have exaggerated the last part a little, but anyway he saw me and when he heard that I was going to you hyenas he cried so hard that I had to bring him—didn't I, Brown-bread?"

"What ever you say," answered Winthrop, grinning.

"What the hell right have ye to have a yacht?" demanded Red. "The last time I saw ye didn't ye get five francs offen me for a bottle of cooney-act?"

"Well, I couldn't help it," defended Winthrop. "My father left it to me and I—"

"Listen to them down there," said Putney. "It sounds like

they were getting down to cases. We'll know who's who darn soon now!"

"They must be ganging up for the finals," answered Grigsby. "Not a soul in sight."

"Which makes the case more deadly," said Cordie, cheerfully, squinting along his gun. "They're framing something on us, I bet you. This is a fine place for me to be on account of you damn idiots. There I was in Yen Yuan's gardens, with everything I wanted and here I am on top of a roof waiting to be killed."

"And that is somepin' else," said Red. "How the divil do you come so thick wid that old hellion that near is the boss of Hong Kong?"

"Me? I'm his buddy."

"Ye are like hell," scoffed Red.

"I am, you red-headed baboon, I bet you. He's the head of the T'aip'ings and says that I am his son—laugh that off!"

"They're bad medicine, Jimmie," said Grigsby, from where he stood looking down on the square.

"Not for me," answered Jimmie, cheerfully. "Me and Yen Yuan are top cutters in that outfit."

"What," shouted Red. "You're a lyin' son—"

"I am not. Anyway he is, and what he is—I am!"

"Listen, Jimmie," said Putney. "You are sure going to hell in about five minutes. What do you want to lie like that for."

"I'm not lying. When Boston Tech had the honor of my presence in—"

"As janitor!" interposed Putney.

"There was a Chinese student there," went on Cordie, paying no attention to Putney, "and he got sick and his money hadn't arrived for the month. He had typhoid fever and I gave him a hand, that's all. His pa is Yen Yuan and he thinks I saved his son's life. What ever I wants, he gets for me."

"Well, get him to—"

A burst of machine gun bullets from a roof to the right, about three hundred yards away suddenly sprayed the stone coping and whistled above their heads, then swept to the side, then back again. Putney, Grigsby and Red Dolan promptly rolled to cover.

Winthrop knelt beside Jimmie Cordie who sent a stream of steel jacketed bullets at the house the fire had come from. He searched every window and opening with bullets, probing them as a surgeon would a wound.

The other gun did not reply as quickly.

"That's the Fightin' Yid on that gun, I bet you," Jimmie said. "I know that baby. He never could hold a gun on the spot for more than a second. I was with him in—"

"You and the bean-eater play with him then, if he's a friend of yours," said Grigsby. "Come on, you two, let's get down and see if we can't take him from the rear. If we let him stay there we're holed up."

"Don't hurt him if it's the Yid," called Jimmie Cordie. "He don't know it's us he's shooting at."

"Ain't that somepin'?" said Red Dolan, crawling along the roof after the others. "If that bird knows it's us whin I get me hands on him he'll wish he never left Jerusalem."

"Why isn't he working her, Jimmie?" asked Winthrop, after they had gone.

"Because, dumb-bell, she's probably jammed on him. He was shooting too fast to last long, the last time. Here they come again!"

THE ATTACK came from all sides, men pouring out from the streets and a large body from the wrecked south gate.

"Heaven send that gun of his stay jammed for a minute," said Jimmie Cordie, as he started firing. "We'll clean up on this side, then take her over. Come on with those—"

The *rat-tat-rat-tat* of the other gun began again. This time the bullets swept the top of the coping in a continual stream. Winthrop laughed.

"Boy howdy, when we take her over he'll get us sure!"

"What do you care?" asked Cordie, his gun sending a rain of death into the now crowded square. "Come on, feed me!"

Suddenly the other gun ceased firing and the men of Tsai Wo appeared, cutting their way through the foes in front of them.

"Come on, Bean," said Cordie. "Now we go. Lift, you poor feeble codfish! That's the boy. Come on—over to the other side! Hot damn, look at them come!"

As Jimmie Cordie opened fire a body of Tsai Wo's men came around the flank and in five minutes it was over, those of Kuan Chung's men left alive were running for the south gate.

A noise on the roof behind them made them whirl, their Colts in their hands. Then the guns were reholstered. First came a little fat Jew, his eyes popping almost out of his head, carrying part of a Maxim, then three Chinese with parts and boxes. Behind them came Red Dolan, his Colt drawn, a ferocious expression on his face.

The little fat Jew saw Jimmie Cordie and dropped the part he was carrying. "Oi—Jimmie!" he yelled. "Oi, such a business! I didn't know it was you, Jimmie! Make this big Irish bum quit pointing that gat at me! He's liable to twitch the fingare!"

"Put that gun up, Red," commanded Jimmie Cordie, firmly. "I knew it was you, Yid, by the way that gun was working. How come you fighting us?"

"George and Putt are down below," said Red, "wid Tsai Wo moppin' up and George says for ye to keep the Fightin' Yid up here wid ye if ye want to save him for anything. I'm goin' to take wan poke at him for damn near killin' me."

"Prisoner of war," said Cordie. "Nothing doing. Come over here, Abie and sit down and tell me how come."

"Kuan Chung hired me in Hong Kong to fight the Maxim for him," said the Fighting Yid, with a grin. "I fight it and all of a sudden ven I don't know who the hell's got the other gun, it rains big Irish bums on top of me and ve get captured. Jimmie, in France once I gave you some help—vell, now you give me some, ain't it?"

"It ain't," said Jimmie Cordie, promptly. "I'm going to have Tsai Wo give you the slicing death. All fighting Yids get that because when a Yid is a fighter, he's a bearcat and better get him out of the way."

"Ain't that somepin'?" demanded Red Dolan. "Have ye anythin' on yer hip, Abie darlin', now that the war is over?"

"I have," said the Fighting Yid, reaching for an inside pocket. "Ve'll all take von, ain't it?"

TSAI WO sat once more in his hall, this time alone with the men who had helped him hold his city.

"This man who fought with Kuan Chung and the Chinese with him," he said to Jimmie Cordie, "is yours—to do with as you please. I know the Clougher syndicate that you represent," he went on to Grigsby, "and I will sign the necessary papers for the concession when they are presented to me. I will send an escort to the coast with you—although," he added, with a grim smile, "I do not think you need one!" He turned to Cordie again. "You will not stay here with me for a little while?"

"I'll come some other time," answered Jimmie Cordie, with a grin. "Just now I've got to put this gentleman back on a yacht."

"You haven't," said Winthrop, promptly. "I'm going to send it home and stick around with you birds."

Tsai Wo smiled. "If I were thirty years younger, I would like to—stick around myself!" he said.

On the way back to the coast Red came up to where Jimmie Cordie was walking with the Fighting Yid. "Hey, Jimmie," he said, "that message ye delivered to Tsai Wo from owld Yen Yuan, what was it?"

"Darned if I know. It was a quotation from Confucius, I know that. Maybeso they belong to the same gang and Yen Yuan was tipping him off that he was backing him up. How did Yen Yuan know where you birds were and where the launch was, tell me that."

"I dunno, Jimmie, how did he? Maybe this guy—now—Confucius, told him."

"Confucius! Boy, that baby's been—" Jimmie Cordie stopped and grinned at the big fighting Irishman. "Maybe he did, Red, old-timer," he added, gravely, "I'll ask him when we get back."

IV

PRIVATE PROPERTY

Three comrades who had seen a lot of action together undertook a Chinese venture to get possession of a vase of fabulous value and found out what American education could do for a Chinese gentleman and his family.

THE TRIM WHITE launch nosed its way along the canal running inland from Kwang-Chau bay on to the South China Sea. Jimmie Cordie stood at the bow, a long pole in his hands, sounding the depth. "By the mark—six; by the mark—five; by the mark—no bottom," he chanted. "By the mark— Hey, you birds, look at that gibboon! He's Red's long lost pappy, I bet you. By the mark—hold 'er, George, she's getting shallow. All right, six foot again, my Gosh, look at that big python—knock him off, Red."

"What are you trying to do—tell all Hainan we're around?" called Grigsby from the engine. "Less wah-wah and more attention to depth."

"Who, me? I can be pilot and talk at the same time. Us Chinese scholars must emote.

"*The bright sun completes its course behind the mountains— Seven.

"*The yellow river flows away into the sea—Seven.

"*Would you command the prospect of a thousand li?—No bottom.

"*Climb yet one story higher—Six.*

"How's that for Chink poetry, you red-headed ringtailed monkey from Cork? No bottom. That was written a thousand years before Christ and—"

"You'll be climbin' wan story higher wid a spear in the ribs if ye don't hush that noise," said the big brawny Irishman sitting

71

forward beside a Browing machine gun covered with an oiled rubber jacket.

"Or several stories lower," said Putney from the stern. "Watch your step, Jimmie. These old canals lose depth darn sudden."

"This one is getting deeper. I bet you that around the bend it'll be a regular lake—seven. What I am doing here with you pirates instead of— Heads up, look who's here!"

The canal had suddenly widened out into a lake of about twenty acres.

AHEAD of them and on both sides were sampans and rafts of bamboo—filled with Chinese. Back of them at the canal mouth, rafts were being launched and as soon as in the water, crowded with Chinese, with long curved swords and sawtooth spears.

Grigsby ran the little launch to about the middle of the lake. "Drop the anchor, Jimmie," he said. "No use trying to do any maneuvering. We'll take what they can give us right here. Putt and I'll take the stern."

"Keep your heads down then," said Cordie cheerfully. "This baby hasn't much clearance. I'll try and shoot between you."

"Try and shoot," echoed Putney. "You better, boy or—"

"Old man Putney's son Archibald will join the angel chorus," finished Jimmie for him. All four laughed.

They had fought together now for ten years, all over the Orient in the places where the old, old rule of might makes right still held sway. Before that, for three years, they had faced death in the Foreign Legion and later in the A.E.F.

"My Gosh!" said Red Dolan, standing up. "We musta got here on a day when all the laundries were on strike. Look at the old lad, Jimmie, wid the long mustaches hangin down, ain't he pretty?"

"Handsome is as handsome does," answered Cordie, swinging Browning idly around in a half circle. "Wait till my baby here gets to talking to 'em. Gimmie me room according to my size and disposition."

"Which is that of a shrimp and a copperhead," grinned Putney. "For Pete's sake, Jimmie, be careful with that thing. What are they waiting for, George?"

"Get down and let me try 'er," said Cordie. "Bet you I can clean those rafts with one round, Red."

"Why not—wid 'em packed that way? I can meself wid a Colts from here, I'll bet."

"Steady," said Grigsby. "Here comes a flag of truce. Keep that gun still, Jimmie."

" 'Tis the old bird with the pigtails in front," said Red. "Look at 'im, sitting on the raft in a chair, fanning himself wid a fan. Sure, Jimmie an me will fan ye, wid lead, me bucko."

THE RAFT poled by six brawny Chinese came to within ten feet of the launch. The Chinese, a fat middle-aged man with a cruel scarred face and little slanting black eyes, set close together, sat in the carved chair under an umbrella, held over him by a man behind.

He looked at the white men and the launch calmly, his face impassive.

"Watch behind you, Putt," said Grigsby. "And you in front, Jimmie. Cut loose at the first move. These babies are rattlers to play with."

"But, at least, they will respect a flag of truce," the Chinaman said calmly in perfect English.

Grigsby laughed. "As they did at Ching-hai and Szech'uan and Yaun-ming-yuan."

"You were there?" questioned the Chinaman, his eyes widening a little.

"Under General K'anghsi. We fought the machine gun for him."

"They were very well fought, killing thousands of General Fei's men. You are American?"

"All but this red-headed ape," said Jimmie Cordie, who with Red was leaning over the Browning. "He is a ringtailed monkey from Borneo and born in a tree."

The Chinaman looked at him gravely. "It pleases you to be facetious. It may please you more to know that you will shortly die by Lingeh'ih."

"Ah, so's your old man," said Red Dolan. "Who might you be and wadda you mean by comin' out here and callin' us names? Get back now before I lose me temper and—"

"I'll attend to this," said Grigsby. "You birds pipe down." Then to the Chinaman, "You have been in America?"

"Yes, at Johns Hopkins. That is the reason I came out to talk to you and see if it might be possible to save your lives. What are you doing here? You are armed in Chinese territory."

"Well," said Grigsby. "I'll tell you—"

"What did he call us, Jimmie?" asked Red, as Grigsby began to speak.

"Nothing, dumb-bell. He said we were facetious."

"That's it—an' to me face, the big piece of cheese."

"It means that we were kidding him, Red. Shut up I want to hear George."

"For a vase," Grigsby was saying. "Incidentally you better wave back some of your outfit, they seem to be inching in a little. That is, if you want to live yourself any longer," and the muzzle of the thirty-thirty in the crook of Grigsby's arm came directly in a line with the Chinaman's heart.

HE STOOD up and looked around at the crowded shoreline, that seemed to be a surging mass of men and boats. "They are impatient," he said coldly, "to begin; but they know better than to start—"

He raised his fan and motioned backward with it and the surge grew still.

"We were sent to get a bronze vase," Grigsby repeated calmly, "from the Temple there on the hill. If you will pull your men back and keep out of our way there will be no one hurt."

The Chinaman looked at him in astonishment, then laughed. "You Americans! You lie here in this little boat surrounded by a thousand swordsmen, with death staring you in the face and you say that—to me?"

"Aw," said Red Dolan, "what's all this wah-wah about. Tell 'im to go back an cut his wolf loose, George."

The Chinaman looked at Red steadily. "You are a big man," he said, "and will take a long time to die."

"Ain't that somepin," said Red in amazement. "What do you want to pick on me for? Go on back to the laundry before I slap you off that chair."

"I think," said Grigsby, "that the best thing you can do, Mr.—whatever your name is is, to go back to your outfit and take them over in the woods somewhere and start a pinocle game if you want to have them all in one piece."

The Chinaman laughed again. "You think so," he said. "I will give orders for you to be taken alive if possible. You will afford me much amusement."

"Yeah," called Red, as the raft started back. "Come and get it anytime."

THE CHINESE attack was swift and deadly but it met a defense equally so. The Browning, operated by Jimmie Cordie and Red Dolan swept the rafts clear of men, the sampan oarsmen and helmsmen going down under the thirty-thirty's of Grigsby and Putney.

The trim little launch lay in the center as deadly as a diamond backed rattler and as poisonous. For a space of two hundred yards in a circle the water was clear, beyond that, it was a welter of rafts and sampans with bodies lying in grotesque positions on them and with men trying to swim ashore.

Beyond to the shore the boats and rafts were in motion, the leaders trying to get their men to attack the little white boat that had looked to be such easy prey.

They came on again—to meet a sheet of steel-jacketed bullets sent to greet them by men who were all entitled to wear the distinguished marksman cross.

There was no mercy shown. It was cold, deliberate, accurate shooting by veterans and the Chinese melted away. The few guns they had did no damage—the owner would put it to his shoulder and shut his eyes and pull the trigger. Generally the ball hit among the trees or went over them.

"Aw, hell!" said Red Dolan. "You don't suppose they've quit already, do you? I thought these Chinks could—look—coming up the canal. Heads down, you birds; cut her loose, Jimmie, old kid!"

UP THE CANAL came a flotilla of sampans, loaded almost to the sinking point with Chinese, a Chinaman with a yellow girdle around his waist in the bow of the first one.

"Hot damn!" said Cordie. "Here comes the daddy of 'em all. That's an Imperial Clansmen. Watch me make his yellow sash red."

This time the attack came from all sides at once. Instead of isolated attempts by three or four rafts or sampans to reach the launch, there was a surge forward of all crafts.

The little launch lay there in the center like Grenville's ship, the *Revenge*, when she fought the Spanish men of war and spit defiance. It was a ceaseless slaughter. The body of the man with the yellow sash hung over the the bow of the sampan that continued to charge straight at the launch.

"Swing her around, Jimmie," called Grigsby. "We can't hold 'em with—that's the boy, that's washing the decks. All right—we can handle 'em now."

It stopped suddenly; what few sampans or rafts that were manned, were fleeing to the shore, being beached and the men disappearing in the jungle…

"Ain't that somepin?" asked Red Dolan, standing up. "Boy we sure mopped up on those babies. Jimmie, what did ye say that bird that's hanging over the bow there was, wid the yellow belt?'

"An Imperial Clansmen," said Cordie, beginning to clean the Browning.

"Clansman is it? Sure I'll—"

"Not the kind you mean, you poor nitwit. That means he's related to the Emperor."

"Which is not so good," said Putney. "There will be hell popping now, no fooling. They don't mind a few of these poor whites but when it comes to knocking off the Emperor's relations, not so good."

"Any kind," said Red firmly. "They all look alike to me. Sure now, Jimmie, why didn't ye leave me take a shot at him, ye cross between a chimpanzee and a hyena?"

"Aw, shut up, why didn't you, instead of going to sleep and letting me do all the work as usual?"

"Yeah? For wan cent now, Jimmie Cordie, I'd knock the can off ye."

"You and what other four micks?" demanded Cordie promptly. He was the smallest of the four but the best shot and what he didn't have in size he made up in chilled steel nerve.

"Conduct your private war outside," commanded Grigsby. "Do you damn fools think this is a time to start playing?"

"Jimmie and me was only foolin'," placated Dolan. "Wasn't we, Jimmie darlin'?" and the big Irishman, whose eyes had been a cold steel blue during the fighting and who feared nothing on earth, grinned at Cordie, who grinned back.

"Let's mop up on George, Red, for interfering with our childish amusements. He's been getting uppity for a long time now."

"Let that job out on contract," said Grigsby. "We better be getting out of here while the going is good. That's the temple up there on the hill."

"Is there a path from the lake, George?" asked Red Dolan.

"The map says so but it doesn't look very nourishing at the minute to try and walk up it. These birds have quit playing with us on the water but it's a cinch that they're ganged up on land."

"Let me call your attention to the fact, Gineril," said Cordie, "that the longer we stay here wah-wahing about it, the more ganging they can do."

"Ain't that somepin?" seconded Red. "Let's point the nose of this hooker at the temple and hit the nearest spot an' then go an' get the damn vase or what the hell ever it is."

"An' then come back an find the launch gone," jeered Putney. "As a strategist you're a fine machine gunner."

"What of it?" demanded Red. "The lake is full of boats, ain't it? We get the vase now, an' come back an' get us wan of these here sampans an' go on wid our knittin'."

"Write a letter about it," said Grigsby. "Pull up the anchor, Jimmie. We'll go back down the canal, as if we were heading for home with our belly full, then when we get around the bend a mile or so we'll pull into that little bayou where Jimmie saw the snake. Jimmie can stay with the launch, being the artillery expert and we'll go and get the vase."

"Well, I'm a son of a gun," objected Cordie, as the anchor came on the bow. "And supposin' you birds gets jumped by the John Hopkins gent that didn't show up after he went back, what then?"

"Why then, James, young feller me lad," said Grigsby cheerfully, "it behooves you to start this warship for the bay of Kwang-chau pronto and in haste."

"Yeah? Well, if you leave me all alone with that big snake, I'll do that little thing soon as you're out of sight, you big apes."

"That looks like the place, George," said Putney a few minutes later. "Swing over to the left."

THE LAUNCH swung idly in the middle of the little bayou, screened from the canal by the heavy, tropical growth along the banks. Jimmie Cordie sat in the stern, a 30-30 Winchester across his knees. The others had been gone two hours. There had been no sound of shots or trouble of any kind.

"It may be," he said aloud, "that those apes got—"

A girl, hardly more than a child burst through the jungle tangle at the edge, her little silk smock torn and bloody and the high satin boots on her feet muddy and ripped. She saw Cordie and the launch and held out her arms in an appealing gesture, then fell, rose and started to run along the shore towards him.

"On that tree trunk," Cordie shouted, pointing to a fallen tree that lay out in the water twenty odd feet. The girl turned and ran towards it, her breath coming in labored gasps. She was a very pretty girl, with long blue black hair, and dark blue eyes, and skin like a magnolia blossom.

Cordie started the launch and nosed it up against the tree. The child ran down the trunk and half jumped and half fell into the bow.

"Quick," she gasped. "Save them. Oh—save them! Li Kwojui has them—my little sister and— Oh, please come and—"

"Come where?" asked Cordie, backing off into the middle again. "Of course I'll save them. Where are they?"

"Li Kwojui has them, I tell you! Quick! He will kill them! See," and she touched her bloody smock, "he beat me with bamboo rods because I wouldn't— Oh—hurry! He has taken them to the temple."

"The quickest way to the temple is by the lake," said Cordie. "Don't worry, we'll get them all right. How come you?"

"We heard the shooting at the lake—my father's a missionary—we were hiding—they drove us from Laichau—we heard the shots—my father and my sister and I— Oh, please do something!

"I'm doing 'er, right now," Cordie answered. "Calm down— you're all right and so'll they be in a few minutes."

HE HEADED the launch out of the bayou. Just at the entrance he slowed down. "Better cover that Browning," he said, cutting off the engine.

"Hand me that cover," and he pointed to the oiled rubber jacket.

"This?" the girl said, picking it up. "Oh, please hurry!"

"I will," said Jimmie Cordie, taking the cover from her, "although—" And he enveloped her head and shoulders with the jacket. Holding her in a grip of steel, he laid her gently down in the launch amid ships. With a coil of rope hanging by the engine, he bound her little feet, then took a couple of turns around her waist, binding her arms to her side, utterly oblivious to the shouting and commotion on the bank.

He jerked the cover off her head and stood up. There on the bank were several Chinese, their long curved swords waving frantically, running up and down, trying to find some way of reaching the launch, a hundred yards from shore. In the water, swimming desperately, their swords held in their mouths, four Chinese were more than half way.

"I'm surprised at Doc," Jimmie Cordie said cheerfully as he drew his Colt's forty-five. "He—*pow*—ought—*pow*—to know better—*pow*—*pow*," and the four heads went under in a bloody swirl. He calmly holstered the Colt's and reached for his Winchester. The Chinese on the bank hesitated for a second, then jumped for cover—not soon enough for one of them, who lay sprawled out, a 30-30 bullet in his brain.

"An' that's that," said Cordie, turning to the girl. She had struggled to a sitting position, and her eyes flashed defiance. "The next time Doc sends his girl friends to talk about being beaten with bamboo rods he should see that their faces were drained of blood and their lips gray," he added severely. "And him a John Hopkins man—double shame on him. I hope I didn't hurt you when—"

"You dog," the girl spat at him. "You dare to touch me and my father—"

"The missionary?" questioned Cordie politely, sitting down by the Browning and rolling a cigarette.

"Li Kwojui," the girl said proudly. "He will give you the slicing death if you dare—"

"It's catching before hanging," said Cordie with a grin. "I'll bet your ma came from Kentuck. My, such a temper!"

"You—she—let me go at once. You can't get away. My father has taken your—"

The sounds of shots came from the canal outside, faint but getting steadily louder.

"That sounds as if they had bit your pa and ran away," said Cordie, starting the engine and running the launch's nose out in the entrance of the canal. "Would you mind working the machine gun while I steer?"

The girl gasped and began to talk to him in mixed Chinese and English.

"I gather that you won't," said Cordie, grinning. "Well, I don't see how I can be a whole machine gun squad and crew at the same time."

He ran the launch out into the canal and along one side, the further one, and pointed it up stream, dropping the anchor. "Keep your head down, Sissy," he said, going to the Browning, "or your pa is liable never to see his daughter Delilah again."

The shots were getting closer now and the shouts of frantic men in Chinese. Around the bend in the canal swept a small sampan. Grigsby was in the bow with one pole, Putney in the stern with another. Red Dolan was kneeling beside Putney, his Winchester throwing a stream of steel jacketed bullets, every one of which found its mark in the crowded sampans not a hundred yards behind them. On the covered stern beside him lay the crumpled figure of a big Chinaman. Putney and Grigsby were poling with all the power of their big brawny bodies and the little sampan was leaping forward at every shove.

JIMMIE CORDIE rose as they swept by. "Hot damn!" he yelled. "You win in a walk! That's racing 'em old kid. Rah! Rah,

Rah! Pontiac Reform School, sis! boom! bah!" And he bent to
the machine gun which began to send a *rat-ta-rat-tat-r-r-r-
r-*of death into the crowded sampans behind.

Red Dolan jumped to the launch as the sampan swerved in.
"Gimme my bums," he shouted. "I'll learn these—" and he dived
for a little storage compartment under the stern seat. "What
the hell now?" he gasped, as he almost fell over the girl. "Did I
hurt ye now, alanna? Jimmy, what—?"

"Come on," shouted Cordie. "I can't hold 'em! Get that big
baby coming."

Red jerked open the door of the compartment, reached in
and stood up, two Mills hand grenades in his hand. A big
sampan, with several dead men in it but still crowded with living
ones, was almost up to the launch when he threw. The bomb
literally tore the Chinese on the sampan to pieces and it drifted
by.

All that was left of the rest of the pursuit was in full retreat
up the canal.

"Be more careful with those damn things," said Cordie, severely. "You didn't count three before you let them go, you big
stiff. You counted ten, I bet."

"I didn't count at all," defended Red. "I held them until I
knew it was time to let them go an' I did that little thing."

"You did," said Cordie grimly, "an' one more split second and
we'd have got it instead of your little playmates."

THE SAMPAN with Grigsby and Putney nosed alongside.

"Here's your boy friend, Red," said Putney. "Were you saving
him for anything?"

The big Chinaman was sitting up, holding his head with
both hands. "Why, Doc!" said Jimmie Cordie. "How come you
here? Come on board, Doc; Miss Doc got here safely a little
while ago."

The Chinaman let go his head and staggered to his feet; he
saw the girl sitting amidships, her hands and arms still bound

and his eyes widened. "Oh, my God!" he said and promptly sat down again.

"Serves you right," said Jimmie Cordie viciously. "You big hunk of nothing—to send a girl to—"

"What!" the Chinaman yelled. "I—send a girl—my own daughter! I thought she was safe at home with her mother, you—you—is she—have you—?"

"An' you at Johns Hopkins for years," said Jimmie Cordie. "If you don't know Americans any better that that, Doc, it's a good thing—"

Grigsby had been untying the girl who, once she was free, had jumped up, clambered out of the launch and thrown her arm around her father, kneeling on the deck beside him. She glared at Jimmie and slowly and distinctly, wrinkled her very pretty nose and ran her little red tongue out at him. The four men laughed—she was only a little girl after all.

"Now I know your ma came from Kentucky and was red headed," Cordie teased, grinning at her.

"Sure now, acushla," said Red Dolan "'tis all right ye are, leave it to owld Red Dolan."

"You birds watch that canal bend," said Grigsby, "while Mr.— while Doc and I talk this thing over. Help him down here, Red. Don't worry, honey"—to the girl. "We aren't going to hurt him at all. In a few minutes you'll be going home with him."

"Come on down and make friends," Jimmie Cordie coaxed. "Think how gently I tied you up and fitted that cap on you. I'll show you how to work this gun, if you will, while your pa is talking."

"You—" the girl flared. "I—" Then she stopped and looked at Red Dolan and Jimmie Cordie, who were both smiling at her.

"Well," she said, "I shouldn't after the way you—" But she held out her little rounded arms for Red to help her into the launch.

"Did you really try to capture me for yourself," Cordie teased, a little later as Grigsby and the big Chinaman were still in close conference at the stern.

"My daddy didn't know I was anywhere around," she confessed. "But I heard the fighting from my garden and I ran down and hid behind a big tree and then when the little white boat went back along the canal I made Kweiliang and some of his men come along with me. I—I wanted it," she confessed. "Then Kweiliang said that if I took off my clothes all but my smock and let him make it bloody with that blood of a pheasant that I could fool you. Then I'd have the boat. He's dead now and—I like fighting."

"Why, you darn little pirate," said Jimmie Cordie. "Your ma come from the Malay chief pirate family, I bet you, instead of from Kentucky."

"She did not, Mister Smarty. She came from Alabama."

GRIGSBY called Cordie and Red Dolan back to the stern, Putney going to the bow.

"Here it is, Jimmie. We didn't make it to the temple. Doc here and his merry men jumped us as we skirted the shore of the lake and darn near mopped up. If Doc hadn't got a little ambitious and led a force to take us in the rear just as we decided to make a rearward movement, he might have nailed our hides to the barn door. As it was, he couldn't get out of the way quick enough and Red creased him with a 30-30. We got on the first thing that was handy and Red brought him along for some unknown reason. Now we've got him, he belongs to Red, and we've got the girl, too."

"Got hell," said Jimmie Cordie, "as far as the girl goes! What's the matter with you, George? Someone must have creased you, too. Count her out of it. She goes home whenever she gets ready; an' what's more Red and I will see that she gets there."

"Ain't that somepin," said Red, "What the livin' hell is comin' off here wid ye an Putt, George, that ye begin to—"

"See," said Grigsby to the Chinaman. "I told you that was the way they would feel about it. You birds are a little quick on the pull aren't you? Whatever gave you the idea that Putt and I— I think," and he rose, "that I'll take you both apart right now and see what makes you go."

"Business before pleasure," said Jimmie Cordie firmly. "Wait until after, then you can try that taking apart thing. We're the ones to get mad, George. You put it up to us to show a Chinaman where we stood. Why didn't you tell him and let it go at that?"

Grigsby stood, his lips tight, his usually laughing blue eyes, frosty. Red Dolan's big lean body was swaying back and forth just a little, in front of him, his eyes, also blue, mere slits. He loved Grigsby and would cheerfully give his life for him. He had fought over his wounded body at Verdun, alone, with clubbed rifle against a German patrol, with no thought of himself; but this was a fight and he barred no living man.

Grigsby was almost as big as Dolan and his body was like steel. He would fight anything, anywhere, any time, but Jimmie Cordie's words, "Why didn't you tell him and let it go at that?" had reached him. He relaxed. "Jimmie's right, Red," he said quietly. "It was my fault. I shouldn't have done it. You can cut your wolf loose now it you want to."

"Aw, George darlin'," coaxed the big Irishman, his body still, "sure it was Jimmie Cordie's fault intirely. 'Tis too quick he is to—"

"Well, you two big apes," said Cordie bitterly, "picking on me. I think I'll start licking the both of you at once. We'll forgive you, George, this time. Let's get the thing settled and get out of here. The ammunition is about all out, me lads. And another thing, George, you tell Red and me not to play, and here you come galumping down the canal racing the neighbors' children, how come?"

GRIGSBY grinned. "He who fights and runs away will live to fight another day," he quoted. "I think we ought to penalize the Doc here for coming between us and the vase the way he did."

"I will pay for my daughter and myself," began the Chinaman, "as much—"

"Wait a minute," said Cordie and he grinned at the girl, who had come aft and was sitting on her father's lap, her pretty, hostile little face peering over his enfolding arm. "When a gentleman receives a call from a lady, can he hold her for ransom? A question of social ethics come in here."

"Ain't that somepin?" asked Red Dolan. "How 'bout that, George?"

"I didn't call on you," said the girl, her eyes on Cordie's lean, bronzed face. "You make me so—so damn mad."

"You wantchee my no wantchee," teased Cordie.

"No, I don't want you," she answered, trying hard not to smile.

"Put your daughter up on the bank, Doc," said Grigsby. "She can make it home all right, can't she?"

"Yes," answered the Chinaman.

"I won't go without my daddy," the little girl declared, and turned in his lap, putting her arms around his neck and her soft little lips to his face. The cruel scarred face became suddenly tender and his arms tightened around the slim form.

"That being the case," said Grigsby gravely, "and the fact that we know that you ma must be looking for you, there's only one thing to do and that is to send your daddy with you, right away."

"Pull that sampan in, Red," said Cordie. "Doc, you take it and pull for home."

The big Chinaman rose and carefully placed the little girl in the stern of the sampan that Red Dolan was holding alongside. He looked calmly at the four men, who grinned cheerfully at him. "Do I understand," he said, "that we are to go and that there is no question of ransom?"

"Devil a question," said Jimmie Cordie. "You heard your daughter say that she wouldn't go without you. Well, we're not hooked up to entertain ladies on this warship, so there you are."

The little girl looked at Cordie and this time answered his smile.

The Chinaman got into the sampan and picked up the pole. "If you will wait here one hour," he said, as he started the first shove, "the vase of T'seng Chung will be brought to you, with the compliments of my daughter. Not as a ransom but as a remembrance of the visit of a young lady to—Americans."

"AND NOW," said Red Dolan, as the launch headed for the bay of Kwangchau two hours later, with the almost priceless vase of the Ming dynasty wrapped up in the bow, "we will listen to Mister James Cordie who will tell us about these here now, social ethics."

THE JEWEL IN THE LOTUS

*Four fighting white men become war lords
for the time being, and ply their trade in a
desperate encounter in a Chinese temple.*

IN FRONT OF the temple built on the sloping bare hill to the south of the city walls the swordsmen of Ch'ienlung were massed, waiting for the High Priest to come to the broad stone steps and begin the sacrifices to the Gods of the High Mountain.

The sun was hot and the air heavy with the perfume from the gardens around three sides of the temple. The warm breezes from the Bay of Tonquin stirred the leaves gently and the flowers nodded as if half asleep.

The High Priest sat in his room in the temple, his cruel old face impassive as the face of Buddha on the inlaid table beside him.

"You will take the box containing the Lord of Death," he said, to the two priests prostrate before him on the floor, "and place it beside the path of flowers. When the maiden comes down the path you will release the Lord of Death and it may be that the daughter of Ch'ienlung will ascend on high and take her place with her most venerable ancestors."

The two priests rose and carefully lifted the long oblong box that sat near the High Priest's chair.

"Master," said the eldest, "has the time come when the Gods punish Ch'ienlung for his contempt of the holy things?"

"The time has come, oh, little brother," the High Priest answered, grimly.

On the two sides of the temple and in front, except for the

space necessary for the stone steps, stood great idols, some of them half man, half beast, some solid stone, some carved and hollowed wood. The idols stood thirty or forty feet apart and between them the flower gardens and little artificial lakes and pagodas.

Standing in front of the swordsmen, a little group of officers with him, was Ch'ienlung, War Lord of the city, pure Manchu of the race that had set his ancestor T'ientsung on the peacock throne of China. His lean, dark, battle scarred young face lighted up as he saw his little daughter come down one of the winding paths, followed by her maidens and bodyguard. The ranks of the priests on the broad steps of the temple parted and the High Priest came forward to the square sacrifice stone at the bottom.

The little girl, gay in her silks and flowered hair, held her little head proudly as she came down the path. A blossom attracted her attention and she stopped and bent toward it, then shrank back, paralyzed with fear. A King cobra rose from beside the flower, its golden yellow body and head towering above her not two feet away.

The deadly head began a slow swaying back and forth. The King was in no hurry to strike.

The little girl stood quivering, the gay flowers in her blue-black hair nodding a little as if in time with the sway of the cobra's head.

Her father stood also, frozen in an agony of fear. He knew that the slightest movement would precipitate the stroke and yet—his face became gray and his hands extended like the talons of a hawk. War Lord of a city and a thousand swordsmen, best sword in Tonquin, Lord of life and death over fifty thousand Chinese and—his daughter in front of a King cobra.

THE SWAY became a little faster, and Ch'ienlung groaned aloud. Suddenly the head went back and the mouth opened. The King was going to strike.

As the head poised, the *pow* of a Colt's .45 came from the

folded arms of one of the big idols, thirty yards away, and the King's head disappeared, blown to pieces by the heavy soft-nosed bullet.

The swordsmen stood as if witnessing a miracle, but in less than two seconds the young chief had his daughter in his arms, drawing his long curved sword as he held her in his left. He knew that King cobras did not release themselves in the gardens of the temple; that the snake had come from India; that the High Priest had chosen this time to settle once for all the supremacy he had questioned on the death of Ch'ienlung's father.

As the priests on the steps drew long swords from their robes and others came running out of the temple. Ch'ienlung snarled an order to the swordsmen.

Some of them ran toward him, but the majority went to the priests, then turned, their swords in their hands, against him.

To the four big white men, concealed under the folding arms of the big idol, it seemed to be as a whirl of leaves in a summer breeze. The long swords flashed and men went down. The priests charged straight across the temple grounds at the young chief— to be met by the swords of those who had come to him. He stood with his little daughter in his arms, shouting encouragement to his men. Slowly but surely, the priests were cutting their way to him.

"Ain't that somepin'?" asked Red Dolan, "after me knockin' off that snake. What the hell is doin', Jimmie?"

"Family fight," answered Jimmie Cordie with a grin. "What did you wait so long for, Red?"

"Did I see it before?" defended the big Irishman. "Sure I was watchin' the little lad wid the—"

"Go on," jeered Jimmie Cordie. "You were the only one that had that angle. You were asleep!"

"I'll knock the can off ye for that, Jimmie—"

"Pipe down, you two," commanded Grigsby. "Damn' good thing for us it is a family fight. Our chances for the ruby went flooey when Red killed the cobra."

"Look at that now," said Red. "They've almost got to him an' him wid the little girl. Sure—" And his Winchester 30-30 came up against his cheek.

"That's the boy, Red," said Jimmie Cordie, following suit. "We don't allow anyone to fuss with the ladies, do we?"

GRIGSBY and Putney both laughed and raised their Winchesters. The four of them had fought together in the Foreign Legion and then in the A.E.F. All of them were dead shots and of chilled steel nerve. They had fought in the places since the war where a bullet or a blade was the only law.

The attack melted away for a moment under the rain of steel-jacketed bullets sent to them by men who killed at every shot. In less than a minute there was a ring of dead around the front of the young chief.

He looked up at the idol and laughed, then called an order and with the few swordsmen left with him, ran to the base made of stone on which the idol was sitting.

"Drive them back into the temple!" he shouted in perfect English. "Here," and he held up his daughter to Red Dolan, who was the nearest. "Take care of the Princess Wu Tse-tien. I will lesson these dogs of priests!"

Red Dolan stooped and reached out a pair of brawny arms for the little girl. She looked up at him for a moment, then smiled and held out her arms.

"Come up here, you!" shouted Grigsby. "Look behind the idols! On the right! Come up here, you damn' fool!"

There, gathering in a compact body, were at least two hundred swordsmen. The High Priest was among them, urging them on to attack.

The young chief laughed again, his face happy with the joy of battle and the knowledge that his daughter was safe for the moment. "Take care of her for me!" he shouted. "I will drive these traitors. I am Ch'ienlung, lord of these curs."

"Reach him up here, Putt," commanded Grigsby, and Putney's big hand clutched the young chief under the armpit and lifted him bodily to the idol base. Ch'ienlung snarled like a fox terrier being lifted by the scruff of the neck from a rat, but relaxed when Putney let him go.

JIMMIE CORDIE, Dolan and Grigsby were meeting the charge with a sleet of steel. The High Priest went down on his face and was picked up by two of the priests and carried into the temple, the rest came grimly on. The charge was also met by the loyal swordsmen of Ch'ienlung, who had won to the idol with him. The long swords hissed and flickered in the sun. Red Dolan had put the little girl gently down and joined in. The four white men were shooting as fast as they could pull trigger, killing at every shot, yet the swordsmen came on. They paid absolutely no attention to the rifles of the four men, their faces grim with the joy of the simon pure fighting man at his trade. Little by little they fought their way, man after man meeting death, to the idol.

Red Dolan, as Putney picked up his Winchester, tossed his Colt's to Ch'ienlung. "Use that, ye bloodthirsty mosquito," Jimmie Cordie laughed and unbuckled his belt with the fifty Colt's cartridges and dropped it at Ch'ienlung's feet. "Here's what goes with it," he said, and watched for a moment until he saw that Ch'ienlung knew how to handle a Colt's. He did, running to the edge of the base with the belt in one hand and the revolver already roaring out his defiance.

"Get the priests," shouted Grigsby. "Jimmie! The priests, you damn' fool. Get them!"

"What do you think I'm doing?" grinned Cordie, reloading his Winchester. "Playing tag with them?"

The swordsmen came on, their swords running blood, to be met with swords. The ground in front of the temple was carpeted with dead and wounded. It was a death fight, no noise, no shouting, just fighting men killing. The only sound was that of the steady *Pow-Pow-Pow* of the rifles and Colts. There were no bows and arrows, no spears, just sword to sword.

Ch'ienlung had stopped snarling and at the edge of the base stood shooting into the thick of his foes, without the aim of the white men, but shooting to kill, nevertheless.

The little girl stood calmly beside Red Dolan, a smile on her lips, her black eyes hard and cold as she watched the swordsmen and priests, that would have given her to a snake, go down. The cobra had scared her, but now—this was something she knew, this sword play, and she was a Manchu princess of the blood. She called to several of the men she knew, telling them to fight hard.

IN TEN MINUTES there was only a thin ring of men around the idol and in front of them fifty swordsmen swirled and struck, Ch'ienlung had shot away his ammunition and had stood a moment, then ran back, picked up his sword and jumped down with his men.

Red Dolan dropped his Winchester and followed him, picking up a sword and charging into the thick of the fight, side by side with Ch'ienlung. The best sword in all Tonquin was at work now, backed up by the two hundred and thirty pounds of fighting Irish, and they cut their way through, then back, then through again.

A priest, his face demoniac in its fury, ran in on Ch'ienlung, his blade like a lightning flashes he swung it around his head. It darted at Ch'ienlung like the strike of a snake to slither off the blade that met it. Ch'ienlung stepped in and his sword flashed up between them. It was the death-carrying cut of the Tartar and the razor-like blade sliced up from the throat of the priest and beheaded him.

"Come back here, you crazy fool!" shouted Jimmie Cordie. "You'll get us all killed. Red! Come—" and he dropped his Winchester, snatched Grigsby's Colt from his belt and jumped down beside Red.

The death of the priest, the arrival of the two white men and the Manchu swordsmen, stopped the fight. There were only twelve men left that broke and ran to the temple steps.

Of all the men who had fought for Ch'ienlung, there were four left.

"Red! Jimmie!" called Grigsby. "Quit! Stop shooting, Jimmie! Red, you fool, come up here!"

His voice finally reached them and the two, with Ch'ienlung and the four men, climbed back on the base. From the city below came a hum, like that of bees swarming.

"They fight for the city," the young chief said calmly. "The High Priest planned well. Two thirds of my men are at Sengan with my cousin, T'ungchih."

THE LITTLE GIRL from the arms of Red, who had picked her up, said something to her father, who smiled and answered, then turned to Grigsby. "My daughter, the Princess Wu Tse-tien," he said, "asks if these big men are swordsmen of mine and if the man with the hair of fire is the one that killed the snake that would have sent her on high with her venerable ancestors?"

"Tell her that we are her swordsmen," said Grigsby, "to command and that the man with the hair of fire is the one that killed the snake."

Ch'ienlung laughed and spoke to the girl. She listened gravely, nodded her little head and then turned in Red's big arms and reached up and patted his red head.

"Ain't that somepin'?" said Red delightedly. "Sure now, alanna, 'tis all right ye are wid owld Red Dolan."

"And it's all right—we ain't," said Putney. "After we get set fixing Red up with his sweetie—where do we go from here?"

"Boy," said Jimmie Cordie cheerfully, "you ain't said nothing yet. After they take the city down there, they'll come up and take us."

"It may be," said Ch'ienlung, his eyes cold, "that my men will be able to hold them. If they can, I will give to the priests the same death that they wished to give my daughter."

"Fair enough," said Grigsby, "but in the meantime, we better be doping something out. How come you to speak English?"

"My father was the friend of the English Lord Howard, and I was sent to Hong Kong to be educated with his son. I stayed five years. This dog of a priest, when my father died before I came back, had ordered things, and now is trying to seize the power forever. My daughter and I are all that is left of the pure Manchu. You white men, what do you do here in the temple of the High Lords?"

"Well," answered Grigsby, watching the entrance, "to tell the truth, we came up the Gulf of Tonkin, then up the Yu River to Sinchau. We gave out that we were looking for a stone that fell from the heavens. Honest and truly, no foolin', we were after the jewel in the heart of the Lotus that's in the temple there."

"You were here to steal the—" Ch'ienlung's eyes widened, then he laughed. "It may be," he added gravely, "that you will not have to steal it. That you may find and keep it. It is a price-less thing to have—the jewel."

"Heads up!" shouted Red, his Colt roaring as he spoke.

THIS time the attack came direct from the temple and seemed to be mostly composed of priests. They came in a wedge shaped mass, silent and grim, their long robes discarded. The four men knelt and coldly shot the wedge to pieces before it had come fifty yards. Six men reached the base, to be met with Ch'ienlung's sword and the clubbed rifles. When it was over Grigsby had a slicing cut on the left arm. Cordie was unconscious on the floor from the hilt of a sword, all of Ch'ienlung's men were dead but one.

"Hold your arm out, George," commanded Putney. "See how bad Jimmie is hurt, Red. Take my canteen. Not so bad, George—long, but not very deep. Wish we had some—"

"Jimmie's not bad hurt," announced Red, "He's got a wallop on the bean wid somepin'. Sure now, Jimmie, wake up and—"

"Let him come to," said Grigsby. "Use my shirt-tail, Putt, that'll plug 'er all right for now. We better be highballing it to some place we can get to water."

"Ch'ienlung," said Grigsby, "we better head for your cousin or somewhere we can hold the fort until he gets to you. They seem to be raising hell down in the city."

"It may be," said Ch'ienlung, "that Chiach'ing, my war brother, is holding them. He must be, or they would be here," he added grimly.

"Yeah? How far is it to your cousin?"

"Twenty miles beyond the mountains."

"Send this man, then, and tell him to come."

CH'IENLUNG gave an order and the man bowed low and slipped around behind the great statue.

"This is a rotten place to do any more standing off," said Jimmie Cordie, who had sat up after Red had bathed his head with a little water from Putney's canteen. "Let's make it up the hill to one of those little pagodas. That one on the top will give us a chance to see all around."

"Ain't that somepin'?" agreed Red. "Come on, let's go."

The little girl spoke to her father. "Wu Tse-tien says," he translated, "that there is water there in a clear spring. She has often been there with her maidens."

"All right," said Grigsby, "Carry the princess, Ch'ienlung. We'll do all the fighting necessary."

Twice on the way they were attacked by small groups of

swordsmen and priests, but they swept them aside with the heavy Colt's as they would kill a snake in the path.

The little pagoda was perched on top of the highest knoll in the temple grounds and the clear cool spring enclosed in a stone basin was inside the walls.

There was no further attack from the temple and the city below was quiet once more.

"Soon we will know," said Ch'ienlung, "whether these dogs who have fed on my bounty have taken my city."

From one of the narrow little streets far below a body of men suddenly appeared and began running up the slope toward the temple.

"Hey, Ch'ienlung!" called Jimmie Cordie, who was perched up on the rail of the veranda outside with the Princess Wu Tse-tien in his lap. Red Dolan was pretending to be jealous, much to the delight of the little girl. "Here come your boy friends now. There's a bunch of priests in front. I guess your buddy got cleaned."

CH'IENLUNG came to the doorway and looked at the men coming to the temple below. His eyes were cold and his scarred young face grew grim. "They are of the priests," he said curtly. "Chiach'ing has taken his place with the Lords on High. We also very soon, now will—"

"Quit callin' the turn like that," said Red Dolan. "Sure, now, it'll be some time before they can knock us off, me bucko. Wid water and shelter and—"

"About fifty shells left," interrupted Jimmie Cordie cheerfully.

" 'Tis so," said Red, scratching his head. "Sure now, I think I'll go down and git me wan of them swords like Ch'ienlung has here. They're grand things to have in a mix up."

"Yeah," scoffed Putney. "Why don't you write 'em a letter and tell 'em we're out of ammunition, you big dumb-bell?"

"Putt's right, Red," said Grigsby. "Better let it ride as it is. They think now that we can handle 'em."

The men from the city reached the temple and went inside. A little later some came out, mostly swordsmen, and sat around the grounds. There was some pointing and gesticulating up at the pagoda, but no effort in any way to come nearer.

"Look at that big baby struttin' his stuff," said Red, his blue eyes narrowing as he watched a swordsman walking up and down in front of a group by one of the idols. The long curved sword was making a blue circle around his head and seemed to flow all around him. He reached for his Winchester. "I'll give ye a chance to try an' parry somepin', me laddie buck," he said.

"Don't shoot, Red," said Grigsby, quietly. "You'd only start the rest up the hill. Let him show what he's got, old-timer."

"Yeah," said Jimmie Cordie, "stick around, Red. Something tells me you'll get a chance at him pretty soon. They'll be coming up to give us the keys of the city or—"

The sound of a sobbing, gasping breath came to them all and they whirled around, their ready hands on their Colts.

A MAN pulled himself up to the little window in the rear of the pagoda. One side of his face was curtained in blood and the front of his cotton blouse was red. "Chiach'ing holds his house, Lord," he gasped, "and sends for help. If the High Priest were—" He fell back. Ch'ienlung translated. "If we could make the city," he said, "we could—"

"Here comes a priest with a flag of truce," announced Jimmie Cordie.

"Yeah? Wave him on, Jimmie," said Grigsby.

The priest stood and looked at them insolently, his depraved, evil face and eyes showing his hatred and fear. He spoke curtly to Ch'ienlung. The little girl turned in her father's arms and answered him, her midnight eyes flashing like the blue steel of a gun barrel.

Ch'ienlung laughed and nuzzled her soft cheek with his nose and lips. "The High Priest," he said in English, "has sent word by this cur dog of his that if you, the white men, will give up Ch'ienlung and Wu Tse-tien to him, that he will let you go in peace with all the jewels you can carry. The Princess Wu Tse-tien has told him to carry back the message that you are her lords of battle and that soon she will come and give him Lingeh'ih for his portion."

"That's a nice girl, now," said Red Dolan, smiling at the little Manchu princess who had given defiance so readily. "Sure, tell the owld stiff that—"

"Steady," said Grigsby. "Ch'ienlung, tell him that the white men will think it over, that already two of them are won over. That they will give their answer in three hours. Add to it for yourself that if you can, you will kill both yourself and your daughter before submitting or any old thing. Putt, you and Jimmie start an argument, quick. You I want to take him up. Hurry up, Red, make it strong."

"Ye won't!" howled Red, sticking a brawny fist under Cordie's nose. "Ye will never give—"

"I say we will!" shouted Jimmie, jumping back and drawing his Colt. "We will—and get the jewels. Wadda you care for them?" And he waved his hand at the chief and his daughter. Putney jumped in front of them and caught Jimmie's gun barrel and threw it up, talking to both of them.

"Not too strong, not too strong," said Grigsby. "Tell him, Ch'ienlung, that already the white men are fighting."

THE PRIEST stood still, his eyes lighting up as he watched the white men. He received Ch'ienlung's message with a sneer, then turned and slowly went down the hill.

"Cut the comedy out," said Grigsby, as soon as the priest was out of hearing. "Something is up down there. Why don't he come up and get us? I thought that one of you birds got the High Priest the first rush. Evidently he came to. Now, why don't they come up? Something has happened in the city or it may be that he don't want to lose any more men. Your buddy must have mopped up on a few, Ch'ienlung?"

"If he is at last driven to his house, he did," answered Ch'ienlung grimly. "This dog of a priest knows my cousin will come. He also knows that with Chiach'ing alive in the city defending his house, he must have something to prove that he's winning. If he can show the city that I am dead and—my daughter also—then there will be but the taking of Chiach'ing and the defense of the city against my cousin, which he has no doubt planned."

"Yeah?" said Red Dolan. "Well, then, why don't he come an' get us, right now?"

"Coming and getting are two different things. That old boy shows sense in trying to make a dicker. He may not be able to pep up his little sword slingers as long as they know that this buddy of Ch'ienlung's is down there alive. We got quite a few of the priests, let alone the scrappers," said Jimmie Cordie, grinning at Red.

"That's probably it," said Grigsby, "and—"

THE LITTLE GIRL turned and said something to her father, who smiled. "The Princess Wu Tse-tien," he said, "asks why we linger here talking. Her war lords are to go and get the High Priest that tried to have the snake bite her, for her to punish."

"Ain't that somepin'?" asked Red Dolan. "Ain't she a reg— Say! Here we sit, the four of us, an' let a monkey faced owld devil tell us what to do. Sure, 'tis right herself is."

"How about it, George?" asked Jimmie Cordie, his eyes shining. "Red's got the dope all right. Let's get to the temple and give him a little dose of his own medicine. They won't be looking for us."

Grigsby laughed. "Suits me. How you feeling, Putt?"

The big man laughed. "Cut yore wolf loose, feller," he said. "I'm ridin' alongside!"

"We'll wait until it gets dark. It's growing dusk right now. Then out the back way and around by the little lake there. Ch'ienlung, do you know the way into the temple from the rear?"

"Yes. There are several ways. We go to take the temple?"

"We go to take the High Priest," answered Jimmie Cordie, smiling at the little girl, "as our boss ordered."

"Ch'ienlung," said Grigsby later, as they crept slowly up to the temple, "what death is considered the most disgraceful?"

"To be hung like a dog with a rope around the neck," answered Ch'ienlung promptly. "That—"

"We'll give the High Priest," said Grigsby calmly. "You are sure of the room? Yeah, well here we are. All right, you birds, let's go! Ch'ienlung, you keep between us with the princess!"

INSIDE the temple there was a scurrying and running and what priests and swordsmen inside flung themselves at the little party, to be killed and tossed aside. The four big men literally shot their way through into an inner room, down a narrow passage.

There, sitting at a table, his face impassive, although he knew that death was coming closer at every shot, sat the High Priest, one leg bandaged and a bloody white cloth around his head. He made no attempt to escape and now, as he saw the little girl safe in her father's arms, he laughed, an evil sneering laugh.

Ch'ienlung's eyes blazed. "Take her," he ordered, holding the little girl out to Putney. Then, his arms free, he stepped forward and his long sword flashed up. "Hold it!" shouted Grigsby. "He's wounded and—"

He was too late, the sword came down and the High Priest's body crumpled to the floor, almost cut in two.

"Make it snappy in there!" called Jimmie Cordie from one of the doors, his Colt rising and falling like clockwork. "There's a lot of these babies coming in."

Red Dolan was at the other door leading to the front of the temple. He had shot away all the remaining shells he had and now was standing with one of the swords he had picked up as he ran through the room.

Ch'ienlung ran to Jimmie Cordie's side and called down the narrow passage a snarling order. There was an instant silence, then the sound of running feet. "I ordered these dogs to spread the news that their master, Chung Wang, he who was High Priest, is dead."

He ran lightly across the room and joined Red Dolan and again called loudly.

"Ain't that somepin'?" complained Red, as the swordsmen who had been grouped at the lower end of the hallway melted away. "Me wid me good sword here an' nothin' to do wid it."

"Keep your shirt on," said Grigsby. "You may have all you want to do with it yet, old settler. Pick that body up and come on with it. We'll hang it over the temple balcony so they can see it. No more killing now, unless necessary. Ch'ienlung, tell them unless they yield here and in the city you will burn the temple and then come down to the city and burn and slay."

USING Red Dolan's belt for a noose, they swung the body over the balcony, where it swung back and fro in the darkness. "Build a fire," ordered Grigsby. "Make it light enough to see in front."

The fire was built from part of the rails of the balcony at the side.

"Now," said Grigsby, "it's on the knees of the Nine Red Gods. We can't hold them off very long without—"

"Listen to them below," said Red, as the noise from the city came up to them. "Sure, the news has got there."

An hour went by, then they could hear the sound of running feet and the shouts of men.

"Get back to the balcony," commanded Grigsby. "We'll stand 'em off from there."

From the balcony they could hear the milling and shouting of men, just outside the firelight, then a man strode into the light, alone. He was a young man, his face smooth and boyish, but his long sword was bloody and his silks red in places.

"Chiach'ing!" called the little girl. "Chiach'ing!"

He looked up at the balcony from which hung the body of the High Priest, at him, at the four big grim white men with their drawn Colts, at Wu Tse-tien in her father's arms, her little face eager and smiling, then turned and called an order. From the shadows came his clansmen, who had helped him defend his house.

"When the news came to the city," Ch'ienlung said later as they were sitting in the High Priest's room, "the priest's men, already having their fill of fighting and knowing that I was being protected by the gods—meaning you gentlemen," he explained with a smile, "decided that as Chung Wang had taken himself on high, there was no use for them to fight, so they submitted to Chiach'ing."

"Well," said Grigsby, looking at Wu Tse-tien, who lay fast asleep in her father's arms, "that being the case and also that it's darn near morning, where do we go from here?"

"To my house for rest and food," answered Ch'ienlung. "Then—"

"Not so good," said Cordie. "These babies we helped you mop up on are coming sooner or later and will pass the word that you brought in foreign devils to help you. We better pull out right now. We can get a good ways down the pass by morning. How much ammunition you birds got?"

THE FOUR MEN counted what was in their belts, Grigsby and Putney having the most, Red not any. Together they had twenty shells for the Winchesters and a few rounds for the Colts. "Not so bad," said Cordie cheerfully. "Red can take the big sword." They all laughed, with no thought of peril on the long journey back to where they had left their launch on the Yu.

"Jimmie's right," said Grigsby. "Better let Ch'ienlung clean house for himself."

"But," said Ch'ienlung, "you have fought for me and if it were not for you my daughter would have been— You came for the jewel in the heart of the lotus? I think you have it already."

"Yeah?" asked Red. "Who got it?"

"Wait a minute," said Cordie with a grin. "I bet you that— He's right, we got it."

"Like hell," said Red Dolan, puzzled. "What the blazes do you mean now, Jimmie Cordie?"

"Why, the jewel in the heart of the lotus—means contentment, you dumbbell. There's no real jewel because—"

"A good many years ago," said Ch'ienlung, "here in the temple a ruby was put into the heart of a carved lotus as a symbol, but for a hundred years now there has been no ruby in the heart of the lotus. It may be that the news of it spread and—"

"It did," said Putney grimly. "It spread so far and so much that the ruby became as big as a pigeon's egg. We decided to come up and get it. That's one on us."

THE LITTLE GIRL stirred in Ch'ienlung's arms. Red started over to her. "Don't touch 'er, Red," said Jimmie Cordie gently. "We're going. Let her think that her war lords have gone back on high to come again at her call."

"Ain't that somepin'?" agreed Red Dolan.

A swordsman came in and spoke to Ch'ienlung, who answered. The man bowed and retired.

"I have just been told that my cousin enters the city at the head of his men and mine. All that I have is yours."

"It may be," said Grigsby with a smile, as the four big men shook hands gently with him so as not to disturb Wu Tse-tien, "that some day we will find the jewel in the heart of the lotus. Until then, Ch'ienlung, we are glad to have been able to help you in keeping yours."

"Tell the little princess," said Red, "that her—now—war lords will come any time she wants, won't we, Jimmie?"

"Yeah, boy!" answered Jimmie.

"If you feel you must go," said Ch'ienlung, smiling at the big Irishman, "my war brother, Chaich'ing will escort you as far as the river."

"We don't need this war brother of yours, Ch'ienlung," answered Jimmie. "Thanks just the same. We can make 'er. Come on, War Lord," to Red, with a grin.

VI

WHEN TIGERS ARE HUNTING

*In the crowded harbor of Hong Kong a man
is taken by force from his own yacht. And that
brings Red Dolan, Jimmie Cordie, and their
buddies into the picture, and sends them on a
chase into the wilds of China—a chase that ends
only on a bullet-swept hill far in the interior.*

JIMMIE CORDIE AND Red Dolan, dressed in immaculate whites, walked slowly down the illy paved and worse smelling narrow street. They were deep in the native quarter of Hong Kong, a section of the city where few Europeans dared to go. In any place Red Dolan's two hundred odd pounds of lean hard brawn, topped by a flaming red thatch of hair, would have been conspicuous. Here he stood out from the slighter, darker Chinese as a giant among pigmies.

Jimmie Cordie, shorter by half a foot, a little leaner, with black hair and eyes, his face deeply tanned, looked smaller than he really was beside Dolan's six feet three inches. They both radiated an extreme ability to take care of themselves under any circumstances.

The Chinese slipped out of their way as they sauntered along. Had not word gone forth from Yen Yuan, head of the Taiping Society, that this dark, always smiling Jimmie Cordie was as his elder brother? Also had not a whisper gone forth that if anything happened him, the ones responsible would very shortly after die, taking a long time to do it?

"Hey, Jimmie!" Red ejaculated. "Look, there's wan of them big curved swords in that shop."

"Where? Oh, yeah, some Malay must have gone broke and—"

A 'rickshaw stopped a little ahead of them and a girl stepped out. She was blonde, slim and boyish, about eighteen, and obviously English. She paid absolutely no attention to the Chinese who began milling around her, forming a dense circle that gave a little in front as she walked calmly along toward the shop where Red Dolan and Jimmie Cordie were looking at the sword. She walked as calmly and unconcernedly as if in the center of a British squadron, her head high, her blue eyes level, showing no fear or hurry. She was alone, in the worst part of Hong Kong for Europeans to be.

Red Dolan looked up as the crowd parted sullenly to let the girl through. Already murmurings and snarls of hate were going up against the "foreign devil woman."

"What the—" began Red, straightening up from a closer scrutiny of the sword and seeing the girl for the first time just as she stopped, staring at the two men. One little hand flew to her heart and her eyes widened.

"Why!" she gasped. "It's Red!" and in another second her arms were around the big Irishman and as Jimmie Cordie said later, she tried to get in his pocket.

"Whist, now," said the embarrassed Red. "Sure 'tis Red, but who the—"

"Red! I'm Betty Wythe! Oh, Red, you haven't forgotten me? I—I—"

Jimmie Cordie laughed and took a step forward that brought him between them and the already much too close Chinese mob. His right hand slipped under his left armpit and came out with a blue steel Colt .45.

"Beat it, little yellow brothers!" he said cheerfully, with a grin. The Chinese didn't understand what he said, but they fully comprehended the big revolver and the backward wave of his hand. There was absolutely no hesitation, the street cleared as if by magic.

"Herself," Red said, lifting the girl up in his arms until the lovely face was level with his own. "Sure, now, allana, I knew ye all the time. 'Twas the sight of the beauty ye have grown to be that dazzled me eyes. See, Jimmie, 'tis herself again!"

"I see it is," answered Jimmie, gravely, "and she's showing the same poor judgment she did eight years ago in kissing you instead of the distinguished Mister Cordie, who rescued her from the Malays and everything."

Betty Wythe laughed a happy, tremulous laugh and kissed Red again.

"Put me down, Red. I want to kiss Jimmie, too. Oh, I'm so glad to see you. Just think, eight years and now"—she put her arms around Jimmie's neck—"just when I need you—oh, Jimmie, I'm so glad!"

"My gosh," said Jimmie, as soon as he could get his breath. "Quit that! Right in the middle of the street, too. I thought the English never showed any—"

"I don't care if it is in the middle of Picadilly Circus," declared Betty Wythe. "Didn't you carry me in your arms? If Putt and Grigsby were here I'd kiss them, too!"

"They're here," said Jimmie, with a grin. "Red and I are on our way to meet them now. How come you down here, Betty? Where's your pa and the yacht?"

"And what are ye doin' down here all by yerself?" demanded Red, sternly. "Sure 'tis no place for ye, at all, and—"

"Oh, I was so glad to see you again that I—Red—Jimmie, daddy's in some awful trouble. He's been kidnapped or—I'm afraid he's dead, Red. He's disappeared and—" Her lips began to tremble a little and her mouth to go down at the corners. "I—"

" 'Tis enough," interrupted Red. "Stop that now, darlin'. Ain't we here wid ye? We'll find yer daddy for ye, machree, won't we, Jimmie?"

"I'm not crying. It's because I'm so glad to see you and—"

"Hold 'er," said Jimmie, firmly. "Let's get out of here, first. Certainly we'll get him for you, Betty. What are you doing down here?"

"One of the stewards brought me a note that said if I would go to the shop of Cheng in the Street of A Thousand Delights I would hear something about daddy. It said for me to come alone."

"Yeah? Well, here is the Street of A Thousand Delights and here is the shop of Cheng. That 'alone' stuff sounds natural. Come on, Red and I will go in with you. We probably won't get anything, but it will give us a chance to look 'em over."

THEY entered the shop and an old Chinaman came forward, his face and eyes impassive.

"You wantee look see?"

Red reached out an iron hand which closed around the collar of the old man's loose blouse, gathering in the folds, holding him as in a vise. He lifted him up from his feet and swung him around facing the light. The Chinaman, never before man-handled, tried to shrink back from the frosty cold blue eyes, his face gray with fear.

From the rear, out of the darkness, there slipped three younger, slimmer men, their bodies, half naked, oiled and shining. The wavy krisses in their hands flickered in the dim light.

Jimmie Cordie laughed and his Colt forty-five seemed to jump into his hand. "Halt!" he commanded, then "No?" and his Colt roared out the backing of the command with the heavy, soft nosed bullets. The room filled with powder smoke and appeared to rock with the three detonations that came almost as one. The three men slumped to the floor, dead before they hit it.

The old Chinaman gasped.

"Let go his throat, you red-headed idiot," said Cordie, calmly, ejecting the three used shells and reloading from the loops of his shoulder holster. "How can he talk when you got him by the windpipe? Stand over against the wall, Betty. There may be some more."

"Me no wantee," squeaked the old man. "Bad men come, take loom, sendee chlit for Missee. Me no wantee. Me velly good man!"

"Ye are," snarled Red, "a velly good man—like hell. What now, Jimmie?"

"Out of here, pronto. Go get George and Putt. We couldn't get anything out of him with a drill, now. Let's go while the going is good. It'll rain Chink cops around here in a minute. I think I got a line, anyway."

They left the shop and walked toward the foreign quarter, absolutely unmolested. The shops on either side were closed, the iron shutters up. The street, near the shop of Cheng, was empty. Both of them knew that the sounds of the shots must have been heard by thousands in the congested district and that there is no more curious people in the world than the Chinese, yet the street was empty.

They reached the end of the street and turned the corner. A few minutes later, just after they had passed out of view, a body of Chinese police came running up and entered the shop. They were out again in a minute with the old man, who pointed in the direction the foreign devils, who had killed as quickly as a cobra strikes, had gone.

The police started to run to the corner, then halted. A big, fat, bland old Chinaman had stepped calmly in their path from one of the shops. He raised his fan, looked at the police, at the sky, at the roofs of the adjoining houses, at his long curved fingernails cased in golden sheaths, at the figures on his ivory fan, yawned delicately behind a thin blue veined hand, then said, in a calm, indifferent voice, "The Master said, 'When tigers are hunting—is it time for jackals to be abroad?'"

The police dropped to their knees and the leader crawled almost to the silken boots of the old man. "Lord," he said, "we did not know. Spare us out of the compassion and mercy of your great heart. We are too insignificant for your honorable notice."

"Do you think, oh little brother," the large Chinaman asked, softly, "that if you knew—you would be alive now? Go back— Cheng is very old and the poppy makes him dream. Tell him so and leave him in peace. The shots were fired by a Pathan—a black man, with a long beard. Is it not so, little brother?"

"Yes, Lord," answered the leader of the police from his knees. "A black Pathan. We saw him running from the shop, but not in time to stop him."

"There have been no foreigners in this quarter today?"

"No, Lord. Had there been we would have seen them."

"That is well. If there had been, and anything had happened to them, I am certain that you and your men would presently die—by *Lingeh'ih!*"

The police drew long, quivering breaths. They knew what the slicing death meant—they had helped give it to others and they knelt, their heads bowed, until the fat, bland old Chinaman had slowly turned and entered the shop, from which he had confronted them.

BETTY WYTHE sat in the living room of Grigsby's apartment with the four big men. She had cried a little in sheer joy and kissed both Putney and Grigsby, much to their embarrassment and Cordie's delight.

Eight years before, a little girl of ten, she had persuaded one of the stewards on her father's yacht to row her ashore while at anchor off the Malay coast. Seized by a band of natives going inland, she had been sold by them to another tribe and when rescued by the four soldiers of fortune, had been selected by the high priest of the tribe as a sacrifice to the snakes they worshipped.

Eight years—and now they were with her again—the men who had saved her. Her inborn English reserve was not for them—they were her big brothers.

She smiled and held out her beautiful arms to them all. "I—I'm so glad. I'm a—"

"You are," said Putney, gravely. "We all admit it. Go on from there."

"And who might ye be," demanded Red, "to be interruptin' herself that way? Go on, allana, pay no attention to him. 'Tis ye that's talkin'."

"It sounds to me as if a red-headed ape from Cork was broadcasting," said Cordie. "Start from the beginning, Betty, and tell us just what happened."

"Why, I don't know where to start. At least nothing happened that I noticed very much. Daddy sent me back home to school after you rescued me, you know, and I didn't join him again until last summer. We lived on the yacht just as we always did since mother died, and everything was the same as before. We'd go to port, and daddy would have a lot of conferences with men on shore and on board the yacht. Three months ago we dropped anchor in Triganu harbor and almost before the anchor left the bow, two men came off to see daddy. He took them below into his library and they had lunch with him there. Then in Singapore last month the same two men came on board again, and they stayed a long time. I was on deck when they came up to go ashore and I thought they looked angry. Then day before yesterday, they came aboard here in Hong Kong—and the next morning daddy was gone!"

"What makes you think your daddy's in trouble, Betty? Didn't he ever go away for a day or two?"

"Yes, lots of times, but he'd go on shore in the launch and it would be in the daytime. I knocked on his door about noon and he didn't answer, and I tried it again later, then about three

I had one of the stewards break in the door. Daddy wasn't there and there was a note on his writing desk that he had started to write to me. The chair was overturned and—"

"Have you the note?" asked Grigsby.

"Yes, I put it in my pocketbook when I came on shore—here it is. See—where the pen dragged down the paper as if someone had taken hold of his arm from behind?"

"Yeah, that's exactly what someone did."

The note read:

> Betty dear:
> Your old daddy is in the middle of a rather serious affair and may have to go away suddenly. Captain Collins has instructions how to proceed in case I am—

The note ended in a blot and a long wavering line to the bottom of the page.

Grigsby looked at it, then handed it to the rest. "What did these men look like that same to see him, Betty?" he queried.

"Big, tall men, with high cheek bones. They looked like Chinese, only their eyes didn't slant up."

"Manchu," said Jimmie Cordie. "Listen, George, I'll ease over and see Yen Yuan. He'll get the inside dope for me if he doesn't already know it. You didn't hear any names, did you, Betty?"

"One of them called the other Dorgun."

"Duck soup," said Cordie cheerfully. "Wait right here for your old Uncle Jimmie."

"You'll get pinched, boy," grinned Putney. "Do you think you can flitter around knocking off Chinese here in Hong Kong without saying 'good morning, Judge'?"

"Certainly," answered Jimmie, with dignity. "As long as old Yen Yuan is my buddy. He's top cutter of the Taipings—"

"Who are a bunch of highbinders," supplied Putney.

"Yeah? What do you care? He insists that I saved his son's life and that he can't do enough for Mister Cordie's son, Jimmie.

His son is on the Hsing Pu also, which I will explain for the benefit of you dumb-bells, always excepting Betty, is the Board of Punishments. What between Wong Li and his pa, boy, howdy!"

"Get going, shrimp," said Grigsby. "Go see your hijacking buddies. We know all about it."

FOUR hours later Jimmie Cordie returned from his visit to the Taiping headquarters.

"Your father," he said to Betty, "is up in Pa-tang, which is in the Szechuen province on the Yangtze Kiang. He's being held a prisoner by Kang Hsi, who is cock of the walk up there at the minute. A steward on the *Mona* named Akwei and the third officer, Larson, were bribed by the two gents you noticed, who were Kang's agents. With the help of Larson and Akwei, these agents got aboard the *Mona*, caught your father writing at his desk, and took him overside into a sampan. They were met at the dock by a party of Kang's men, transferred to a junk, and the whole outfit highballed out for Pa-tang. This Kang Hsi was high up in the army of the North, and all of a sudden he gets thrown out by General Li. Yen Yuan thinks that Li caught him in some dirty work at the crossroads and that your pa is mixed up in it someway. How, when or where he doesn't know at the minute, but says that he will by tomorrow morning, no foolin'. He'll know if your pa is all right, also. He was, up to the time they left Hong Kong, and was being treated with respect. So that's that, young fellers me lads. How's that for M.I. stuff?"

"Now, how the h—heavens did ye get all that, ye shrimp of the world, Jimmie darlin'?" demanded Red.

"Boy, I told you who my buddy was, didn't I? Those babies can get all the dope, anytime. They brought the steward down to Yen Yuan and a couple of more. You're going to be shy a third officer, Betty. Last seen of Larson he was making the last hundred yards to the squarehead concession in nothin' flat."

"All right, Jimmie. Can the Taipings pry him, Wythe, I mean, away from Kang Hsi for us?" asked Grigsby.

"Yen Yuan says no can do without a regular war. He's got some members scattered around up there, but this bird Kang is in the White Lily Society, and they and the Taipings aren't taking tea together at the moment. Yen Yuan says that he will pass the word for all this bunch to ease off for Wythe as much as possible, and if they get a chance, protect him. He says that he'll give us a junk and as many men as we want to man it, and that if I say so he'll declare a tong war on the White Lily outfit, who are stronger than horse radish up in the country, but not near as strong as the Taipings in the cities. I told him to lay off because I figured that if Kang Hsi got in a jam he'd blame it on Wythe and he'r scrag him on general principles."

"Which is just what he would do," said Grigsby. "He'd find out the reason for the war and—"

"What the h—heck do we be doin' sitting here for?" demanded Red. "We know where he is, don't we? Well, then, what more do we want—a map or some wan to lead us by the hand? Let's go and get him and have done with all this wah-wahin'. Sure, herself is worried bad and—"

"That's right, Red," grinned Jimmie Cordie. "There's only about twenty million Chinese between here and Pa-tang. What's a few million Chinks to—"

"Nothin'," said Red, firmly. " 'Tis many of them we've slapped outa the way before now—and well ye know it, Jimmie Cordie!"

"We'll go in light," said Grigsby, "and pack all the ammunition we can. We'll get the Boston Bean and the Fighting Yid to go along—that'll give us another machine gun. Tell Yen Yuan to have the junk ready by noon, Jimmie. Betty, you go back to the yacht. You're in no danger now."

"Not after word has been passed that the *Mona* is under the wing of Yen Yuan," said Jimmie. "Take her back, Red."

"**WHAT!**" said Betty Wythe, sitting up very straight. "I—go back! Well, I will not. With my daddy in danger and—" she stopped, seeing the glint of steel begin to come in the eyes of the four men and at once changed her tactics. "Please," she began to coax, "Red—you can take care of me. I can shoot a rifle now, and a revolver, too. Daddy taught me. Honest I can, Jimmie. George, you know that you and Putt can take care of me, you know you can. I—" Her lovely lips began to tremble and go down at the corners.

"Sure now, darlin'," began Red, sternly. " 'Tis well ye know that we can't take ye along wid us. Wid men now, it's different. What would the likes of ye be doin' along wid us roughnecks? 'Tis hard goin', acushla, and there'll be hard fighting and—"

"But—don't you see?" pleaded Betty. "It's you that I want to go with. Anybody else—it wouldn't matter. But you did have me with you—and you did take care of me—and I'll wear a boy's suit and my hair is short now—and— Please take me! You and daddy are the only people in the world I care about—so why shouldn't I go?"

Jimmie Cordie laughed.

"Putting it the way Betty does, I vote we take her!"

"You two," said Grigsby with a grin of warm understanding, "are a couple of darn idiots. Once for all—no females of the species allowed. I give Betty credit for being game and I also think we could take care of her, if we had to—but no man in his sane senses would take a woman into the interior of China at the moment. Betty—you go back to the yacht like a nice girl."

"That's cold turkey," said Putney. "I vote with George."

"Let's compromise," said Jimmie Cordie. "This junk of Yen Yuan's can be loaded to the guardrails with the best fighting men of the Taipings and, by gosh, if I ask him he'll send another to lead the procession and one to act as rear guard. It's fairly safe on the river and no outfit unless they're stark crazy will jump a bunch of Taipings going on about their business. Supposing we take Betty with us, leave her on the junk at Pa-tang, take a little pasear into town, bring back her daddy, which shouldn't take long, and all come down the river? I'll guarantee that with Yen Yuan's highbinders looking out for her that she won't be touched."

"If that's the case and they're so good," asked Putney, "why not land them and mop up?"

"Because on the river and on the land are two different things. We won't be in sight on the river, and whoever could jump the Taipings would be to blame. If they openly backed us up on land it would be the same as war, nitwit. Besides if they started in with us the Chinese would think it a tong war and all rally around. On the river we would only have to fight what junks were launched against us, Archibald, me son!"

"Jimmie's right," said Grigsby. "Well, if Betty will pass her word of honor that she won't ask to land, and will stick close to Jimmie's buddies, and he can get Yen Yuan to furnish the junks, I'll vote that she comes up the river, anyway."

"I won't," said Betty, promptly, her eyes shining. "Word of honor, I won't ask. Oh, I'm so glad."

"Let's go," said Red, standing up. "What's all the yappin' about, anyway?"

"Plenty of time until morning," answered Jimmie Cordie. "I've got to go and see Yen Yuan about the junk's and get the latest news from the front. Want to go along, Red?"

"Who, me? Wid herself to look after? Go tend to yer knittin', ye shrimp."

"I didn't want you along, anyway," said Jimmie Cordie from the door. "You're much too ladylike to mix with us highbinders!"

MANY days later, three large junks flying Taiping house flags made their way unnoticed into an old disused canal and threaded their way along its silent length until it brought them some distance from the river toward a range of hills. Beyond those hills lay the city of Kang Hsi.

Shortly after the junks had come to anchor, a body of men disembarked, traversed the flats near the river, and began the steep ascent of the low mountains. From a distance the little column toiling up the slope looked as any other party of Chinese laborers would. They were bent over, carrying heavy loads, and they were dressed as ordinary coolies.

"Sure now," panted Red Dolan, leader of the men dressed like coolies, putting a hundred-pound box of machine gun ammunition down on a rock at the side of the trail, just at the summit, and peering down into the valley revealed, "Jimmie, ye shrimp, why the hell ye couldn't have had some of yer friends along to pack this, I dunno."

"Because, dumb-bell," answered Cordie, grinning, putting down the part of the Browning machine gun he was carrying, "I told you that if the Taipings got into a scrap with us along it would mean a war. Now, they can claim that they didn't know what we were after or that they never saw us at all and we weren't on their junks."

"'Tis too high politics for me," grunted Red. "I've carried that damn' box until me back is broke."

"Stick around, old kid," said Putney. "From the looks of things down there, it won't be long now before you have a chance to get rid of some of the weight."

"Ain't that somepin'?" demanded Red, looking down at the sprawling Chinese city in the valley below. "Some one must have told those babies we was comin'."

At the foot of the mountain and running out into a cultivated valley was a Chinese city of a thousand houses or more, a walled city with small canals running through it to the valley beyond. Thousands of Chinese were in the fields and on the walls and outside the walls on the mountain side. There was a good deal of running back and forth and a parade of troops out of the main gate looking toward the mountain.

Grigsby looked at the scene below through his field glasses. "Not so bad," he said. "Darn few guns, mostly swords and spears, and a lot of bows and arrows. We can get through all right, if we don't stay too long. The countrymen won't fight. It'll be Kang Hsi soldiers that'll stay with us. Get those guns hooked up and let's go."

"First," said Red firmly, "I shed this nightgown I been wearin'. What kind of clothes they are for a man to wear, I dunno."

"That's Kang Hsi's palace up on the little hill in the center," said Jimmie Cordie. "According to the dope, Wythe is up in that little pagoda on the left. Come on, Yid, get that gun set. Game is to shoot our way to it, get him, turn around and start back, pronto. No lootin', Yid, you hear me?"

"Oi, Jimmie," expostulated the Fightin' Yid. "For vy you tell id to me only. Tell id to the Irisher by you."

"All right," said Grigsby, unslinging his thirty-thirty Winchester. "All kidding put over until tomorrow at three o'clock. Right down the trail. Jimmie, you and Red first, I'll back you up. Putt, you take the rear guard with the Yid and the Beaneater. Let's get down as far as possible before we start. Maybeso they'll give him up without trouble."

"What?" said Red, starting down the narrow trail. "After all this packin'. The black curse of Shielygh be on ye, George Grigsby, for even thinking such a thing."

THE MILLING and running about stopped on the plain between the city and the foot of the mountain and the Chinese lines stiffened as they stood and watched the approach of the little party. There was no forward movement as yet. Not until they had reached the level, five hundred yards away. Then there was a sudden drawing of swords and the flash of spears and a body of four or five hundred Chinese charged straight at them. A ragged volley of gun fire came from both flanks. The Fighting Yid and the Bean having no rear to protect as yet, promptly swung their gun around, and Putney stepped up alongside of Grigsby. The two deadly little tubes swung idly for a moment, manned by men who were unafraid and second to none in the handling of them.

Four hundred yards, then three, and Grigsby raised his thirty-thirty to his cheek. The machine guns set up a *rat-tat, rat-tat, rat-tat!* and the steel jacketed bullets tore through the crowded charge, cutting wide lanes. The charge halted, half blown to pieces inside of ten seconds.

But these were the simon pure fighting men of Kang Hsi,

and the eyes of the city and their master were on them. They reformed and came on, their faces set and grim. They knew what machine guns were, these men, and yet they faced them without fear. It may have been that they feared what Kang Hsi would do to them if they failed, more than they did the guns in front.

Jimmie Cordie picked up the leading-groups and swept them out of existence as calmly and coldly as if watering the garden at home. The Fighting Yid and the Bean were firing into the mass. Grigsby and Putney were shooting as fast as they could pull trigger. Shooting to kill, which they did at every shot.

The few Chinese that were left by the time the charge had come another hundred yards, turned and ran or threw themselves on the ground to avoid the death that hissed and whistled around them everywhere.

"Let's go," commanded Grigsby. "Straight through to the city gate, then in. Clear the way, Jimmie. Get back with that other gun, Yid."

The Chinese in front of the gate were fighting men and stood their ground. A company charged across with fixed bayonets, led by a young man in a natty khaki uniform. From the wall, an old brass cannon roared, the ball sailing far overhead. The Chinese are good men with a sword or any kind of cold steel, but with a gun their idea is to put it to their shoulder, shut their eyes, point it upward and let it go.

Cordie swung the Browning, spitting steel down the line of bayonets from one end to the other, slowly and carefully, going back to pick up any groups he missed. When he came to the end, the line was no more. He had wiped it out.

"That's giving 'em hell and repeat, Jimmie darlin'," said Red. "Sure 'tis yerself that can—"

"Less talk and more fast with those belts," answered Jimmie. "What are you doing, taking a nap?"

"A nap? Sure, you shrimp of the world, I'll knock—"

"All right, let's go," said Grigsby. "All the way this time. Mop up on the sides, Yid, as we go along. Cut her loose, Jimmie, old-timer."

They fought their way slowly toward the gate. Slowly, because they had to halt and fight off charge after charge. The bullets of the old trade guns were whistling closer now, but most of the opposition was in the form of massed charges by swords-men. If the Chinese had spread out and started to attack in waves and groups they could have overwhelmed the white men in a matter of minutes, but they didn't. There would be a waver-ing and a milling around, then a charge by two or three hundred, which was met and swept out of existence by the two machine guns. The Chinese are brave, good fighters, whatever may be the general belief, but they also fully believe that 'he who fights and runs away, will live to fight another day.' Already, there was a steady ebb out toward the valley below around the city walls.

"Look out!" suddenly yelled Grigsby. "They're going to shut the big gates! Shoot 'em away from it, Jimmie! Jimmie! The gate—you fool!" and he stopped to make Jimmie hear.

"I got you, stiff," answered Jimmie, cheerfully, and began pouring a stream of bullets through the gate and around it. By now they were within one hundred yards of it and the machine gun worked by Cordie and Dolan literally blew all signs of life away from the big wooden gates.

The gun in the rear, with the Fighting Yid at the trigger, was as merciless and accurate. Those of the Chinese left between the city and the mountain, charged in or tried to bring down the men of the deadly little column with their rifles. Putney, who could wear the distinguished marksman's badge, stood calmly beside them, picking off man after man with his thirty-thirty.

THEY fought their way into the city, through the gate, up the narrow climbing little street toward the palace of Kang Hsi. Cordie would sweep the roofs and the upper story of the houses lining the street with the machine gun, the Fighting Yid keeping the road to the gate clear in the rear. There was very little opposition until they got to the palace of Kang Hsi. Then they met with a charge of swordsmen and with rifle fire from the windows. Grigsby spun around, dropped his rifle and went down. The Boston Bean fell across the machine gun the Yid was fighting.

"With me, Yid," called Jimmie Cordie. "Mop up on the house!"

The two machine guns rapped out the answer to the sudden attack. The Yid cleared the front of the palace and the roof, sweeping the windows clear. Jimmie Cordie shot as closely and as accurately as with a rifle, and the charging mass went down.

"Red!" Cordie shouted, "get to the pagoda! Get Wythe! Go with him, Putt. Come on, Yid! Feed me—let that gun go to hell for a minute! Get goin', you two. I'll shoot you a path."

Up the hill ran the two big white men, their rifles discarded, their heavy Colt forty-fives in their hands. Up and to the pagoda. As they came close to it a Chinaman slid around from the rear, put a big key in the door, unlocked it and disappeared again. Evidently the Taipings, though not actively taking part in the raid, were standing by with help of a very useful kind.

In they went, there was the sound of several shots, then out, with a gray haired white man between them.

"Got him," said Jimmie Cordie, cheerfully. "Feed me, Inkenstein, feed me!"

"Is George dead now, Jimmie?" asked Red, when they got back. "Sure it's a black day for—"

"Take this gun for a minute and I'll see," answered Cordie. "No, he's got it in the shoulder and through the leg and a damn' bad scalp wound of some kind. He's breathing all right. Pick him up, Red. Putt, you pack the Bean." Wythe had already stooped and picked up Grigsby's rifle and unbuckled Cabot Winthrop's cartridge belt with the Colt forty-five hanging in the holster. "The Yid and I will fight the gun. Mr. Wythe, you pick off any gunmen you can. Let's go."

"Right," said Wythe cheerfully. "You chaps came just in time, I fancy."

Red Dolan, carrying Grigsby over his broad shoulder, stalked along, his Colt in his hand. Putney followed with the lighter Winthrop, then Wythe, then the Fighting Yid and Cordie. One Browning they left where it was after taking the firing pin and breech mechanism. Their way to the mountain was absolutely unopposed.

"Not so good," said Cordie, when they reached the bottom of the mountain trail and stopped to rest. "That bird has too many men left to let us get away with it like this. He'll bushwhack us somewhere en route, I'll bet you."

"Wadda we care?" demanded Red. "We can do some of that bushwhackin' stuff ourselves. If George now is only alive and—"

The Beaneater stirred and tried to sit up from where Putney had put him. "What happened?" he asked, opening his eyes. "Did I—are we—"

"You did—and we are—" answered Cordie, grimly. "Don't tell me you've only been taking a nap."

"Nap?" Winthrop felt his head gingerly. "I must have been—must have been—"

"You were. Let's get going. Can do, Red, up the hill?"

"Wid George?" asked Red, amazed. "Sure, I could carry himself all the way to Hong Kong. I wish now that he'd be comin' to. 'Tis too much like he's hurt bad."

"Hop to it then," said Cordie. "Yid, you go out in front a little ways. Mr. Wythe will give me a hand with this gun. Easy does it, now. How about it, Putt, got him?"

"Yeah boy," answered Putney, with a grunt, as he heaved the now protesting Bean on his shoulder. "Cut your wolf loose, old settler."

UP THIS narrow trail, in easy laps. A hundred feet or so, then a rest. The Yid was acting as scout. They made it to the top and started down, the lake and the junks in sight, some three miles away. Grigsby had become conscious and they had stopped to bandage his wounds and to examine the Bean's head. It looked as if he had been creased by a bullet, and they bandaged him up also with their handkerchiefs and parts of the tails of their shirts.

Wythe told them that Kang Hsi had threatened him with torture in the morning unless he produced the papers or told where they could be found. He said that the papers had been sent to England for safe keeping and that Kang Hsi had refused to believe it.

They started down, the Bean insisting on walking now. Red and Putney alternating on packing Grigsby. Jimmie Cordie couldn't pack the Browning by himself, so Wythe gave him as much help as he could. There were not many rounds left for it and those few Wythe and Cordie carried.

Halfway down the trail ran between two narrow walls, then widened out into a little canyon or gorge. The Yid got about half way through, climbed up a little ways, and then came to a halt, drew his Colt, fired the contents of the chamber, and ran back up the trail as fast as his short little legs would carry him.

"Oi, Jimmie," he began, as soon as he got near enough, "der is a million of dem down below mit guns and everything. Now ve get it some regular fighting, vat?"

"Hold 'er a minute," said Putney. "Looks like they got us in a trap, old kid. See up on the top, behind."

There on the top of the mountain behind them, massed on either side of the trail and on it, were hundreds of Chinese, keeping under cover and as low as possible, but there, just the same.

Cordie laughed. "Trap is right, Archibald. We've only got about a dozen rounds left for the baby here. They'll last as long as a snowball in hell. We'll have to hole up here on this side under that hanging ledge and let them bring it to us, I guess."

And bring it they did, from above and below at once. Up the trail and down it charged the Chinese, this time in mass formation that reached from wall to wall. Jimmie Cordie shot away the last rounds for the Browning first up and then down without doing any more than plugging the trail up for a moment or so while the rest climbed over the bodies.

The Bean had recovered enough to use his rifle and now, with Wythe, who was almost as good a shot but not so fast, who was using Grigsby's rifle, they poured a steady stream of death up and down the trail. It was fast shooting by men who were all veterans, but it served only to check and slow down the Chinese, who came on regardless of losses. Red was kneeling beside Jimmie Cordie now, their two rifles throwing out an almost continuous stream of steel jacketed bullets. The Bean, his long legs stretched apart, far from his millions and yachts and town houses, stood with a grin on his face and threw lead with the best of them. Wythe stood like a sportsman at a pheasant drive in England, his gun a little slower but just as deadly. The Fighting Yid was talking to himself and the rest and the Chinese all the time his lever was working.

"Oi, such a biziness! I got you, feller! Oi, Jimmie, ve gif dem hell, ain't it? My—der is a million, I bet you! I vish dat de old gang vas here mit de guns. I got you too, feller, likevise."

Nearer and nearer came the massed Chinese, now within a hundred yards. Sixty or seventy men going down every ten seconds, the rest not stopping longer than to hurdle the bodies and come on.

Jimmie Cordie exhausted his thirty-thirty shells and drew his Colt, a minute later Red followed suit. "Jimmie, will the Taipings take care of herself, now?" he grunted, as he raised his Colt.

"Yeah, boy," answered Jimmie, cheerfully, "or they'll lose their heads. Don't worry, Red, old kid."

"Stay wid 'em," Red answered. "Jimmie, darlin' sure it's a good way to go out wid—"

"None bet— Look coming down the sides. They'll—Holy Mackinaw! It's the Taipings and—look at that little devil sliding down in front of them!"

DOWN the steep sides of the hills poured and slid the best and most deadly fighting men in China. The Kang Hsi men promptly stopped, turned and ran, those that could. Those that were caught in the middle stood and fought until cut down.

Betty Wythe ran up and threw herself in her father's arms, "Oh, Daddy! Daddy! You're safe—you're safe!"

Yen Yuan's captain, who commanded the junks, came up with the interpreter to Jimmie Cordie, his cruel, scarred young face still lighted with the lust of killing, his sword red, and bowed low. "Lord—my insignificant head depended on your safety."

"I'm darn' glad it did," answered Cordie with a grin.

Grigsby sat up and looked at Betty Wythe. The sick feeling had gone and he knew that his wounds were not serious. "Didn't you promise not to leave the junk?" he demanded.

"No, I didn't. I promised not to ask if I could go with you—and I didn't either. I made Shih-kai bring me. Oh, George—you're wounded—and for me!" she slipped out of her father's arms and knelt beside Grigsby, her slim young arms going around his neck.

"So am I wounded," said the Boston Bean, firmly.

THAT FISH THING

*"Shall not a friend act as a friend always?" Red
Dolan and Jimmie Cordie thought so—and
when a friend sought their aid, he found them
heeled and ready for what turned out to he the
wildest adventure of their wild careers.*

"**WAIT A MINUTE**, Red," said Jimmie Cordie, swinging in toward the window of a native shop in the Street of Benevolent Wisemen, Hongkong. "I want to see those jades."

The big Irishman grinned and turned with Jimmie to the window. "Look at that now," he said. "Let's go in and see them closer."

A young Chinaman, who was talking to the old proprietor looked up as the two white men came in.

"Led! Jimmie!" he shouted, running to meet them, holding out both hands. His clean-cut young face, with its aristocratic features, was lit up with joy.

Jimmie and Red both smiled.

"Hullo, Liu-hsia!" Jimmie said, shaking one of the hands held out, as Red grasped the other. "What are you doing down here, oh honorable cadet of the magnificent house of Yin?"

At the same time Red Dolan was saying, "Sure, 'tis me little fighting cock of the North, himself. What the devil now—are ye here steppin' out, ye omadhaun?"

Liu-hsia, prince of the ancient house of Yin, smiled and patted Red's big arm. "I come for blizness—stlictly blizness, Led."

"Business? And what the hell kind of business do a sprid-houge like ye—"

"Give Liu-hsia a chance to talk a little, you big ape," interrupted Cordie. "Use your mouth more to eat with!"

135

"What? Sure I'll take four shrimps like ye—"

"See, there you go—still talking. Take a rest, then you can tell me how many Cordies you think you can take."

"That's right, Jimmie, alanna," grinned Red, who loved Jimmie Cordie better than anything on earth. "Go on, ye little bantam!" to Liu-hsia.

Three years before, Jimmie Cordie and Red Dolan, with Grigsby and Putney, the other two members of the quartet that had fought together in the French Foreign Legion, in the A.E.F., and for the years after in the Orient, had fought for Liu-hsia's father in North China. His father had been one of the generals in the Army of the North and had been educated in England. Liu-hsia could understand English better than he could speak it, although when not excited he could speak very good English in the way his father had taught him.

Now he smiled and said, "We go somewhere and I tell you, Led and Jimmie. Maybeso, now I flind you—can do much better."

"All right, Liu-hsia," said Jimmie. "Come on, we'll go to Grigsby's—Putt is there also."

He called the proprietor up from the rear. "One thousand li," he offered, pointing to some of the jades.

"Won hundled tlosand li," answered the old man, indignantly, "Jlade of Tzu-kung."

"You have my royal permission to keep them," answered Jimmie gravely.

The old man evidently intended to do so as he promptly removed himself to the rear once more, talking to himself.

Liu-hsia's story of how he came to be in Hongkong was briefly told after they reached Grigsby's apartment, where they found both Grigsby and Putney.

His father had sent a trusted retainer to Hongkong with money for additional guns and ammunition. This trusted retainer had arrived—and seemingly dropped out of sight like a stone in a well. Then, a polite message had come from the Chi

Huan Society—a message which meant, stripped of its verbiage, "We got your man Friday and unless you come through with a million li he will die very soon—and take a long time to do it!"

The father of Liu-hsia did not know what to do. The last thing in the world that he wanted to do was to antagonize the

Chi Huan, although he lived and fought far in the north. He recognized that the kidnapping of his man was strictly a matter of business. He would have—and had—done the same. But what puzzled him was not knowing whether or not the Chi Huan had scragged the old man and were asking for a million li on general principle afterward—or whether he was still alive and the message was a true one. His own connections in Hongkong were too weak to attempt any sort of a rescue—even the ascertaining of correct information. He needed the man—and the guns and ammunition more. Whether his man had deliberately sold out to the Chi Huan and was helping to mop up on him was another thing.

Grigsby listened to all Liu-hsia told. "You are sure that the headquarters of the Chi Huan are where you say?"

"Yes, in the Street of Much Wisdom."

"Then the chances are that you will find your man there, or word of him. They won't be looking for attack at headquarters. Can you ease in there without them knowing you or—"

"Aw, what the hell," interrupted Red. "Let's go and take the damn place apart. What's the use of so much talkin'? Jimmie and me will go in the front and you and Putt come in from the rear, won't we Jimmie?"

"Yeah, boy," said Jimmie, "and right after all of us will come nine million yellow brothers."

"Jimmie's right, Red," said Putney. "That's bad medicine down there. Better let Liu-hsia do some scouting first and find out if his man's there. I've been within a mile of that street and boy howdy, they're thicker than flies around a molasses pot."

"We could get in all right," said Grigsby, "the mere fact of our coming in cold turkey as if we owned the place will hesitate them for a little while. We can't lick a million Chinese, that's a cinch, and they'll all come rallying around the flag, irrespective of who's who—once it starts."

"What?" said Red, in honest amazement, "Sure, Jimmie and me will shoot a road for ye lady-fingered old women, won't we, Jimmie, darlin'?"

"Two roads, one for each," said Jimmie, promptly, smiling at the big Irishman, "let's take a couple of Browning submachines along, Red. We'll guarantee a safe trip to these weak sisters, won't we?"

"Let Red take 'me good sword,'" jeered Putney. "Why fuss with carrying machine guns?"

"While you apes are telling how good you are," said Grigsby, "will you pardon me if I go away somewhere and frame this thing with Liu-hsia?"

"We will," said Jimmie Cordie, gravely, "with pleasure."

THE HOUSE OF ENJOYMENTS was about as safe a place for a white man as a den of copperhead snakes would be in August. The Chinese guides, who piloted tourists into what they alleged was the native quarter, knew better than to bring any party within half a mile of the Street of Much Wisdom. It was the headquarters of the Chi Huan Society, which came nearest of all the Chinese secret societies in rivaling the Taipings in numbers and ruthlessness.

Grigsby had arranged with Liu-hsia that if he found his man there and was uncovered doing it or needed them that he was to get a message to them if possible, if no message was received inside of six hours, they would come and get him—or take the House of Enjoyments apart. The message had come, delivered by a little singing girl who had flitted into Grigsby's apartment, spoken a few words to Grigsby's house-boy and away again.

The message was *"Liu-hsia prisoner at House of Enjoyments, come quick."*

And now they sat there, sipping tea and nibbling the little cakes as calmly as if in Grigsby's apartment in the American quarter. They were all big men, lean, browned, hard bitted, with muscles trained to coordinate instantly. All with the chilled steel nerves that must go with the makeup of men who follow the Lost Legion's trail and they were all firm believers in "what is written, is written."

Jimmie Cordie, the slightest of the four, was the best shot, if it were possible to pick the best out of four men who were all entitled to wear the distinguished marksman bar and pendants. Any one of them would have gone singing to his death for the rest, collectively or individually.

They had calmly sauntered down the Street of Much Wisdom, the Chinese giving sullenly way. There was something about the four big men, clothed in immaculate white linen, something the natives sensed as infinitely dangerous. The absolute air of confidence and indifference to surroundings helped them gain the House of Enjoyments without interference. Once inside they had been served without comment. The room was fairly well crowded with Chinese of various stations.

One of the singing girls drifted from table to table, finally reaching the one at which the four men sat. She sat down cross-legged beside Jimmie Cordie, tuned up the singing guitar and began to sing softly, leaning forward a little.

"Phoenix, bright Phoenix,
Thy glory is ended!

Think of the future;
The past can't be mended.
The court is today
With danger attended."

Just as she finished several Chinamen came into the room from the rear and the little singing girl rose and fluttered away.

"Heads up!" said Jimmie, calmly reaching for his teacup, "The young lady has just tipped us off that it's going to rain."

"Yeah?" asked Red. "How did she? It sounded like a lot of nothing to me."

"It's the 'Phoenix song'—the song with which Chieh-yu tipped Confucius. Yen Yuan translated it for me."

"Ease over a little, Red," said Putney. "I need a bit more room."

"We'll force the play," said Grigsby quietly, his eyes on the advancing group of Chinese. "Red, when the man in the lead gets within reach, and I raise my finger, gather him in. Jimmie, you and Putt shove your guns in the ribs of the next two. I'll attend to the rest."

THE TALL, gaunt Chinaman strode haughtily up to the table followed closely by two others. When he halted he was within a foot of Red Dolan's back. Red had not turned, sitting there as if totally relaxed, his eyes on Grigsby's left hand which was resting idly on the table.

The Chinaman stood there, his little piglike eyes venomous as he stared at the lean, browned face of Grigsby, who looked at him with steady inquiring eyes.

"My house is no place for foreign devils," he snarled. The man beside him translated the Chinese into English. The crowded room suddenly became quiet and tense. Here and there a hand slipped under a blouse.

"And you are?" questioned Grigsby, not changing his position in the slightest.

"Kung Chu," the Chinaman answered, "and—"

One of the fingers of Grigsby's hand rose an inch from the table. Red rose and turned with the quickness of a grizzly bear in action, one iron hand closed on the Chinaman's throat and the other slipped between his crotch. He heaved once and the Chinaman spun around like a pinwheel in the air, then Red crashed him down on the table, from which the rest had promptly stepped back, holding him face up, with one brawny hand.

"Here he is, George," he announced.

As Red lifted him from the floor, Jimmie's Colt forty-five automatic was digging into the ribs of the man who had translated and Putney's was in the right ear of the other man before the Chinaman hit the table.

There was a long hiss of astonishment from the room, then absolute silence. Grigsby stood, with his big blued steel Colt in his hand, a smile on his face. It was a frozen little smile and it told the Chinese in the room plainer than words that the first man that moved would die.

"Watch the rear, Red," said Grigsby. "Translate, you!" to the man Jimmie Cordie's gun was on. "Kung Chu dies at the first move. You two also. We came here for a friend—we will take him with us and go. Those that stand in our way die also."

There was no slacking of the tension in the room as the man translated, just an intent watchfulness.

"Take him by the scruff of the neck, Red, and start out the rear. You birds take your two playmates along. The lad that Red's got knows where Liu-hsia is, I think. I'll cover—get going."

Red lifted the Chinaman on the table like a fox terrier would a rat, and shook him once or twice the same way, also. The Chinese between them and the rear door, made way for them, not too far back on either side—but far enough to give them a clear passage. The sight of Kun Chu in the hands of the big Irishman with the cold blue eyes seemed to paralyze any thought of action for the moment at least.

Just as the first two, Putney and his man, had nearly reached the door, it slid back and the opening filled with Chinese, swords in hand. There was a quick bunching together—then a swift charge directly at the four men and their prisoner.

Putney pushed the man he was with away from him, then as the man's hand came up from his blouse with a knife, shot him between the eyes. As he did, Red slipped the struggling Kung Chu under one arm, drew his Colt and rapped him smartly over the head with the barrel, "Be still now, ye baboon," he said, and then began firing into the face of the charge.

Jimmie Cordie's man slipped like an eel to the floor and reached for Cordie's legs. Jimmie laughed and his knee caught the Chinaman under the chin, knocking him out.

There was a surge forward now, all over the room and a knife sunk deep into the wall within an inch of Putney's head.

Grigsby shot from the hip, Red turning to help drive the rush back in front. They stopped it—with six dead Chinamen on the floor. The firing had been so rapid and merciless that the Chinese, brave, as they were, shrank back, seeking cover wherever they could find it.

PUTNEY and Jimmie Cordie had made the doorway look like a shambles. One moment crowded with lithe, eager fighting men, the next, a writhing twisting mass of wounded and dead.

"Get in the hall," shouted Jimmie Cordie. "Hold 'em back, George. You and Red! Putt and I'll go through."

Grigsby and Red backed to the doorway, jumped the pile of bodies—Red with Kung Chu hanging limp under his arm. The hall was a fairly wide one, with passageways leading off both right and left.

"Put him down, Red," Grigsby ordered. "Take the rear. I'll stop 'em this way."

Red eased the unconscious Chinaman to the floor and straddled him. "Where the hell did that shrimp get to, I dunno!" he said. As if in answer to his question a burst of shots came from the passageway on the right and two Chinese ran across the main hall. As they reached the center there were two more shots, so fast that they sounded like 'powpow' and both China-men spun around like tops then fell on their faces.

Red grinned and yelled, "That's the boy, Jimmie, ye scut! Stay wid 'em!"

When it had started, just before the first rush, someone had called an order and the big iron gate of the compound had swung shut. The Chi Huan Society felt fully able to conduct its own wars without outside help. This had stopped the popu-lace from pouring in. Outside the street was an excited, milling mass of men, being increased every second by those within hearing of the shots.

As the two shots came from the interior, there was another rush from the big room. This time guns began to spit lead at the foreign devils who had dared to come and kill in the Chi Huan headquarters.

Again it was met and halted by the cold, accurate shooting of Grigsby. Red had leaned against the wall so that he could still see down the passageway and joined in. When it was over, Grigsby had a bullet in his left shoulder and a thin trickle of blood was running down Red's face where a bullet had grazed his forehead.

What saved both men was the fact that the Chinese were shooting guns of poor workmanship, not clean, and most of all, the almost universal habit they have of shutting their eyes when they pull the trigger.

"Did ye get hit, George, darlin'?" asked Red, as he reloaded, "I got wan across the mug from the feel of it."

"In the shoulder," answered Grigsby, "not very bad, I guess. Jimmie and Putt better be getting a move on. We can't stay here all night. These birds will let some more of the gang in."

"Why not?" demanded Red, "what the hell is a few Chinks? I'll take the butt of me gat here and go through a million of 'em."

"Why not 'me good sword'." grinned Grigsby, leaning a little against the doorway. The pain of the torn nerves and flesh in his shoulder was beginning to make him feel a little sick.

Two of the tables in the room seemed to rise as if by magic and come rushing at the door. Neither Red nor Grigsby fired at the tables. They knew that the men behind would have to drop them as soon as they reached the pile of bodies, or raise them up.

Both of the big men stood tensed, their Colts held loosely in their steady hands, waiting. One of the wounded men on the floor precipitated the action. As he saw the table coming toward him, he rose to his knees and tried to crawl out of the way. Instead he fell against the legs of the men pushing it, who stumbled over him and the table fell forward, uncovering the five men behind it, who also fell. Grigsby shot them off the overturned table, one after the other as they tried to roll to safety.

THE OTHER TABLE stopped, wavered, retreated a little, then came on with a rush. When it reached the pile of dead in front of the door, it was lifted, thrown to one side, and six of the Chi Huan charged home across the bodies of their brothers. They had no guns, but the bright steel blades of their long knives flickered in the light of the many lanterns hanging from the walls.

Grigsby was reloading when the second table arrived and Red stepped forward to check it. The first two men plunged forward, dead before they fell on the bodies under them. Grigsby snapped a fresh clip into the butt of his Colt and killed the third. The other three won through to the hall, two of them twisted by Grigsby and jumped at Red, their knives out like the tongues of snakes. Grigsby parried the knife thrust of the other with his Colt and with a continuation of the swing and a right moulinet, beat him to a second thrust with the barrel of his gun across the temple.

Red's gun roared in the face of the first man to reach him and he took the knife of the other in his left forearm. The man with the knife had lunged forward and now was close to Red, whose gun rose and fell twice and the man went down like a poled ox.

"Come here with me, Red," said Grigsby, calmly. "I'm getting pretty sick to the stomach for some reason. They'll rush us again in a minute. It'll help stop the—look out! Your Chink is crawling away!"

Red pounced on Kung Chu who was crawling down the hall, like a big tiger would on a wounded deer. "Come back here," he said sternly, "I'll let ye know when to go away, ye monkey faced gorilla," and he flung him back under his feet and once more straddled him, part of the Chinaman's blouse in his hand. "What now, George?"

Grigsby finished reloading and grinned. "Considering I have only two more rounds," he said, "I think James better be showing up pronto!"

"Let's go and find them and—"

From the side hall into the main came a compact little party, first Putney, then Liu-hsia, with a long curved sword in his hand, his robes torn and dirty, blood clotted on the side of his head. With him was an old Chinaman and the singing girl that had sung to Cordie. Back of them was Jimmie Cordie. "Come on," he called, "Get in front of us down the first hall."

"They'll pile in on us from the doorway, Jimmie," answered Grigsby. "Lots left out here."

"I'll hesitate 'em if they do. Come on, Liu-hsia's girl friend knows a back way out."

Grigsby emptied his Colt into the room, then turned and ran down the hall after Red, who started down as Jimmie called.

"Gimme that sword," Red demanded of Liu-hsia, "an' Jimmie and me will mop up on these Chinks. I have no more shells for me gat."

"I told you to fill your pockets, you red-headed ape," said Cordie. "Give him nothing—get in front, you and George. Gimme room accordin' to my size and disposition."

THE SINGING GIRL led the way through dark halls and rooms, then down a flight of stairs, Jimmie Cordie walking about ten feet back of them, shutting door after door behind him. Suddenly Red stopped and started back.

"I forgot me Chink," he said as he got to Cordie.

"What were you saving him for?" asked Jimmie with a grin.

Red looked puzzled for a moment. "Damned if I know," he admitted. "I thought George wanted him."

"Why don't you ask him if he does?" suggested Jimmie, gravely.

"Tiz a good idea. Hey, George, did ye want the Chink I had? If ye did I'll go back and get him for you."

Grigsby turned and looked at Red. "Why—no, Red. Thanks just the same," he said politely. He knew that if he had said otherwise, that the fighting Irishman would have gone promptly back.

The singing girl said something to Liu-hsia, who translated. "No can do—stay here. This way not known to many—only girls—lunnin' away—make noise—get all Kung Chu men here."

"Where does it come up, Liu-hsia?" asked Grigsby.

"In a house that is friendly to the singing girl on the Street of Blossoms. There are iron gates to close, she says, that will stop any following."

"Get going," said Cordie. "Stick around with me, Red."

"Where'd ye find him, Jimmie?"

"In one of the rooms to the right, way back. The little singing girl came up after we turned and showed us. He was tied up alongside of the old bird he was after. The Chi Huan must have spotted him about as soon as he got in. The little girl's father was a brave of the House of Yin a long time ago and when she heard that one of the house was in dutch, she got to him, alle same one clansman to another."

"Yeah? Did he have the jack on him yet?"

"What a question to ask. Hold your arm out." Jimmie pulled up his soft white shirt and tore off a long strip. "I hate you like hell," he grinned, "but not enough to see you bleed to death, you poor fish."

Red held out his arm, "Hey, Jimmie—it won't be very nourishin' for her when she comes back, will it?"

"Just about as nourishing as kissing a rattlesnake. She won't go back, dumb-bell. Liu-hsia will take her north with him."

"Yeah? See what I got off the Chink I was packin' around thinkin' George wanted him!" and Red held out a little dull gold carving about as thick as his hand. It looked like three fish, all joined together, their tails, each in another's mouth.

"Put it away," answered Cordie, as they began to climb some stairs. "We'll look it over later, you darn pickpocket."

"I am not," defended Red. "When I reached for him the last time some of the coat come away in me hand—and this was in the piece."

They came up into a house, through a trap door and were met by an extremely scared old Chinaman, who protested volubly to the little singing girl, who answered him, then spoke to Liu-hsia. He turned to Grigsby, "Must go—quick! No can stay till morning. Old man lun, too. He stay now—Chi Huan kill him."

"Take a look out, James, me good man," said Putney, "and see how many of the neighbors's children are around."

"Yessir, your lordship," grinned Cordie.

"I'll go wid ye, Jimmie," said Red. "Maybeso we'll find some more of 'em in here."

"Not a soul in front or down toward the street of the Peacocks," Jimmie reported. "Hell of a hurroosh going on over in front of our late host's place of amusement. If we start right now we can get to Peacock Allee all right and from there on it's duck soup."

The old man whose house had been used as a sort of underground railway for singing girls and other ladies, promptly fell in with the party. The Street of the Peacocks was more or less deserted and the little party was not challenged. Any Chinese, after one look at the four white men and the scion of the House of Yin, who still had the long sword in his hand, decided that a whole skin was much better than gratified curiosity and dived into any place offering cover.

ONCE out of the native quarter, Liu-hsia laid the sword down on a window ledge and the entire party walked calmly to Grigsby's apartment in the breaking dawn without further excitement of any kind.

The little singing girl and the two old men were made comfortable. A British army doctor called to treat Grigsby's shoulder and Red's arm, and the four men with Liu-hsia sat in a council of war.

Liu-hsia told them that the old man had been brought to the Chi Huan on pretext of getting arms, his money taken away from him and that the message sent north was on the square.

"Well," said Putney, "we've got him back for you, anyway. But that's not much good in helping you mop up on this bird that's fighting your father. What your father needs is the guns and ammunition."

"And another thing," Grigsby supplemented, with a grin, "he better get organized pronto to take a battle from the Chi Huan."

"Aw, hell," said Red, "Jimmie'll get some of his highbinder buddies to clean that gang up, won't you, Jimmie?"

"I won't!" answered Jimmie, promptly. "Do you think they got nothing else to do but run around wiping my nose, you big piece of cheese? My gosh, since when have we had to holler for help?"

"Maybe ye think I'm afraid now?" asked Red, his eyes getting steely, "ye half baked shrimp of the world, I got a good—"

"You have," interrupted Grigsby, "you're all good—you and Jimmie both, with a copper on the bet. Take your private war outside, you big hunk of nothin'. We got some figuring to do and damn little time to do it in. Any time you think the Chi Huan are going to sit down and sob on each other's shoulders about what we did to them, you're fooled, boy. There's a price on our heads, right now, so far as that goes."

"Now," went on Grigsby, "lets get down to cases. How much money did your father send down?" he asked Liu-hsia.

"Thirty thousand tael in money, and some jewels worth about twice as much—altogether about ninety thousand taels."

"What's a tael worth now?" Grigsby asked.

"About seventy cents," Jimmie answered, "Maybe a little more. You can figure it about sixty thousand dollars, George."

Grigsby's house-boy knocked and after Grigsby called, entered. "China topside man come," he announced, "velly poltant man," he added, proud of his English.

"Show him in here," Grigsby answered, then as the house-boy retired—"Our Chi Huan friends are starting it off quicker than I thought."

THE MAN that the house-boy ushered in was a Chinaman, about forty-five years old, dressed in immaculate European afternoon calling clothes, cutaway coat, striped trousers, top hat and all. He was smooth shaven and wore a little pair of nose glasses, platinum rimmed.

As he came in, the four men rose. Liu-hsia remained seated, his eyes tightening a little. A prince of the House of Yin does not rise to greet a stranger—unless he knows the stranger's rank.

The Chinaman looked at the four big men, at the bandages on Grigsby's shoulder and on Red's arm, at the torn and be-draggled gold brocade on Liu-hsia's coat; and the arrogant look in his eyes was replaced by the more courteous expression of a man treating with his equals. He straightened, and his heels snapped together. He had received his military education in Germany, this Chinaman, and he showed it in his bow from the waist and the way his heels, cased in neat patent-leather shoes, hit each other. When he straightened up from his bow, he announced in perfect English, "Tzu-lu, of the Board of Foreign Affairs, Pekin."

Grigsby bowed in acknowledgment. "I am George Kenneth Grigsby, formerly Major, United States Army," he stated.

Grigsby then introduced the others, giving their names and service ranks.

The Chinaman bowed as each man was introduced. As Grigsby finished, Liu-hsia spoke from where he sat.

"And I am Liu-hsia of the insignificant, miserable, poor House of Yin."

The Chinaman bowed low to Liu-hsia. "My House of Wei is too much beneath the notice of the magnificent House of Yin to be spoken of in the same breath."

"And now that we know each other," said Grigsby, "I suggest that you be seated, Tzu-lu. Will you have a drink before you start to tell why we are honored by a visit from one of the Board of Foreign Affairs?"

"Hey, Jimmie," whispered Red. "What the hell is the Board of Foreign Affairs?"

"Same as our State Department," whispered Jimmie. "Keep still, I'll tell you later."

"I am not here officially," answered Tzu-lu, with a smile as he sat down. "And thank you, no; I do not drink this early in the day."

"You meant of course you are not here officially for the Board of Foreign Affairs. But you are—for the Chi Huan."

Tzu-lu leaned back in his chair and laughed, a real laugh of amusement and admiration. "You Americans," he said, "I spent eight very happy years in Washington as First Secretary of the Embassy. I admire the American people above all others save the Chinese. Yes, Major Grigsby, I am here officially, very much officially, for the Chi Huan Society. Will you tell me from the beginning, just what happened this morning?"

Grigsby smiled—"I think Captain Cordie will be the one to tell you about it. He was in the matter from start to finish."

Jimmie looked at Liu-hsia and grinned. "Any reason why I shouldn't?" he asked.

"I see none," answered the young Chinaman, grinning back at him. "This man of the honorable, most powerful House of Wei very plobably knows the beginning, oh, elder Mother."

Jimmie began at the point where he and Red met Liu-hsia

in the jade shop and told Tzu-lu all the way through up to the arrival at Grigsby's apartment.

"I see," said Tzu-lu, after he had listened carefully all the way without a single question. "You went there to protect a friend at his request. You were attacked and defended yourself. You rescue your friend and in the doing of which—some twenty of the Chi Huan die. But all that is honorable warfare and to be expected. You went there for that purpose only?"

"That is all," Jimmie answered, simply.

The Chinese diplomat looked at him closely, then sighed. "It is time I retired to my flower garden," he said. "My eyes have deceived me at last."

"What do you mean?" asked Jimmie.

"Because, Captain Cordie, while your story is quite full—you neglect to tell of one thing. It is true the Chi Huan took the old man, as the honorable father of the resplendent prince who honors this house, has done to many men. It is true that you rescued him—shall not a friend act as a friend always? That is as nothing, the Chi Huan can take the loss honorably, both the man—and their men—but that which you have taken, Captain Cordie, cannot be replaced and the stain cannot be washed out even with much blood. You have taken the heart of the Chi Huan and—"

"Wait a minute," interrupted Jimmie Cordie, a puzzled little frown showing in his usual laughing eyes and on his forehead. "It's too fast for me. First, let me tell you I have the greatest respect for the Chi Huan. They are fighting men—I can't say anything higher. Will you believe me when I say that frankly I don't know what the hell you are talking about?"

TZU-LU looked at him, a puzzled frown on his own brow. "You ring true—and yet— So— I will—what is it you say in America, oh, yes, I will come clean! More thousands of years ago that I know the Duke of Chi, who was Chien, established the Chi Huan. Ever since, the three sacred fish, made by his own hands, have been the heart of the Chi Huan. All vows are taken to them. The miserable Kung Chu, who is now dead, and some of his followers were entrusted to transport the sacred fish to the inner shrine. Two of his men before they died told that he had put the sacred fish on his person to carry them to the shrine when the alarm came that you four men were there. That is what I mean, Captain Cordie."

"Well, for Pete's sake!" and Jimmie grinned. "Now I got it. Red, what did you do with the thing you got when you grabbed for that big Chinaman?"

"What—them little fish?" asked Red, who had been regarding Tzu-lu with cold, hostile eyes. "It's in me coat over there on the chair. Is that what this guy has been wah-waning about?"

"That's her," Jimmie grinned. "Get it."

Tzu-lu's eyes widened in astonishment as Red got up and went over to a couch where his coat lay, carelessly tossed in a bundle.

They widened more as Red came back and handed Jimmie the three gold fish.

"This is it?" asked Jimmie, holding it in his hand.

"Yes," answered Tzu-lu rising.

"Sit down again for a minute," commanded Jimmie curtly. "There are one or two little matters to talk over. First, Red—tell Tzu-lu just how you got this thing."

"He crawled away from me," said Red grimly, "and I reached for him, the scut. When I pulled him back, part of his coat came away in me hands. In the piece I had in me fist was that fish thing. I put it in me pocket because I was due right then to get busy. I showed it to you on the way out, Jimmie, darlin', don't ye remember? Ye said ye'd look it over later. Is that what he wants now?"

"I guess it is, Red. Well, Tzu-lu?"

"I have put myself in your hands, Captain Cordie, in telling you of the value of the sacred fish to the Chi Huan."

"We are not hard to deal with," answered Cordie. "Red, it's your play, you got it."

"Do it for me, Jimmie," coaxed Red. "Whatever ye say, now, suits me."

"The matter of the ninety-odd thousand taels that the retainer of the House of Yin brought with him?" asked Jimmie.

"Every tael shall be returned."

"And as a penalty for—shall we say, losing the game and to salve his wounded wrists where the cords bit deep?"

"Whatever amount you mention."

"We will say another ninety thousand taels?" said Jimmie.

"It shall be paid with the rest."

"And—Liu-hsia goes to the north with guns and ammunition. Might it be possible the Chi Huan could, shall I say, help make the way smooth—after they know that in no way have we dishonored the sacred fish?"

"In many ways, with all their power shall the Chi Huan help smooth the way."

"And the little singing girl who goes with him?"

"Shall be stricken off the rolls of the songbirds with all honor, and a scroll presented to her, together with gold enough for her to retire. What is all this compared with the sacred fish?"

"Enough for us," said Jimmie, cheerfully. "Those terms of ransom satisfactory to you birds?"

Grigsby, Putney, Dolan and Liu-hsia all nodded and Jimmie stood up. With a bow Jimmie handed the little gold fishes to Tzu-lu.

"The money shall be here inside of two hours," said Tzu-lu. "You trust me?"

"Why not?" asked Jimmie Cordie gravely. "Wouldn't you—trust me?"

Tzu-lu looked at Jimmie for a moment, then smiled.

"Yes, I would," he said.

VIII

RIGHT SMACK AT YOU!

Somewhere up in Turkestan, in the desert of Kyzyl-kum, beyond Famine Steppe, lay the tomb of Jagatai Khan, son of the Earth Shaker. Rotten rich with loot it was, so the tale ran, and rumors that deadly peril shrouded this old lost tomb but added to its lure—a lure that drew Jimmie Cordie, Red Dolan, and their friends up into the distant, forbidding hills.

CHAPTER I

THE SON OF JENGHIZ KHAN

"**THE YID BELIEVES** it," said the Boston Bean, "And he wouldn't lie to me!"

"Why not?" asked Red Dolan lazily, from the couch in Grigsby's apartment in Hong Kong, China, where his two hundred and thirty pounds of bone and muscle lay sprawled out. "And why wouldn't he lie to the like of ye, Beany, darlin'?"

"Well, I saved his bacon once and—"

"Never mind those apes," interrupted Putney looking up from his game of solitaire. "Tell it to me; I wasn't listening when you started."

"I met the Fighting Yid and another man this morning," began the Bean, whose aristocratic sorrowful looking face concealed a reckless happy-go-lucky heart and chilled steel nerve. "They just got in from Chinese Turkestan. They met a bird up there that had been run out of Samarkand, they said—he had gone in up in the northwest by the Famine Steppe and the desert of Kyzyl-kum and—"

"Enough!" said Red sitting up, "tell us no more. Them names is plenty. 'Famine desert,' says me bold Beany and—"

"Pipe down, Red," commanded Jimmie Cordie. "Go on, Bean. I've been in that neck of the woods."

"All right, I will. In the year 1219, to begin at the beginning, Jenghiz Khan came down from Mongolia with his youngest son, Tule, and mopped up on Bokhara."

"Correct," affirmed Jimmie Cordie. "And when he got in the

said Bokhara, he stood on the steps of the principal mosque and shouted to his horde, 'The hay is cut; give your horses fodder!' Then they looted the city."

"Well," went on the Bean, "after the looting of the town, Jenghiz Khan started back to Mongolia by way of Samarkand. One of his generals came from the Kara-kul Oasis—"

"Wrong," said Jimmie firmly. "All wrong—and you from Boston. What happened was this. He had several sons who used to lead the hordes, one of whom was named Jagatai. That baby had been jazzing around with some of his pa's men, and going through the pass of Taras, had taken Otrar for the old man. At Kara-kul he called it a day and kicked the bucket. His pa decided to bury him there with all the honors of war because he, the said Jagatai, loved that neck of the woods. So they took him out in the rocky hills that the desert of Kyzyl-kum is crossed by, and after scragging all his personal servants and concubines and what not, they buried him. Proceed from there, Beaneater!"

"You seem to know so damn much about it," said the Bean. "What else did they bury with him. You ought to know—I suppose you were there?"

"No," grinned Cordie. "The day he was buried I was in a stud poker game with the Khan of the Tartars. I know what they put in the hole with him though. All the loot that was his share was put in!"

"Exactly," answered the Bean. "And from that day to this, it's been right there—waiting for whoever finds it. This lad that the Yid met said that—"

"Too many 'he said' and 'the Yid said,'" interrupted Grigsby. "Go and get the Yid and this Sootchman, if he's still around. We'll get at it first hand."

"I'll be back in an hour," said the Bean. "I left them down at the place of One Million Delights."

"And that's wan hell of a fine place to leave anyone!" yelled Red as the Bean closed the door behind him.

"WHAT do you think about it?" asked Putney after the foot-falls of the Boston Bean had died away.

Jimmie Cordie laughed. "It's just one of those things. No doubt there's a raft of those tombs scattered all over the lot up there, but nine-tenths of them have been looted five hundred years ago. And also, young fellers me lad, the amount of stuff they had in 'em was exaggerated."

"I suppose, now, ye have looted some, ye grave robber," jeered Red.

"Not more than six or eight," answered Jimmie with a grin.

They all laughed, the four men who had fought together in the Foreign Legion, the A.E.F. and afterward, wherever there was need of machine guns and rifles. They had fought for War Lords—and for themselves.

"You say you've been up there, Jimmie?" asked Grigsby.

"Yeah—years ago though. I was with my pa when he was special agenting. To tell the truth I don't remember much about it, being a youngster at the time, but I do remember this—that's no country to go jazzing around in hunting any man's tomb. We were at the oasis of Kara-kul. That's where I got the dope about Jagatai, Jenghiz Khan's son. It's not like China up in that man's country. You can't slap a few out of the way and see the rest run. Up there they'll run—but right smack at you, old kid."

"Wait a minute," said Grigsby, "I thought that there was only a few Kirghiz tribesmen up in that country."

"You better take a few more thinks," said Jimmie. "In Samarkand there are over one million people. My gosh, it's 26,000 square miles. Man, they've got mountains up there 22,000 feet high. Not in the Famine Steppe or the desert of Kyzyl-kum, which is in the northwest, but in other parts. Darn right there are a few Kirghiz up there—and also, my fair dumb-bells, if you or any other white man go jazzing around there you'll find that more than a few Afghans, Tartars, Uzbegs and Tajiks will come rallying around the old flag."

"And what the hell do ye care, Jimmie Cordie?" demanded

Red. "Is it ye now that is sittin' there and trying to tell us, what wid a couple of machine guns and the rest, that we couldn't slap all them guys you do be namin' outta the way?"

"Listen, you red-headed bum from Cork, these birds have guns, *sabe?* And they think when they die on the field of battle they go to Paradise."

"All right," interrupted Grigsby. "What I want to know is— if it looks like the real thing, what's the best way to go in?"

"We can get in easy enough," answered Jimmie. "But getting out is something else again. But far be it from me to frighten you delicate young ladies off. I just wanted to tell you what's doing up there. We can go up the Persian Gulf to Bushire, then to Teheran and then to Astrabad. I know a lad up there—if he hasn't been bumped off before now. He'll pass us on to Bokhara. That is unless you gents had rather take a little walk through Afghanistan."

"Never mind the kidding stuff," said Grigsby. "Go on from there."

"Go on from there? From Bokhara we go over into Samarkand, that's all. We walk up to the tomb, open it, take the stuff, turn around, walk back to Bokhara and come home. Simple isn't it?"

GRIGSBY'S Chinese boy ushered into the big living room the Boston Bean, the Fighting Yid and a tall, gaunt Scotchman.

"Come over and sit by me, ye Yid beneath notice," said Red, after the introductions were over and the house boy had put bottles and glasses on the table. "Then ye will be right handy for me to play the 'Wearin of the Green' on the coco of ye, do I think ye are about to tell the truth!"

"Big Irish loafer!" promptly returned the Yid, sitting down alongside the big Irishman who would make three of him. "Me and Jimmie vill kick the slats from you, gondiff? Ain't it, Jimmie?"

"Darn right it ain't," answered Jimmie. "You can do it easy enough by yourself—why drag me in for a kid's job."

"Let's dispense with any more foolish remarks," said Grigsby, "and get down to cases on this thing. Mr. Macintosh, will you tell us just what you know of this chap van Johann and what he told you?"

"This I know about Johann," answered Macintosh grimly. "When he was to the lee-side of a bowl o' whusky, there was nae raising him. He wadna' lie for the mere sake of the lie, ye ken. What he was doin' way up yonder is no my affair. What he says he saw, I believe he saw—but I'll go no further!"

"He told it to me, George," said the Yid. "He vas up dare mit some fellers who vos lookin' for some ruins mit writtin' on dem, for some society vat is in Germany. Vell, he vanders avay some day and up on de side of a hill what has caved in, is dere a place vot looks like a hole in the ground, ain't it? He goes in, all by himself, und he sees a big room in de back und dare is skeletons und gold und diamonds und everyting. He takes it a handful und goes out to go back und get his gang und just ven he is tellin' dem about it—bingo—dey is jumped by all de people. Dare is a runnin' fight und finally he und von odder chap vins clear out of all of dem, und comes down through Tagharma into Turkestan, where ve met him. He vanted us to back mit him und get a outfit togedder. Ven ve vouldn't—he goes down into Kashmir. I got it from him just vare de place is."

"Where it was, you mean," said Jimmie Cordie, with a grin. "You poor fish, what do you think the bunch that jumped him are doing—letting it stay there?"

"Vate a minute, Mister Viseguy," grinned the Yid. "De hole vas only a small von, und before he vent back he covered it up mit dirt und everything. Ven he vos jumped dey come from de odder side."

"Yeah? My mistake, Mister Cohen. Did he tell you how to get to it?"

"He did—und also he got it a promise from me that did I go und find dem, he vould get it his share."

"Fair enough," said Grigsby. "He will. Want to go along, Mr. Macintosh?"

"I do not!" said that gentleman, rising. "I ha' heard full many the time of the four of ye, and would I be wishful of goin' anywhere it is with ye I'd be glad to go. As it is—no, all the time, not up there, for no man or money!"

"Well, if we go—and we find anything, we'll save some for you," answered Grigsby. "How's that?"

Macintosh grinned. "If ye come back—with anything—ye can leave my bit with the British Consulate. I'll bid ye all good day!" He took up his hat and, without another word, stalked out.

"Vell," said the Yid, after the door closed, "do ve go up and take a look-see?"

CHAPTER II

"RIGHT SMACK AT YOU!"

THE TIGHT, COMPACT column advanced slowly into the Kyzyl-kum. They had come up the way Jimmie Cordie had outlined, as English scientists, going in to investigate an archaeological find reported to the Royal Geographical Society of London. Jimmie Cordie, who, as Red said, "could projuce anything at any time," had, in an afternoon in Hong Kong, gotten credentials signed and gold-sealed by everyone but the President of China. Yen Yuan, head of the Taiping, the most dreaded and powerful secret society in China, whose son Jimmie had saved from death in the States, when they were students at Boston Tech, had furnished them with two hundred fighting men, ostensibly to act as bearers, but in reality to serve as fighting men when necessary. If the outfit seemed unusually heavily loaded, it was explained that the bulk of it comprised scientific instruments and digging tools. There was very little trouble made, though. The credentials, the presence of the Taiping—

whose members were scattered through the Orient, wherever there were Chinese—was generally sufficient to pass them along. Incidentally, the hard-boiled look of the entire outfit discouraged any unwarranted investigation. It would have taken more of an army than any lord of a city had, to have stopped them, and as a result they were passed along, paying for what they got promptly, until they reached the Kyzyl-kum Desert. Once in, it was a different matter. It was no man's land there, and whatever a man held and wanted to keep, he had to protect for himself. The first day out, there had been whirlwind attacks by the Uzbegs and Tajiks. Attacks that seemed to blow up suddenly, like a sandstorm, to be beaten back as promptly. The second day, at break of dawn, there had been a rush by Afghans, attracted by promise of loot. It had lasted all day and Jimmie Cordie's statement, "they'll run right smack at you, old kid," was fully verified.

Now, the third day, twice since dawn, there had come an attack on all sides at once, made by Afghans, Tartars, Kirghiz, who came pouring down from the bare ragged hills, and all the rest, who seemed to have combined.

The Fighting Yid had been wounded the second day and was being carried in an improvised hammock slung between gun barrels.

The Boston Bean limped alongside of Jimmie Cordie, his head almost concealed by a bloody bandage, using a rifle as a crutch.

"Do you think we'll make it, Jimmie?" he asked.

"Darned if I know, Codfish," answered Jimmie Cordie cheerfully. "We're almost to the place, according to the Yid. All the water we have is what we got on us. Here's a problem in higher mathematics for you. We start out with two hundred men—in three days we have half of them left and two of us out of commission. If we reach it, how long will it take us to get back—and with how many men?"

"Why is a mouse that spins?" grinned the Bean. "I think the

answer is that before long the angel chorus is to be increased by several new faces. My head feels like there are two or three boiler factories operating inside of it."

"Hold 'er down here, you long-legged giraffe, and I'll pour some water on it for you."

"You will like hell! What'll you do, you poor fish?"

"Fish is good—I don't drink water. Hold 'er down."

"Heads up, Jimmie!" Grigsby shouted from the left flank. "Get to your gun!"

THE ATTACK came on all four sides and the little column tightened in, then formed into a four-pointed star to meet it, machine guns at each point. Red Dolan with two Chinese at one, Jimmie Cordie, Putney and Grigsby at the others, with Chinese to feed them. They were all machine-gun men, taught in the hard school of the Foreign Legion and the equally hard one in the A.E.F. and the guns were perfectly handled.

The bearers knelt or stood, forming the lines between the points of the star, and fought as calmly and as coldly as the white men. They knew that if the smiling, black-eyed one, who was the "honorable elder brother" of Yen Yuan, did not come back safely, they had much better meet death with him. It would be a much shorter and easier one.

It was a deadly attack, delivered by men who counted death as an entrance into bliss. Men that knew nothing else but fighting and whose ancestors had charged home against all comers for centuries. But it was met by men with equal courage—and better weapons.

The Boston Bean sat down and began using a thirty-thirty rifle, his lean, aristocratic face as impassive as ever, even if pale now and drawn with the pain of his wound.

The Fighting Yid had promptly ordered his bearers to set him down, rolled out of the hammock, staggered to his feet, took a rifle from one of the men and, with a bullet in his left leg, high up, joined in. He used one of his bearers to lean against, much to the Taiping's disgust. The Yid, when engaged at his trade, which was fighting, always talked to himself or anyone in sight, whether they listened or not.

"Vate, mister vid de viskers," he began. "I get to you in a minute. Dare is yours—und dare is yours—and here is von for you—Oi, Jimmie! Vatch Popper knock 'em off und learn you sometings. Und dare is yours—"

Twice the horde almost reached the lines and always men who had been wounded or those whose shaggy little ponies had been shot out from under them, were crawling in over the hot sand, like wounded snakes—and just as deadly. They would be met with the long curved swords of the Taipings, which had appeared like magic from the packs.

It was a grim, merciless fight to the death, waged there on the sands of the Kyzyl-kum Desert. A fight between men who were fighters, irrespective of race, creed or color. The machine guns cut wide swathes and piled up tangled heaps of men and horses, and the rifles poured a stream of steel-jacketed bullets into the horde. But from all sides, out from behind the sand hills and out of the passes of the barren hills that towered almost four thousand feet, came the attackers. And from the top of the hills and the sand dunes there was a steady volleying of the trade guns and quite a few modern rifles. The trade guns, carrying lead slugs, were more to be feared, as the slugs smashed through bone and muscle, tearing and crushing. Those in the charge would fire as they started, sling their gun, draw sword or level lance, crouch in the saddle—and charge directly in the face of the guns.

And the charge was met by the tight-lipped white men, all but the Yid, who talked all the time, and the equally grim, hard faced Taiping, led by Wang Li, one of Yen Yuan's most trusted captains.

The sand between the hills and the star was covered with men and horses, mostly in groups where a burst of fire had caught them. There was a sudden lull, although the horde was massing again in a circle a thousand yards away and the sniping went steadily on. Every once in a while a man in the line would pitch forward on his face—his arms and legs twitching. The Bean got up and came over to where Jimmie Cordie was.

"Hullo, Codfish," grinned Jimmie, busy cleaning his gun. "How'd you like to be in your pa's barn just about now?"

"In my pa's barn," answered the Bean, sitting down on an ammunition box. "There is a stream of cold water flowing all—"

"You say 'er," said Jmmie firmly. "Go on, I dare you. One peep out of you about cold water and you'll be sitting on a damp cloud playing a harp, right after."

"Did you say a damp cloud?" grinned the Bean. "Gimmie a cigarette."

Red Dolan came up. "Hey, Jimmie—George says to break it up as soon as they start and never mind any cross fire stuff. Hand over them pills, Beany darlin'. How's the head of ye?"

"Go tell General Grigsby that he's teaching his grandma how to fry eggs, Mister Dolan. You better be getting back to that popgun of yours, you red-headed ape—it looks like the band was going to start playing. And don't leave it all for me to do this time, either. Tell Putt and George the same, also. And likewise, keep your eyes open when you're shootin' that gun!"

"What? Keep my eyes open, is it? I'll knock the can off ye for that, once we get home, ye shrimp!"

"Take the Beaneater on, he's a crip," answered Jimmie. "One Cordie can lick ten—get back, Red! Here they come!"

THE HORDE meant to wipe out the outfit that had invaded their territory, in this one charge. After that they could fight each other for the little guns that spit a continuous lance of death.

As they got in motion, the machine guns began to rattle. Jimmie Cordie, who could hold a machine gun almost as closely as a rifle, waited a moment until he saw how far Putney's fire was reaching, then picked it up from there and brought it to Red. It was a merciless defense, put up by men who were all veterans. They fought for their lives there in the Kyzyl-kum Desert—and they all knew it. Nearer and nearer came the attack, great gaps now between bunches of riders. They came steadily on, their lances and swords gleaming in the sun.

Red Dolan stood up from his gun. It had jammed on him after the fifth burst of fire. He picked up a rifle and began using it. Of all the Taiping, there were only forty-odd left on their feet—the rest were dead or wounded.

Putney's gun jammed also a moment later and he drew his Colt. Whenever Putney became hard pressed he began to croon some old song. This time it was "There is a fountain filled with blood, drawn from Emanuel's veins," and between every two or three words, his Colt raised, he threw down, and a man dropped.

The Yid stood as before, only now two of the bearers, both slightly wounded, held him up. His rifle was worth more than their two—and he was still talking. "Oi, vat lofely shootin'. Von-two—three—und von for you—vat? Am I missing? Vell, vell, you decided to fall, vot? Hold me tighter! Give me anoder gun. My, dey eat dis stuff, vat?"

The Boston Bean had begun firing with a rifle, but the constant recoil had made his head seem to burst open and he had put it down and drawn his Colt, standing there with it in his hand, trying to rally strength enough to clear away the mist before his eyes.

Grigsby and Cordie still worked their guns methodically, swinging in a radius to take care of the half circle. Wang Li untouched, stood out in front a little, with a long curved sword in his hand. Any man that had crawled up to the line on his side unscathed, met his death. Wang Li's sword would flash out once—never twice.

Suddenly, just as it seemed that the little star would be wiped out, the charge broke, as charges do even when delivered by men who are fearless, and those that were left, wheeled their ponies and fled to the shelter of the sand hills.

As they did Grigsby shouted an order to Wang Li and stood up. The firing ceased and the six white men and those of the Taipings that were able, stood up.

"My gosh," said Cordie, "it was about time. What happened to you, Red?"

"Nothin'—she jammed on me, that's all. Are ye hurt at all, ye spridhogue?"

"Only in my feelings," answered Jimmie with a grin. "When I look around and see what's left of the ammunition. How are you, Codfish?" he went on, turning to the Boston Bean.

"Not so bad—if I could make this damn head of mine quit turning around so fast."

Red looked at him, "Goofy," he said, with deep conviction. "Never mind, Beany, acushla—I'll carry ye on me back."

"All right," called Grigsby. "Get busy."

"His master's voice," grinned Jimmie. "Stay and take care of the Duke of Boston, Red. Get the Yid over here first. He looks all in."

"He is," agreed Red, looking over to where the Yid was sitting, swaying back and forth. Red went over to him. "Come to daddy, ye fat omadhaun. 'Tis like a mattress ye are, tied in the middle. Up ye go, Abie darlin'," and he lifted the Yid, as a mother would a child, in his brawny arms.

"Big Irish bum," jeered the Yid, as he rose in Red's arms. "Me und Jimmie vill from you knock—Oi, I am down and out and all in. Easy mit de leg, I esk you."

"Shut the trap of ye," commanded Red. "Or I'll roll you across the sand for the wildmen to play wid. Are ye hurt bad, Abie, acushla?"

Jimmie, with Grigsby and Putney, counted ammunition and collected all the water bags. "I'm of the personal opinion," Jimmie said with a grin, "that this is rapidly getting to be a place that is not so good. If they come once more, the ammunition will be most distinctively all, gents!"

"And that's the time, Mr. Cordie," answered Putney, "that you showed if you load only fifty per cent more brains, you'd be half human. George, I think the best thing we can do is to back trail, *pronto* and in haste—and keep on that way as long as possible. I hate to crab the party, but it don't look as if we could get much further."

"What?" demanded Red. "After lickin' them scuts? Are ye goofy too, Putt?"

Grigsby grinned. "If we've licked 'em, Red, they don't know it. We better go on, Putt. No water on the way back and there may be—"

"On, the fire!" called Jimmie Cordie, jumping for his gun. "On the left! Give 'em hell, Wang Li!"

THIS TIME there was no attempt to encircle the remainder of the horde, about two hundred men, charged in a wedge shaped column, led by an old man with a long flowing beard. He was riding a big stallion and loomed above his followers who mostly were on the shaggy Mongolian ponies. He stood in his stirrups like a Cossack, his sword held as in the position of "right cut against infantry." Back of him, spreading out on the lines of the wedge, about ten deep, came the Afghans,

Tartars, Uzbegs and Kirghiz, brother fighting man now, until the loot was secured.

Grigsby and Putney were at their guns almost as soon as Jimmie. Grigsby fired one belt—reached for another—but there was no Taiping to hand it to him! Both had been reached by the snipers on the hill tops. Grigsby stood up for a second, to step clear of the bodies, and reached for an ammunition box, looking over to where Jimmie Cordie was working his gun with Red. The Boston Bean still stood with his Colt in his right hand, his left holding his head as if to stop it going around. Grigsby saw the Fighting Yid, lying prone on the sand, still pumping his Winchester and still talking. As he stooped for the box, he saw Putney, standing as if on a rifle range, using a 30.30, his face as calm as ever. The Taiping were lying and kneeling as before, among the bodies of their brothers. Wang Li was standing in the middle of them, watching the advance of the horde.

As Grigsby straightened up, the side of his face suddenly became curtained in blood and he fell sideways over the bodies of the men at his feet.

One machine gun left in commission now—Jimmie Cordie's—and he was shooting it with all his skill. He had seen George Grigsby go down out of the corner of his eye, as Red hooked on a belt for him and now, the smile was gone from his lips and he shot, bringing all he had ever learned of machine-gun work to bear, coldly and accurately. He started at the point of the wedge, ran down the side opposite to him, as a gardner would send the water from a hose on a border of flowers. Then back and down again. But even a machine gun bullet must stop when it hits and these men were chunkily built, hard-muscled, and wore heavy sheepskin clothes. A bullet would not go through them and into the next man, as it would through a half-naked, illy-nourished, savage or a much slighter, thin-bodied Chinese. Men would go down, as did their horses, carrying other horses and men with them. The men if they could, would crawl out of the welter and continue the charge on foot.

The rest never faltered but came on, to ride over these strangers who had killed so many of their tribesmen.

The rifles of the Taipings were taking toll, and every time Putney or the Yid shot, a man fell from his saddle. The old man leading, by one of the strange freaks of battle, was not touched. He came on, followed now by less than fifty men and as they got to within a hundred feet, he shouted in exultation and waved his sword over his head. The stallion he was riding was stark crazy and was running, his head far out, his lips curled back, the long yellow teeth showing through the foam.

JIMMIE CORDIE fired one burst—then another, almost under the hoofs of the horses, and stood up, drawing his Colt.

Red Dolan sent a bullet through the brain of the stallion when he was within ten feet of them and the big horse, killed in the middle of a jump, turned a complete somersault, throwing his rider over his head. The old man lit behind Jimmie Cordie, and as Red parried a blow from the sword of the next man, whose horse had been killed by the last burst, and closed with him, Jimmie turned to where the old man had fallen. There was no one on his front, most of the horde left had hit the line further down and were being met more than halfway by the Taipings, who were as fight crazy as the tribesmen.

As Jimmie faced him, the old man, dizzy from his hard fall, raised up on his elbow and his sword swung in an arc like a flash of blued steel lightning. But Jimmie Cordie had been raised in a hard school, where men were taught that a wounded man was often more dangerous than a man on his feet. As the old man's wrist turned, Jimmie stepped back a half step. As the blade point passed him, he stepped in, his Colt hammer beginning to rise. Now he was on the old man's right side, so close that the sword arm could not be brought back. The grim face of the old Tartar glared up into his, unafraid, and he tried to twist the sword so that he could thrust sideways with the point. Jimmie Cordie, who had fought and killed for years, without a thought if the man killed was a fighting enemy, did a surprising thing. The hammer went down again from almost half cock and he struck the old man across the side of the head with the barrel. It was not a hard blow, but hard enough to knock what remaining sense he had out of him and he sank back on the sand.

Red Dolan had parried the blow aimed at him and had crashed the butt of his rifle squarely between the eyes of the Afghan. The Boston Bean, his head cleared by the shock of the hand to hand fighting, was using his Colt. The Yid, hit by the fallen body of a man, was lying still. Putney was beside Wang Li, he had dropped his Colt after emptying it and was using a sword.

Jimmie Cordie stood in a practically cleared space. "Shoot 'em away from Putt!" he said calmly. "Red! Drop that gun! Use your Colt!"

"Colt hell!" snarled Red. "I'm goin' meself," and with the rifle, its butt now shattered, Red Dolan ran to the milling mass of men, in the center of which was Wang Li, Putney and ten of the Taiping. Around them eddied thirty-odd of the horde—all that was left.

The Bean started to follow. "Stay here, fool," Jimmie shouted, raising his Colt. "We can do better—" and his Colt began to send death to those of the horde on the outside. They fell, one by one, as he fired. The Bean stopped and joined in. They were both men who could put six bullets in a playing card at revolver range and now they were shooting to clear Putney.

The men pushing in paid absolutely no attention to those falling beside them. They got into striking distance and killed or were killed. But the two deadly revolvers could not be withstood and the tribesmen melted away. As Jimmie started to reload for the second time, there was a flurry, a flashing of sword blades, a surge forward and Putney, Wang Li and three of the Taipings staggered across the dead bodies in font of them, their swords dripping blood.

Putney came slowly up to where Jimmie and the Bean were.

He had been wounded in several places and was carrying himself on his nerve. He stopped and looked gravely at Jimmie Cordie.

"Old kid," he said, slowly and distinctly, "I just wanted to tell you that you were plumb right. They run right smack—" He pitched forward and would have fallen if Jimmie hadn't caught him and eased him down.

"Steady does it, old settler," said Jimmie. "Hang tough, Putt. You'll be—my God! Where's Red?"

"Under the pile, probably," answered the Bean, weakly. His head was beginning to turn again, this time worse than ever.

Jimmie Cordie started over to where the bodies lay the thickest, to be halted and turned by a yell from the Fighting Yid, who had come to under the bodies of the men who had fallen on him, and had wiggled his way out to a sitting up position. "Oi, Jimmie! Look! Oi! Dey got Red! Over dare! Knock 'em off, Jimmie!" and the Fighting Yid tried to get to a rifle.

CHAPTER III

"LOOK WHAT THE REDHEADED APE WAS PACKING!"

FOUR HORSEMEN, LEADING another horse, across which there sprawled the big form of Red Dolan, were almost in the shelter of a hill, a thousand feet away. Red had reached the fight, been swung around in the milling to the side away from Jimmie and the Bean, killed the first two men that struck at him and the next second had gone down from the heavy hilt of a sword on the temple. The men nearest to him had promptly quit trying to get in to the fight any more and had crawled to where they could pick up horses, dragging Red with them, thrown his unconscious body across a pony and were heading for the hills. They knew that the prospect of loot had disappeared, and without question figured that a ransom would be paid for the man they carried. If not, they would have something to show for the loss of tribesmen and if Red remained alive, something to make pay by torture.

Jimmie Cordie and Wang Li picked up rifles and Jimmie shot twice. It was all he had time to do. Two saddles were empty as the little party turned into the hill, out of sight. Wang Li had either missed or hit the same man Jimmie had.

The sniping suddenly ceased from the hills and Jimmie knew that they had come down to see what kind of a man it was that had been brought from the battle.

"I will get horses, oh honorable elder brother," said Wang Li, "and we will go for the war-lord of the flaming hair."

"No we won't," said Jimmie calmly, although his lips were gray. "There's wounded men here, Wang Li. If the war-lord is alive, he won't be hurt, yet. We will see that all is done here that we must do—then we will go, you and I. But for that offer, oh captain of warriors, you are my brother always. Get water and open up the package marked with the red cross."

Jimmie went over to where Putney lay and lifted him up, then over on his back, putting a gun butt under his head. There was a deep cut on his left arm up near the shoulder, two not so deep on his left forearm, a glancing sword had laid his scalp open on the right side and there was another cut straight down his ribs on the left side that ran from his collar bone to his shortrib. None of them were serious, except for the amount of blood they had let out of him.

Jimmie, with the help of Wang Li, gave him first aid, put a coat under his head and left him there on the hot sand. There was no place to take him. "I got it some brandy mit my pack," said the Yid, crawling over. "I gif it to him, Jimmie."

"You will? Come here, you Yid wildcat, and get fixed up yourself. My gosh, how many holes have you got in you?"

The first-aiding of the Yid was accompanied by many voluble protests. "Oi, Jimmie, easy mit de iodine! Oi, my persecuted race! Quit vid de fingar! Oi, gif a drink before you cut it ouit, Jimmie, I esk you!"

One of the bullets had gone through the fleshy part of the forearm and was just beneath the skin on the other side.

"Sit tight then," Jimmie said, opening a bottle of whisky that was in the Red Cross case. "Here, drink hearty, while I sharpen up the knives and the saw."

"Vat?" yelled the Yid. "A saw? Oi, for vot, Jimmie?"

The Boston Bean came over and stood gravely watching Jimmie operate on the Yid.

"Cut his head off just below the ear," he suggested. He had stopped holding his head and his Colt was holstered, but his eyes showed that the real Winthrop had gone away somewhere. Jimmie looked at him for a second, then said, "I will in a few minutes. You go and see if you can find a pail or something to hold the blood."

The Bean considered this for a moment. "That's a good idea," he said. "Then after you cut it off I'll use it. The top of mine has gone, see?" and he bent his head.

"Sure you can," said the Yid, game to the core. In spite of his pain, he was trying to help Jimmie Cordie. "Go get it de pail."

The Bean turned away without saying anything else and began pawing over the equipment.

"Vell," said the Yid, as Jimmie tightened the last bandage, "now ve got it a goofy, ain't it?"

"He'll come to," answered Jimmie. "Put this bird down by the other one, Wang Li and then we'll—well, for Pete's sake! Welcome to our fair city, Mr. Grigsby."

GRIGSBY had come up to them, still a little uncertain on his feet, white of face, with caked blood on his neck and head, but otherwise sane and all together. The bullet, a steel-jacketed one, fired at long range, had hit him, glanced from his skull, torn it's way across his head, laying the skin open and out. The result was just as if he had been creased. It had knocked him cold for a long time.

"It looks to me more like a cross section of hell," Grigsby answered, with a rather weak grin. "Where's Red?"

"Gone on a visit with some of our recent playmates," answered Jimmie. "Wang Li and I are going after him as soon as I get the hospital organized. Step up, you're next."

"You go easy," commanded Grigsby. "My head feels like if anyone touched it, it would break up in small pieces!"

Ten minutes later, they sat by Jimmie's gun, which was ready to hurl out defiance at any further attack. Putney was conscious now, the strong brandy taking effect. He was sucking on concentrated beef cubes and already the color was coming back in his face. The Yid was propped up against a box also with a bottle near him. Grigsby's head felt better and he was able to sit down on a box alongside of Jimmie Cordie.

The Bean had come back to them and after announcing that he couldn't find a pail, sat crosslegged in the sand, at Jimmie's left.

Jimmie looked at him. "Never mind," he said, "I'll find one for you. What's that on your Colt butt?" and he reached over and took it from the holster. "Oh—nothing but dirt! I thought it was a gob of something!" and he held the Colt in his hand, swinging it around by the trigger guard. He did not return it to the Bean. Wang Li and the three Taiping were busy among their own wounded. All of a sudden the Yid said, "Oi! vat—" then stopped. He was facing in the direction of Wang Li.

"What's the matter with you?" demanded Jimmie. "Bandage slip?"

"No—it vos—I got it a pain, ain't it. It's gone now."

"Yeah? Well, keep your pains to yourself while we dope something out. We can't stay here, that's a cinch."

"Collect all the wounded," said Grigsby, "and get to the nearest hills, fight our way into water, and hole up!

"That's all we can do—and the quicker we do it the better. We might dig in here but it would be a case of no water pretty soon and the wounded would catch hell in this sun. They'll gang up again. It's a thousand yards to that baby over on the right."

Wang Li, leading ten of the Taiping, all with roughly bade bandages on their arms or legs or heads, came slowly forward. The three men that came through the fight walking with him.

"Lord," he said, bowing to Jimmie Cordie. "Give orders. These brothers of mine can still use a rifle—and it may be a sword for a few minutes." He was a pure Manchu, this young war captain of Yen Yuan, and had been much with the English in Hong Kong and Pekin. "The rest," he added calmy, "have ascended on high, taking their seats with their venerable ancestors."

"Mit your assistance," muttered the Yid, as Jimmie spoke. It was just as well that Wang Li did not hear him. He had done what was considered his duty, both by himself and the men who were so badly wounded. He had put them out of their misery and started them in all honor on their journey.

"We have here two wounded men, Oh brother," answered Jimmie, "and we must make the hills. We must carry one machine gun, rifles ammunition, food and water. Sit down with us in council."

WANG LI bowed, his face lighting up with pride. He knew what that invitation meant—and the Taiping with him knew also. It meant that if they got back, his place among the million and more Taiping would be among the highest. "Lord, I am not worthy to sit in your magnificent presence."

"You have my permission," said Jimmie gravely, handing over an empty box. Wang Li sat down, his followers standing beside and behind him.

"I am not of the brotherhood," went on Jimmie. "But these men who are wounded? Are they not my fighting brothers? Let them sit on the stand!" Up to that time Jimmie Cordie had been protected and guarded because of Yen Yuan's orders, but from then on, all through the Taiping, which ranged from the highest to the lowest in China, he was served for himself also.

Wang Li snarled an order and the wounded sat down, the three unwounded standing back of him.

"Get going," Putney said, suddenly. "Never mind any more talk. I can walk if you take it slow."

"Und I can crawl," declared the Yid. "Mit von more drink I can fly, I bet you."

"Make up light packs," said Grigsby, "food and water, fill our belts, each man take a rifle. Take your gun down, Jimmie, Wang Li's men can pack it. You take as much ammunition as you can pack. We advance a hundred yards, stop, go back and bring up Putt and the Yid, then forward again for another. Wang Li and I will do the bringing up stuff and you can cover us."

"All right, except that taking down business. We'll carry her as is, until we get in the clear. Make a portage of it—a hundred yards at a crack. We can get more stuff into the hills that way."

The Boston Bean suddenly pulled his legs under him and crouched, half up from the ground. "Gimme my head!" he snarled, and launched himself straight at the Yid. It was fast but Jimmie Cordie's action was faster. As the Bean's body shot past him, he twisted the Colt he still had in his hand and the barrel struck the Bean just above the ear. There was force enough in the blow to throw the Bean off his lunge and roll him unconscious on the sand a foot away from the Yid.

"What the hell's coming off?" demanded Grigsby.

"Nuts," explained Jimmie calmly. "He's been that way off and on all day. If he'd hit the Yid he'd have busted open his wounds."

"So you apply a counter irritant?" Putney grinned.

"Yeah boy, and save the Yid's bacon all at the same time. The Bean was knocked goofy—maybe that'll knock him all right."

"Anyway, it's given us one more to carry," said Grigsby. "Let's get going."

"Look!" the Yid shouted. "Behind you, Jimmie!"

Jimmie Cordie turned, as did the rest. The Bean's Colt was again ready for action.

The old Tartar that had ridden the stallion and been knocked out by Jimmie, was staggering to his feet. His hands were groping aimlessly at his belt for a weapon that was not there.

"Don't shoot," Jimmie Cordie said, getting up and starting over toward him. The old Tartar saw him coming and made a desperate effort to clear his befogged brain. Jimmie halted when he got to within four feet of him.

"Put 'em up!" he commanded, at the same time raising his left hand above his head. That command, delivered in almost any language, when backed by weapons, is understood, and the old man, after a quick glance around, slowly obeyed. Jimmie motioned with the gun toward the others and the old man promptly started over.

When they arrived, Grigsby said, "What are you going to do with your boy friend?"

"Darned if I know?" admitted Jimmie. "Maybeso swap him for Red."

"Yeah? Well, let's get going. Load him up with ammunition."

THE OLD MAN made no objection, and after watching the rest for a moment, he lifted one of the one hundred pound boxes to his shoulder. As he did, one of the Taipings brushed against him, very slightly. The old man turned and snarled something. The Taiping put down the box he was carrying and drew his long curved sword. The Tartar grasped the box and raised it above his head, ready to throw. Wang Li, who saw it, shouted an order and the Taiping sheathed his sword, picked up his box and started. After a minute, the old man lowered the box and stalked along.

At the first halt, Jimmie Cordie went back with Grigsby and three of the Taiping, The Yid, Putney and Wang Li staying. When they returned with the Bean, who was still unconscious, Jimmie Cordie had the Tartar's sword. He went up to the old man, bowed and held it out, hilt first.

"Oi, such a business," said the Yid. "For vat you do dot, Jimmie? Now, go und find a rattler und gif him first two bites."

"Shut up, nitwit," whispered Putney, beside him. "Jimmie's up to something."

The Tartar looked at Jimmie, then at his sword, then held out his hand and took it. Jimmie motioned to one of the boxes, sat down himself for a moment. The old man watched him grimly until he had risen again, then went and sat down on the box Jimmie had pointed to, his sword across his knees.

"Vat is it?" said the Yid in a stage whisper. "Jimmie makes him a passenger, ain't it. Maybe he comes over here at us? Ven he does, I crocks him before he gets started mit de pig-sticker."

It was a long, hard job, the bringing up of the stuff and transferring the wounded, but they stayed grimly with it. From the first time on, Jimmie stayed with the machine gun. But there was no need. The hills were still and there was no attack of any kind. The old Tartar made no offer to help, neither did he show any hostile intent. He advanced when they did, and sat on a box near Jimmie when the rest went back for more. He ignored the Taipings and they him. That was all. It was late in the afternoon when they came to the hill, not even dusk yet, but rapidly getting that way. As they came close, they could see a cut or gorge running in, with side walls about a thousand feet high.

"Hold 'er," commanded Grigsby. "Heap plenty fine place for an ambush. Maybeso that's why our little playmates have been so quiet and let us get this far. Somebody's got to take a look see."

Wang Li volunteered to go, with the three unwounded Taiping, two on each side. As they started, the rest sat down to wait. The ten Taiping spread out, those that could handle rifles took them, the rest with their swords. The man the Tartar had spoken to, had evidently told the rest something as there were a good many black looks cast in his direction and quite a little talk. The old man ignored it all.

"We can ease in—"began Jimmie—he stopped, being interrupted by a yell from the Yid.

"Oi look! Dar is de castle over dare! See, on de little hill in de middle of de two big vons on de right. See, he said it was by a hill mit rocks on de top dat looks like a castle!"

"My gosh!" said Jimmie Cordie, looking in the direction the Yid was pointing. "It does look like a castle at that—or I'm getting goofy too."

"You always were," answered Grigsby with a grin. "Well, when Wang Li gets back, we'll ease over that way. If the tomb is there we can—"

"If de tomb is dare? Oi, George, vat a vay to talk. Sure de tomb is dare—und if it isn't, vat a swell place to make it a stand."

"You said something that time, Yid," agreed Jimmie. "If we can win to that hill where the castle is, all hell couldn't pry us loose."

"Until our water and ammunition are gone, you mean," put in Putney.

"Naturally, I mean until that happens," said Jimmie curtly. So curtly that Grigsby looked at him in surprise, then said gently, "Easy does it, Jimmie. Red's all right, and we'll go get him."

"I don't know whether he's all right or not," answered Jimmie. "But I do know one thing, and that is as soon as I get you birds in out of the wet, I'm going out and find out."

Wang Li and the men with him came came back. "No one on either side, Lord," he reported to Jimmie Cordie. "We went to the top."

"All right, then—let's go," Grigsby said. "What are you going to do with the seven Sutherland sisters brother, Jimmie?"

"Pack him right along. He can talk so that one of the Taiping understands. Wang Li can translate. I may be able to get a line on where Red is."

THEY made it to the hill where the rocks on top looked like some medieval robber baron's hold. It took quite a while. No attempt was made to hurry, plenty of time taken out to rest and never for a moment was the vigilance relaxed. As they came into a little valley, the hill loomed up ahead of them, a little on the left.

There on one side of a smaller hill, almost in front of the castled one, about fifty feet up, in the middle of a bare swath that was plainly made by a landslide, was—the black mouth of a hole going in! It was a climb of about forty-five degrees angle and by the time they made it, carrying the Bean, Putney, who had collapsed once more and the fighting Yid, plus the fact that Grigsby played out halfway through, it was dark.

THE OPENING was about ten feet high by twelve wide and the solid blocks of stone that made what was the roof were set on upright stone blocks, set tightly together by some kind of cement or mortar. The floor was made of square blocks of stone and as even as a billiard table. It was absolutely black after the first ten feet and the floor seemed to take a sharp pitch downward. The air was much cooler than outside and seemed dryer.

"Hole up here in the entrance," commanded Jimmie Cordie, as the last load was brought in. "We can do all the exploring later. George, can you work this gun with the Taiping to help you?"

"Yeah, boy," answered Grigsby. "Putt will be all right again in a little while and the Yid can do some shooting right now if necessary, can't you, Yid?"

"Vot, can't I?" answered the game little Jew. "Esk me und vatch Popper. Prop me up by de opening und vatch."

"I can also," said a faint voice behind him. "I wish someone would tell me just what happened."

"Oi," yelled the Yid. "Beaneater, you is back, vat?"

"Back, hell," said the faint voice. "I haven't ever been away."

"Fair enough," said Jimmie. "The Codfish is returned. Now, Wang Li, lets you and me go outside with my friend here and see what we can get. You take the deck, George?"

"I got it," answered Grigsby. "Come back before you start, Jimmie."

"I will—and before I go to administer the third degree to my new found friend I want to ask the Yid what he thinks now about the bunch that jumped Johann not finding this place. Look at the mess around in front. She's cleaner than a rabbit, I bet you. Your Dutch friend didn't throw enough dirt over the hole, Yid."

"Vell," admitted the Yid. "It looks dat vay, Jimmie—mit dose cart tracks und de busted veels und vat not. But anyway ve found it shade and coolness und a place to rest, ain't it?"

"That's right," answered Jimmie as he started, "and right now all that's worth a damn sight more to us than all Jagatai's loot."

The old Tartar accompanied them without any objection, and as they went out in the semi-darkness, the Yid called, "Jimmie—keep the finger on the Colt und vatch de big sword!"

Five minutes later Jimmie and Wang Li came back. Grigsby had given Putney a drink, and now Putney was conscious once more. "Where is he, Jimmie? Did you kill him?" asked Grigsby, not seeing the old man.

"No, we let him go. He could speak Chinese. He is or was top-cutter of an outfit, but we mopped up on most of them. He said that there is no regular village around here and damn little water. He doesn't know where or who got Red. I think he's a damn liar myself, so I turned him loose."

"Why?" asked Grigsby.

"Oh, hell!" answered Jimmie. "Figure it out yourself. Where's Red's pack? He's got a flashlight in there I want."

"Over there by the gun," Grigsby answered. "I suppose you know you are going to your death, Jimmie?"

"If my number is up—and not unless," answered Jimmie, pawing over Red's pack. "And I don't give a damn if I am. Red will be looking for me to—well, for Pete's sake," and for the first time since Red was taken, Jimmie Cordie grinned. "Look what that red-headed ape was packing!" and he held up four Mills bombs. "My gosh, with these and—come on, Wang Li. Take a rifle and a Colt."

"Load your belts, Jimmie," said Grigsby. "You may need all you can carry."

"Give me yours, Yid. You got a full one. Hurry up, he's getting too far ahead of us. Let's go."

"Who is?" asked the Yid, as he passed over his full belt, having had one of the Taipings fill his up with shells right after the last attack.

"Why the old man, you damn fool. Why do you think I let him loose?" answered Jimmie, as he disappeared.

CHAPTER IV

"HERE'S A LITTLE LIGHT FOR YOU!"

WHEN RED DOLAN regained consciousness, he was lying on the ground on what felt like bare rock. That it was some place way up on the top of a hill he could see by the moonlight which was just strong enough to distinguish large objects. His hands and feet were not bound, and save for a dull ache at his right temple he was unhurt. His iron body had withstood the jarring of the ride across the back of a horse without strain or bruise.

Around him in a circle sat men most of them crosslegged. Back of them stood others. There was a cleared space about ten feet across in the midst of the encircling figures that neither moved nor spoke as Red first sat up, then got to his feet. Where he was or what had happened after he had killed the man in the fight and then felt something as if the heavens had suddenly dropped and hit him, he didn't know. That he was alone, surrounded by enemies and unarmed made no difference to Red Dolan. His one thought was to get to the man nearest to him, take his sword away from him and fight the rest. As he tensed his body for the rush, the circle around him melted away, as far as sitting men went. It was as if they sensed that the big red-headed man standing, there was as dangerous as a sabre-toothed tiger and was only to be met by men with weapons ready and on their feet. A man, big almost as Red, whose body seemed to be great rolls of fat, with long drooping mustache, his sheepskin coat removed, stepped in front of the others, and faced Red. He was a Tartar and the sword held in his fat, hairy right hand was a Persian talwar, whose blade showed, even in the moonlight, the damascening of a sword of price.

Suddenly the moon, what there was of it, went behind a cloud and it became dark, with the black velvety darkness of the north. There was a moment's confusion, a shouting of orders in different tongues and with it the crash of falling bodies and the tinkle of a blade on rock. Red had crouched and sent his two hundred and thirty pounds of hard muscle with all his strength in a flying tackle at the big man in front of him. His shoulder hit just above the knees and his arms went around the legs of the Tartar like the closing of the jaws of a vise. The man went down as if struck by a shell, his sword dropping. The force of the tackle sent both of them rolling over and over into the milling feet of the men nearest to them. Red's weight, plus that of the Tartar, plus the force with which they were rolling, made them like some old Juggernaut car. Before they stopped rolling there were three or four men knocked down and one or two across them.

Red, having played football in the old days when they played football, and not a ladylike game of throwing a ball around and tagging each other, let go of the Tartar, who was completely out, heaved at the bodies of the men on him and came out of the pile like a Jack-in-the-box, only to dive for the nearest legs to him and gather them in.

Mr. Dolan formerly of the Foreign Legion, the A.E.F. and points west, was in his element. As a rough-house battler he was, as the Yid had once said, "a dirty fightare," and at the moment he was not holding back anything he had, either. The men trying for him were handicapped. They didn't know that kind of fighting, it was dark, they had to be at least a little careful as to who they cut at, if they didn't want a blood feud afterward.

RED was handicapped by no such considerations, and as he heaved up with the legs he had gathered in, he let go, kicked at a man, butted another, reached out an arm, felt a body, drew it to him, jabbed up with his two fingers held stiff to where he thought the eyes might be, let go, jammed his knee up hard in another man's belly, went down on his knees and dove straight through the surrounding legs, which faded away on either side.

The men against him were good men, all fighting men and all eager to close with Red. Any one of them could and would have ended it with one cut. But doing that in the dark, with a two hundred and thirty pound Irishman, who loved fighting, throwing himself around like a wounded boa constrictor, was not easily done. After the last bucking of the line, Red felt that he was through the press. It was dark and he couldn't see, but he no longer felt—and smelled—the bodies around him.

He got on his feet—and fight drunk, turned to charge back. As he did, some one bumped into him. Red promptly gathered the newcomer in, and as his arms went around him, his hand closed on the hilt of a sword, over another hand. The man strained against Red, at the same time yelling loudly. He had been sideways to Red when he bumped him, but in reaching for him, Red had turned him so they were face to face. Red's left hand closed on the man's throat and his right slipped down over the hand on the sword hilt to the wrist. His hip came against the hip of the struggling yelling man and he heaved up, once. The yelling and struggling ceased and when Red let go, the man's sword had dropped and he followed it, his head way over on his shoulder. Red had broken his neck with a twist as the weight of the body had come on it. He stooped, picked up the sword and jumped into the darkness. His feet hit solid rock the first time, sloping down and he crouched and ran down the side of the hill. About thirty feet more he ran full tilt into a ledge that stuck directly up and the only thing that saved him from a cracked skull was the fact that he was holding his sword hand out a little. As it was it stunned him and he stumbled to his knees. As he did, his left hand, flung out to break the fall, went into an opening in the rock. He just had sense enough left to feel around. It seemed to be a crack of some kind, big enough to hold him and Red crawled in. It ran back about five feet and was not quite long enough to allow him to stretch out The height was barely sufficient to clear his shoulders as he lay on his side.

Torches had been lit now, up on the hill top and there was a lot of running around and loud talking.

"Talk on, me buckos," Red said aloud. " 'Tis clear of ye I am. As soon as I get me head to stop buzzin', I'll take me good sword here and come up to ye and then—and then—I'll go find Jimmie—the—" Red's head went down on his arm and he passed out of the picture.

Hence he did not see that there was a bunching together of the torches on the hill. Several that had been farther out, as if the holders had been starting a search, came back in. The whole thing, from the time Red stood up and was confronted by the fat man, had not taken five minutes.

INTO the light cast by the torches strode the old Tartar that Jimmie had released. Several other Tartars at once closed in behind him. The Afghans, Uzbegs, Tajiks and Kirghiz, to the number of about thirty, got together also.

"Where is he?" snarled the old man, in a bastard mixture that they all seemed to understand.

"Lord," answered one of the Tartars, "he was here, lying quiet. Then suddenly he became possessed with a million devils. See, Lord, what he has done to us. Then, in the darkness when we could not see to strike—he flew away!"

"Fools!" shouted the old man. "He was worth many rifles and they would have given the little guns that spit death for him. Out and search—shall he hide from a hill-man and a rider?

Get fresh torches. Go far out and drive in—soon it will be light! Go without fear. His friends are driven into a hole."

"Here's a little light for you!" said a mocking voice from behind, on the same side the old man had come up the hill.

The old man, with no thought of being followed, had gone slowly up in the hills, still dizzy and shaken from his fall and Jimmie's blow on the head. Wang Li and Jimmie had caught up with him without trouble—and arrived with him, a little while back.

At the sound of the voice, which they could not understand, the entire party on the hill top turned, and hands went to sword hilts.

Even as they did so, a Mills bomb detonated almost in the center of the massed men. It blew them literally apart, men falling away in all directions. Before the flash of the first bomb had died out, another landed and exploded among the remnant of the tribesmen. The old man pitched forward, half of his head blown off. The torches were down now, some burning on the rock, but none held up. Just enough light for those left, now frantic with fear at the devils that had appeared to burn and tear them, to see two forms come over the how of the hill, one with streaks of fire coming from an outheld arm, the other, with a long curved blade that shimmered in the flickering light.

Ten or twelve tribesmen—all that were left—yelled in an agony of fear, turned, and fled blindly down the hill. Just then the dawn broke, clear and lovely.

Jimmie Cordie and Wang Li stood for a moment, looking down on the dead bodies, and the wounded who were trying to roll out of the sight of the demons who had the form of men.

"Turn some of those piles over," said Jimmie. "Red may have been killed before the—"

A wild Irish yell of exultation came rolling up the hill and following it came Red Dolan. He had been brought to consciousness by the two detonations of the Mills' bombs, and on cautiously peeking out of his hole up, had seen Jimmie and Wang Li just as the dawn came.

"Jimmie!" he yelled as he came. "Jimmie, ye scut!"

Cordie's grim, tight-drawn face became once more calm and smiling. It was as if some magician had wiped it clean. He holstered his Colt and stood there, one hand on his hip, and waited for Red.

"We didn't wake you up, did we, Mr. Dolan?" he asked, as Red got up to them.

"Ye did, ye shrimp of the world," answered Red. "And damn glad I am ye did. Sure now, 'tis once I'm glad to see the homely face of ye. Are ye hurt, Jimmie darlin'?"

"I am not. Everything is all right now—you damn red-headed baboon. My gosh, you look like the curse of Brian Boru, you big cheese. What do you mean by—"

" 'Tis right," interrupted Red. "I feel the same about ye, Jimmie, alanna. Where do the rest be now?"

"At a summer resort near here. Let's get going."

"Right away, Jimmie. Sure now, Wang Li, ye highbinder. I owe ye wan, for comin' wid Jimmie. 'Tis me that will pay it some—"

"Cut the wah-wah out and move out," said Jimmie. "They may rally and we've got a hell of a way to go."

"Wait till I swap me sword here for that wan wid the pretty handle," said Red. "Sure now, ye stole me bombs, ye robber!"

"Stole hell," grinned Jimmie. "We hoped you were dead and divided up your kit. The Yid got your shaving set."

"He did—and it will be about wan minute after I get back that he'll keep it. Come on wid ye—wait a minute, do ye know which way to go now, Jimmie?"

"Yeah, we made trail sign. Carry these belts, you big moose—and this rifle, as well as 'me good sword.' I'm about all in."

"Jimmie! Now why the hell didn't ya say so, ye grinning gibboon. I'll carry you, wid all the—"

"You will not—go first, Wang Li."

CHAPTER V

"I'LL PACK 'EM ALL THREE!"

A LITTLE AFTER daylight, the Yid, who was sitting propped up against one of the big entrance stones, let out a yell.

"Oi! Come see! Here comes Jimmie mit Red! He got him! Und Wang Li mit dem! Now, by golly, ve give dem hell vonce more, ain't it?"

Grigsby and the Bean, who had been sitting further back, came to the entrance. Putney, whose clean, hard, well conditioned body, helped by the dry, cool air, was rapidly rallying from the effect of the cuts, turned and inched himself over so that he could see the three men coming up the hill.

"Mr. Dolan didn't want to leave his friends so soon," said Jimmie, as they came up, "but we persuaded him to come and visit us for a little while."

"Yeah?" said Grigsby. "Well, we are glad to see Mr. Dolan— all in one piece. I think, in honor of his arrival, we will all take one small drink."

"After which," Jimmie Cordie went on, "Mr. Dolan will entertain by explaining just why he quits work and goes horseback riding in the middle of the shift."

"And so would ye, shrimp, if ye knew no more about it than I did. Here I was, havin a fine time, and all of a sudden somepin' hits me and—"

"There you wasn't!" finished Jimmie for him.

Later, Jimmie and Grigsby sat outside the hole, while Red was telling the rest about what happened to him and Wang Li was doing the same with the Taiping.

"I don't want hang any crape on the festive proceedings," Jimmie said to Grigsby, "but let's get down to cases. Putt is coming along all right; so is the Yid. The Boston Bean is sane at the minute but liable to go bats again any time. Neither one of the three can stand the gaff. The Taiping are all shot to hell except Wang Li. That leaves you, Red, Wang Li, and Mr. Cordie's son, Jimmie. You follow me, Mr. Grigsby?"

"I'm ahead of you, Mr. Cordie—keep right on!" answered Grigsby gravely.

"As you urge me to do so I will," grinned Jimmie. "We have enough ammunition to last about ten minutes for the Colt plus what we have for the small arms in general, which isn't more than two thousand rounds all told. The food question doesn't enter in—there is plenty. But the water question is sticking up like a sore thumb. You agree, Mr. Grigsby?"

"Fully, fully—continue with your remarks, me good man."

"I will. We are now some three days' march in Kyzyl-kum Desert at the tomb of the late Mr. Jagatai Khan. It is quite obvious, Mr. Grigsby, that some one arrived before us—after the said Mr. Johann left. When we started we had two hundred perfectly good Taiping fighting men, four machine guns, and what we thought would be plenty of ammunition, water and sich-like. Plus that we all had good health. I'll bet nine dollars that this place is as bare as Old Mother Hubbard's cupboard. Question in front of the class—how long can we stay here before we start to fight our way back? Our late playmates will come to call on us again and—"

"You are slipping, teacher," grinned Grigsby. "They have already come. Look on the surrounding hills. Cut the comedy, Jimmie. Only thing I can see to do is to hole up here until the wounded are better, then strip down to fighting weight and shoot our way out. We got all the water bags and there's enough to last a week. If you ask me, we're damn lucky we got here."

Jimmie grinned. "What we got handed to us up to date is like the gentle patter of a summer shower on the old tin roof, old kid, compared with a tornado, when they really get ganged up—which they will do now. George, no kiddin', we got just as much chance of cutting our way out of here as a snowball in hell."

"What do you care," yawned Grigsby. "We're all together and it's a cinch we got to go sometime. Why not now, Jeems?"

"No reason—except I've got a few heavy dates to keep first, if I can—well, something may break. It's on the knees of the Nine Red Gods, anyway. Let's get in and take a look-see down the hole."

"I'LL GO wid ye, Jimmie," announced Red promptly, when they went in and told the rest they were going to explore down the sloping shaft.

"I'll go too," said the Bean firmly.

"You will not," said Jimmie, just as firmly. "You are liable to go goofy any minute, you poor piece of brown bread. Hell of a nice thing if you jumped at us down there and tried to take the tops of our heads for yourself, wouldn't it? You stay in the hospital, you hear me?"

"You and Red go," Putney said. "George can stay here as chief nurse and be ready to knock the Bean cold. Don't you try for my head, Beany, if you"

"Oi," yelled the Yid. "Dot only leaves me und vonce before he did it?"

"Aw," defended the Bean, "I was nuts then. Now I'm all right."

"If you are," said Jimmie, as he and Red started with two flashlights, "you are promoted to be chief cook and bottle washer. Get busy on those tins. If you birds hear three shots, rally around the old fireside—and we'll do the same. Come on, horseback rider!"

They went slowly and cautiously ahead, their Colts ready and flashlights in their left hands. The passageway narrowed considerably, but was still high and wide enough to allow them to walk abreast. It went down on the same angle for about a hundred yards, then took an abrupt slope upward. The walls and roof were of stone, underfoot it seemed to be of tiles or squares of stone set close together, the same construction as the entrance. The slope up continued for a hundred feet, opening out here and there in chambers, and then the passage became level for a few feet and suddenly opened out into a square room about twenty feet square.

All the way along the passage there were bones and pieces of copper and old time-eaten blades of swords and axes—but nothing else.

"Whoever got here," said Jimmie as they entered the chamber, "sure mopped up. See those overturned slabs, Red. That's where his—"

"Mary, Mother!" interrupted Red. "Something crawled in here and died by the smell. Devil a thing here, Jimmie. The black curse be on that Yid for—that's what smells, Jimmie, over in the corner."

Jimmie's flashlight joined Red's. "Yeah, it looks like a snow leopard—my gosh," as they walked toward the body of a magnificent leopard. "She crawled in here to die, Red. Look at the dead cubs. She brought them in or she had 'em in here, I bet. See the place she has hollowed out for a den. Look at the stones pawed to one side. Her old man must have got knocked off outside and—what are you doing?"

"Nothin'," answered Red, who had knelt close to the head of the mother leopard. "I never seen one of those babies before. Hey, Jimmie, look at them teeth? How'd you like to have them sunk into ye."

RED had drawn back a little and put one hand down on the side of the hole. No sooner had he done so than he grunted jumped up, and drew his Colt, stepping back. As he did, Jimmie promptly stepped back also, and his Colt seemed to jump in his hand.

"What is it?" he demanded throwing his light into the hole.

"I put me hand *on a man's nose!*" answered Red. "There— where I rested it!"

"*A man's nose?* Come on, goofy—come and join the Bean. Sure, you're the Czar of Russia and I'll lick anyone that—"

"I am not," said Red firmly. "And bad luck to ye, Jimmie

Cordie, for even suggestin' such a thing. I put the hand of me on a man's nose, I tell ye!"

"Too bad he didn't bite you," grinned Jimmie stooping down where Red's hand had rested. "You mustn't get so damn familiar with—by gosh, Red, it is a nose! When your friend the leopard here kicked out in her death agony she uncovered it." As Jimmie was talking he was pawing the loose dirt from around what looked like an iron knob sticking out of the ground.

"Keep away from that damn thing," said Red. "It may be a trap or—"

"Trap? It's a statue, dumbbell. Buried, see—that's the reason the birds that beat us here didn't find it. Say? Are you a passenger on the liner? Get down here and help me clear it!"

"Get up here," commanded Red, "ye poor weak sobsister! I'll dig it out for ye!"

Jimmie got up. "Hop to it. There'll be more digging than you think, old timer. From the size of the face, that baby is nearly man size!"

Red dug with his hands, his heavy boot-toes, and his heels.

" 'Tis loose," he grunted finally. "Give me a hand, Jimmie, alanna."

Together they brought the figure up out of the ground and carried it almost to the entrance of the room before setting it down. "Holy cats," Red said as they did. "It weighs enough. What the hell is it, Jimmie?"

"Darned if I know. May be a statue of Jagatai, or one he looted and thought a lot of."

They stepped back and put their lights on it.

It was an effigy of a man, short, thick set, standing erect on a low square block, with what looked like, as Red said, a towel around his waist.

Red flashed his light up on the face, "Holy smoke!" he said, " 'Tis the Fighting Yid!"

"What?" asked Jimmie, who was looking at some characters

carved on the stone base. "Where's the Yid?" and he turned to the entrance.

"This statue," answered Red, with deep conviction, " 'Tis the livin' split of him. Take a look, Jimmie."

JIMMIE laughed and threw his light up with Red's. "Boy howdy, it is at that. Black the Yid up and he could—wait a minute. I thought the darn thing was made of iron or bronze but it might—" Jimmie reached in his pocket and brought out a pocket knife. He dug into the leg of the statue nearest to him. The knife scrapped through a layer of verdigris and then a yellow streak showed. He dug deeper, then sat down on the stone and laughed.

"What the hell now," demanded Red. "Are ye goofy, ye laughin' hyena?"

"Goofy hell!" answered Jimmie. "My gosh, it is funny, though. Here we are not able to carry ourselves out and we find a—oh, my sainted aunt Mandy!"

"Find a what?" asked Red. "If ye have gone bats now, Jimmie Cordie, I'll—"

"Oh, for Pete's sake, you nitwit. What do you think that thing is made of?"

"I dunno, what?"

"Gold, my boy, gold—and we can't pack an—"

"Who can't?" interrupted Red. "Gold, is it? Sure I'll carry it meself, ye poor feeble peanut. How much do it be worth, Jimmie darlin'?"

"What? What good will it do you to know. Man, you got to pack ammunition and water, not gold."

"I'll pack 'em all three!" answered Red firmly. "How much gold is there, Jimmie?"

"Well," grinned Cordie, "given that the Yid weighs around one ninety and this baby is a little thinner, we'll say one seventy-five for him. He certainly isn't solid, or we wouldn't be able to lift him. Must be a thick shell of gold. Gold is worth around say twenty dollars an ounce at the mint—and let me call your attention to the fact, my fair red-headed nitwit, that you are one hell of a long way from any mint at the moment. Well, at twelve ounces to the pound that's two hundred and forty dollars a pound. Two hundred and forty times one seventy-five—holy smackers. I'd need a sheet of paper and six pencils. It's somewhere around forty thousand dollars, Red."

"Is that all? Sure wan vase we—"

"Let's go back. We couldn't take it, Red, if it were worth forty million. I'd swap ten of them right now for some of the old gang with machine guns. Gold is good in some places, boy, but right here it isn't worth a tinker's damn."

They went back, and after Jimmie had told about the statue, the Boston Bean asked, "Did you say it looked like our distinguished friend here on my right?"

"It did," answered Red. "Could be himself!"

"And there was some inscription carved on the stone?"

"Yes," said Jimmie. "What's on your mind, Codfish?"

"Why, it may be that—could you get it up here where—"

"Sure, Red, go down and bring it up for the gentleman."

"Who, me—by meself? I will not. Lemme have three of the Chinks—an I will!"

The three unwounded Taiping went with him but only after Wang Li agreed to accompany them. They hadn't lost anything down that dark slope underground and they didn't like tombs anyway.

CHAPTER VI

"IF THEY GET TO YOU, YID—"

WHEN THE STATUE was finally brought up and placed a little back from the entrance of the tomb, so that the light of day could play on it, the resemblance to the Fighting Yid was remarkable, as far as the face and general outlines of the body went. He came over and looked at it. "Oi, Popper! How come you here vid only a napkin on? If dot ain't a statue of my old man, I eat it!"

"What's the inscription, Yid?" asked the Bean.

"Vat? How the hell do I know? Vait a minute—it's Hebrew, ain't it? It is—vat de—und me de son of a rabbi, mit a million lickin's behind for not learning it—vaite; it is, *This—is—*now, vot de hell is dot damn curlycue—*a*—dot's it—*a* Und dem comes it—*F*—und dat baby is *G*, und dat baby is *H*—now I get it back—'*A-F-G-H-A-N-A*' it reads. '*This is Afghana*' and under it reads—'*The son of Jeremiah,*' who was de son of Saul, de King. How's dot for reading, mistares?"

"Very good," answered the Bean gravely. "Darn good. This is Afghana, the son of Jeremiah, who was the son of Saul the King. Fair enough, my brave Hebrew scholar—fair enough. Now we will go home, in state."

"Goofy again," said Red, moving over alongside the Bean. "Be easy now, Beany, darlin, or I'll floor ye wid a right swing to the jaw."

"Lay off, Red," warned Jimmie. "You're the goofy one. Go ahead, Codfish—tell us!"

"Let's go out where we can sit in the sun," answered the Bean.

"I've got a toehold on an idea. Now," he went on after they were all seated about a yard outside the entrance, Putney as well as the rest, "here it is—that's a statue of Afghana, from whom the Afghans claim descent. How the hell it got in there, I don't know—and I don't care. But here it is for a guess. Jagatai did a lot of promiscuous looting and he didn't care where or when. He ran across that statue in some temple or shrine or whatever the hell the Afghans call their dumps—and he promptly assimilated it. Why, he only knows, and he isn't around to tell us. Not a doubt in the world that the Afghans have some tradition about it—and that it has been handed down that

Jagatai had it. Now, question is—how much do they think of
it—and would they recognize that old gent?"

"Good way to find out will be to set him out in front here
and see what happens. It's a pipe they won't stay away from us
very long," said Jimmie. "In fact, gents, if you will notice, it's
getting time for the party. Cast your eyes over on the top of the
next hill and down in the valley, and you'll see the guests beginning to arrive!"

The hill they were on was more or less a detached one from
the spur that jutted out from the disconnected, broken-up range,
going into the next higher one with a ridge not more than a
hundred feet high. It stood out like the point of a broad bladed
spear. Attack could come from any direction, down the hill as
well as up and in the sides, but to reach the entrance it must be
delivered squarely in front.

"If we do set the old boy out," said Grigsby, "and they recognize him, it will start something off and we're not in shape
to take advantage of it. Any hard play and Putt and the Yid go
south. The Bean's head is an unknown quantity. They won't make
any attack yet, knowing damn well they've got to pull us out of
this hole."

"That's right, George," agreed Jimmie Cordie. "They'll try us
out to see what we've got, then they'll sit down in front and try
and starve us out. Those gents have nothing to spend but their
time. Go ahead, Codfish."

"Well, here's what I thought—if we could show them we—"

"Show who?" demanded Red. "Them chimpanzees? 'Tis all
mixed up they are. What wan knows the rest—"

"How did you happen to think of starting wah-wahing?"
interrupted Putney. "Put a jaw tackle on. They'll be starting up
here any minute."

"Do I have to ask the likes of you—" began Red, hostly.

"Send him a letter about it," interrupted Grigsby. "Pipe down,
Red. Go on, Bean."

"I'VE BEEN TOLD to do that several times," sighed the

Bean, "and have tried without much success. Well, here it is—if the Afghans recognize the statue, they'll want it. They are the best fighters and can mop up on the rest. I thought we could show the darn thing—hole up, fight 'em off until they get sick of it—then make a deal with them to escort us back to safety in return for the statue."

"Boy," said Jimmie gravely, "the old bean is hitting on five of the six once more. But, Lord Boston, you've slipped on one or two little details. The first one is, you can't make these birds sick of fighting. They'll carry the fight to us, free, gratis, and for nothing. Second, if they see the statue it will only be like adding a little T.N.T. to a charge of 60 per cent. gelatin powder—we won't notice the difference, old-timer. We may make 'em pause long enough to listen to a compromise, but any dicker you make with Afghans, my learned friend from Bosting, is nix with them at the first chance. Of all people, they are the last to make an agreement with—unless you have the whip hand."

"If we put it out for a minute—or long enough to give them a chance to take a good look, then stand them off, all that are here of them, what happens?" asked Putney.

"Easy," answered Cordie. "They go home or to wherever there are more of them, leaving enough here to keep us holed up, then come back with a crowd and mop up, if it take until Christmas."

"Which gives us the time we are looking for," went on Putney. "Then when they get back with enough Afghans to mop up and take care of the rest of the mixture, we can put the statue out again, only this time it will be the Yid blacked up—the darn thing is almost black and—"

"Vat?" yelled the Yid. "Oi, Putt! Vat did I ever did to you? Me, mit a towel on, outside und mit dem—"

"I'll cover you, Yid," grinned Jimmie. "There won't any more than four or five reach you."

"I got it!" shouted the Bean. "The Yid can come to life, wave them back and— and—we can hold the Yid as prisoner and make them keep away from us—no, we'll—"

"Inside!" Red bowled, jumping to his feet. "Here they come!"

It wasn't much of an attack, really it was more of a feeling out. A party of fifty or sixty men trotted up to the bottom of the hill, dismounted, and scattering out, rushed the slope. If it were a feeling out, it succeeded in doing that thing. It fully demonstrated to the onlookers that the men left alive and holed up were able to put up a fight. The .30.30's stopped most of them, the rest were met by Wang Li, Red, and the Taiping and wiped out. Several of the wounded, those who had been shot down first, rolled back down the slope, and one or two got on their horses and rode back the way they had come.

"Let 'em go!" shouted Jimmie Cordie, as the Yid stepped out, his deadly rifle already at his shoulder. "You damn fool, come on, set His Joblots out—Come on, Red, you big moose, take hold!"

THE STATUE was set out about three feet from the entrance and the men slipped back to cover. Two of the scouting party were Afghans and had been wounded as the rush started. They were facing the other way when the statue was brought out, both of them half-sitting, half-lying on the ground. One of them staggered to his feet, turning as he did so. He saw the statue, let out a wild screech of terror, fell forward on his face. The other, from where he sat, turned at the yell and saw what the first had yelled about. He had been shot through the chest and a bloody froth was on his lips, but he jumped to his feet, raised his hands high above his head, took two full steps forward, then crumpled to the ground, dead.

"There is no doubt," said the Bean softly, "but what they recognize it."

"And there is also no doubt, John Cabot," answered Jimmie Cordie, "that news has reached the rest of our playmates. Look at 'em come—all Afghans this time. Help me get this gun out here, Red. Leave the damn think where it is—no time to bring it in. This is the one we've got to stop!"

They stopped the rush but all the machine gun ammunition was exhausted before the Afghans drew off, those that were left. The sight of the statue made them literally stark crazy. There was no drawing off of whole men, only those who were wounded so badly they could not use their weapons. The fire this time from other hills was not so bad as the range was longer and those in the charge had trusted to swords. Jimmie Cordie, as he shot the last burst, got a lead slug through the right forearm. Fortunately, however, it did not touch the bone.

"Velcome to the hospital," said the Yid, after they had taken the statue inside. "Now if Red gets a nice little von, ve all got it, ain't it?"

"Well, ye Yid ape," said Red bitterly. "I've got a good mind to take you apart."

"Get one more mind," said Grigsby, from where he was fixing Jimmie's arm, "and get to the front. They may be coming over the hill."

"They are not," answered Red, as he stepped to the entrance. "Holy cats—there go all the different kinds of wildmen—come and see, Jimmie. Look—all divided out. See—there goes them damn hyenas that the Yid belongs to!"

"Not all," corrected the Bean. "See that bunch over there and that one on the top of that hill? They're making camp, boy. We're going to be policed until the rest of the gang get here."

"Ain't that somepin'?" demanded Red. "Them few hold us! Come on, the rest of ye, sure we can dance through that many."

"Hold 'er, Red," Cordie answered. "They wouldn't fight us— they'd tail along and run the rest up to us. We're better off here. They'd get us before we'd gone a day's march. The plan—holy mackinaw! What are you trying to do, twist the arm off me, you big cheese?"

"Stand still, Mr. Cordie," answered Grigsby with a grin. "Full many a time you've worked on me. Don't begrudge me a chance at you."

"When you get through, hand him over to me," said Putney.

"Oi, und den to me," put in the Yid. "Vat I vouldn't do to dot monkey. He poured de iodine, a quart at de time—"

THE DAY went by, then the next day and night. They could see camp fires on the hills now, when darkness came. There was a ring of them, some far out on the desert.

"Ridin' herd on us," said Putney, one night, as he relieved Red, who had been on guard. His wounds were healing fast, aided by the beef cubes and jerked beef, and thick broths made for the wounded by Jimmie Cordie. The Yid's wounds were better, and Grigsby's head had almost healed. The Bean was normal once more and Jimmie's arm, though painful was not serious. Of the Taiping wounded, eight were practically well, the other two were in a bad way. They were all a clean living, hard muscled bunch, who had never abused themselves and had lived in the open air, on good plain food. The dry air and the prompt first aid had prevented blood-poisoning.

Another day and night went by, then at the break of dawn on the fourth day, they saw filing down through the passes and around the hills onto the desert, an orderly array of riders—all Afghans. The men on the hills and further out came down to meet them.

"Curtain, first act!" Jimmie Cordie said, as they stood in the entrance, watching them. "Now's the time for the Yid to strut his stuff, while it's still a little dusk. Get ready, Yid. Red, get the stone upon the skids and—"

" 'Tis ready long ago," interrupted Red. "Strip, Abie darlin', and let daddy black ye up wid the burnt wood."

"Oi," protested the Yid. "Vait, I esk you. It's cold und I must sit dare mit nodding but a towel on."

"You sit, you polecat," warned Jimmie. "You stand—and no matter what happens, don't you move an eyelash, you hear me?"

"Do I hear you?" groaned the Yid. "I do, plenty. Vat if dey reach me, Jimmie?"

"If they reach you, old kid," grinned Cordie, "from what I see of those big knives you won't have to worry much longer than a minute about it. Remember now, Yid, don't get so carried away with your part that you forget your cue. When George and Red come out, you wait till they get on each side of you, then you reach out a hand and put it on their heads—"

"One hand on each head," interrupted the Bean firmly. "Go on, Mr. Cordie and be a little mere explicit, please."

"Then," Jimmie went on, not paying any attention to the Bean, "you step down, put one arm around each of their shoulders—how's that, you hair-splitting piece of brown bread!—and walk back to the hole and in, with them."

"Und if dey gets to me first, de deal is off, ain't it?" asked the Yid, with a grin as he started back with Red and the Bean.

"If they get to you, Yid," confirmed Jimmie gravely, "the deal is off—several ways."

The Afghans seemed to be holding some kind of a conference among the chiefs, the rest standing or sitting on their horses quite a little ways back. And not until Red, Wang Li and three Taiping set the Yid, now an almost perfect duplicate of the statue of Afghana, standing on the block of stone, just outside the entrance and about in the middle did the conference break up.

"If you see it's a real come-and-get-it," instructed Jimmie Cordie to Red and Wang Li, "get your men and go out and bring it in. But—"

THE AFGHANS had seen it and there was a surge forward which was checked by shouted orders. Then a party of twenty or more mounted their horses and trotted briskly for the hill. There was no attempt at a charge and the riders were old men, most of them. "We got a nibble," said Jimmie from the Colt machine gun, "let 'em have all the line they want."

"Who's going to talk to them?" asked Putney.

"I think that most Afghans speak Pushtu," answered the Bean, "and the educated ones speak Persian. I can speak a little Pushtu and—better halt 'em, Jimmie!"

"I'll do that little thing," answered Cordie, and the machine gun began to rap out the warning. A line of sand spurted up about a hundred feet ahead of the riders. It ran from the extreme left to the right and was laid down as if by a ruler. There was not a foot of over or under shooting along the whole line. It told the Afghans to stop before it and they knew it did and stopped well on the far side. From where they were they could see the statue plainly and several were out of their saddles, kneeling on the sand. Three of the older men rode up to the imaginary line, dismounted and stood, their right hands held up, palm forward, the universal sign all over the world of peaceful intentions.

"Get out, Bean," commanded Grigsby. "You with him, Wang Li. You say you know Persian, they may speak it. When you get halfway down, wave them up to you."

The three Afghans advanced without hesitation to where the Bean and Wang Li halted. The rest of their party dismounted and joined those kneeling in the sand.

"What do you wish, you men who are our enemies?" asked the Bean, speaking Pushtu.

The oldest man spoke readily in the same language. "All men are our enemies who come unbidden into our lands. We come for our ancestor, Afghana, who has been hidden from us many years."

"This is not your land," answered the Bean. "Your land lies to the south and east. Your ancestor came to us of his own free will—and will stay with us, until we go back to our land."

The grim old Afghan laughed. "We will come and get him," he answered. "And you dogs, sons of dirt eating mothers, will die —slowly!"

The Bean laughed. "Before that happens, oh father of many dogs, Afghana will be lost to you forever. We will burn him up and send his spirit back to hell. But first, oh blind fools of the north, see for yourselves, that he will fight with us!"

The Bean took off his sun helmet and reached for his neck cloth, as if to wipe his face. As he did, Grigsby and Red Dolan came out and stood, one on each side of the Yid, who slowly raised his hands and put one on each head, according to instructions. The three Afghans gasped with astonishment and those on the sand, stood up. Then, the Yid got stately down from the stone and Red came around to the other side. The Yid reached up, he had to, to get to the shoulders of the two big men, and put one arm around each of them, as far as he could. They walked slowly up to the entrance and went in, disappearing in the semi-darkness.

"Afghana is our brother," said the Bean, "and will go with us. Tonight we take him through the ground to a new resting place. If you think you can get him to go with you, unless he wishes, oh robbers of widows and orphans, come and try it—and never see him again!"

The three old men, all of them Ghazi, men who devoted their lives to the extermination of all other creeds but Mohammedan, stood, their eyes and mouths wide open.

"Go back to the slaves quarters," went on the Bean. "Or come—and be smitten with his wrath."

"Lord," said the old man who had spoken. "Do not go with the most holy one until we have made report. Upon what terms, Lord, will he come to us, his children?"

The Bean was too clever to fall into the trap. If he had announced terms, the Afghans would have become suspicious and would have begun to figure coldly. "How do I know?" he demanded. "Am I to speak for a Lord such as he? Get back to your kennels and it may be that at dawn tomorrow, he may speak. If before, we will signal you."

The three old men turned without a word and walked down the hill and the party rode back to where the thousand-odd warriors waited for them.

"**WELL,**" said the Bean, after he had told the rest what had happened, "what now?"

"This," said Jimmie Cordie. "It's a pipe they'll fuss about it all today and tonight, then in the morning we'll bring out the real thing and signal them to come back to where they were just now. Then, Beany, you tell them that Afghana has spoken. He is to go with us, his friends, until we reach the border of Bokhara. His children are to follow and guard on all sides—but far away, beyond range of a gun—"

"Wait, dumb-bell," said Putney. "How the hell does Afghana know what the range of a gun is—also how does he know what a gun is?"

"Well, you world's biggest fool—do you suppose the Afghans will figure that? If they could, they wouldn't believe a statue could come to life. Nut, they think it perfectly natural that he knows everything. To continue—tell them he says that if they close in, or allow any other race or breed to come between them and him, that he will at once go back to his underground home or Paradise, whichever sounds best. When he is ready for them to come and get him, he will appear alone."

"I am forced to ask you some questions, Mr. Cordie," said Grigsby gravely.

"Go ahead," answered Jimmie generously. "We've got all day."

"The first one is—do you think the Afghans, once we are in the clear, will obey that rule of out of range, or will they come galumping in and take their great grandpa away from us?"

"Ain't that somepin?" said Red. "How about that, Jimmie darlin'."

"The answer to that is, God he knows, and no one else!" said Jimmie with a grin. "Personally I believe they will do exactly as they think he wants them to do. If it were us alone, they'd agree to anything and then scrag us, but with him—I doubt it, Their holy men wouldn't stand for it, taking the chance of losing him."

"Well, at that, we can't stay here. The second question is, Mr. Cordie, when we get to the said border, just what do you expect to find? A traffic cop on the corner to shoo them back? What is to prevent them from getting their relation and then hopping merrily on us? What's the difference in being killed here and killed there?"

"Not a darn thing," agreed Jimmie. "What I thought was, the last night out, we'd set the old bird up on top of the trench, soon as it gets dark and take it on the lam, having told them not to show close until they saw him alone. By morning we ought to be far on our way. "None of them will want to leave. His Royal Joblots and chase us much further."

"You mention trenches—is it your idea that we dig in?"

"Yeah boy, every night—some of the Afghans might get a little ambitious to take a good close look at him and come sneaking up. Those babies can crawl up to a cobra and get first bite before she knows anything about it."

"I see. Now, one more question and I'm done. Does the Yid do his famous impersonation on the march?"

"He do," answered Jimmie, with a grin.

"Vat?" said the Yid. "I go out mit a towel und all blacked mit burnt vood? In de sun I sveat und it rolls off me. Und mit bare feet? Oi, Jimmie, such a business!"

"Don't holler before you're hurt," answered Jimmie. "You're carried in an elegant hammock, Yid, with bearer and a fan and everything."

"What?" shouted Red. "And who the hell is going to carry that fat omadhaun for three days?"

"You, for one," answered Jimmie.

"I am? Like hell I am, Jimmie Cordie. Take shame for yeself, ye—"

"All right, delicate—then I'll take your place. If four men can't pack a hundred and eighty-five pounds of live weight, taking it easy, for four days, they better go to the old man's home—where I'll send you, you red-headed ape, just as soon as we get home. I'll do your packing for you and carry your gun also!"

"Sure now, Jimmie, darlin'," soothed Red. "Ye know I was only foolin'. Sure I'll pack Abie, all by meself if ye say so."

"Yeah? Well, just for that you can be one of the other four that pack our new buddy along—that will be heavier."

"For Pete's sake, Jimmie," said Putney, "what do you want to pack that damn thing along for?"

"Why—to leave for them—but at that, it isn't necessary—we can leave the Yid just as well."

"Vat? For dem? You leave me? Not vile I got it a pair of legs—vounded or oddervize. Jimmie! Ain't it you und me is buddies? Black up the Irisher und leave him—he likes dem und goes on visits mit dem."

"Never mind now, Red," said Grigsby as Red started to say something. "Go on, Jimmie, make it plain."

"All right—the Yid is carried in state, sitting in a hammock— is that plain? Then, we cover up His Joblots, without the base, with whatever we have got—we may have to make a long box out of ammunition cases—and we pack him also. There are eight of the Taiping that can lend a hand plus the three whole ones, and Wang Li, Red, the Bean, you and I in commission to do a little packing. We'll strip down to our rifles and gats and four days' chuck and water. We'll have to leave the Colt machine, which I'll put out of service. Now, on the line of march they can see the Yid being carried. If they start in he can wave them back and—"

"If they keep right on coming, Jeems?" grinned Grigsby.

"Then, gentlemen," answered Cordie firmly. "We will be forced to first scrag the Yid, then fight it out."

"Try und do it," protested the Yid. "If my children don't obey popper's orders, I gets it a rifle und joins in."

"Then," went on Jommie, "if they do leave us alone, the last night out, we will stick the real Mr. Afghana up on top of the trench and execute a masterly retreat to the rear, as fast and as far as we can."

"What," said Red, "and him all gold? Leave him for them scuts!"

"Boy, you'll be lucky to get out of this man's country with your skin, let alone a shirt tail," answered Jimmie.

THE REST of the day they sat at the entrance and watched the Afghans. There seemed to be several conferences going on at the same time and twice fights swirled up, to be scattered out by the rest. In the morning, at break of day, the three old men came up once more. The Yid, arrayed as Afghana, came to the entrance and stood with one arm around Grigsby, as the Bean and Wang Li went down to meet them. The bandage on his left leg had been pulled tight and smooth, and he looked the part even better than the day before. The Afghans looked a little closer also, but what they saw only confirmed their belief. The Afghans have distinctly Jewish features and without doubt their descent is from a Hebrew origin.

After the Bean had given them Afghana's message, adding to it just what the white men would do at the first sign of a rush, among which was that they would cut Afghana up in little pieces and eat him. the three swore by the Prophet that Afghana would be obeyed in every particular. And to prove it, after they got back to the main body, the Afghans spread out, in an ever widening circle, until there was a mile on either side—and nothing in between.

Jimmie Cordie led, then came Wang Li, then the Bean, then four of the Taiping carrying the Yid, who lolled back in the hammock made from discarded coats and web belts, and hung between interlocking gun barrels. Then four more of the Taiping carrying what looked like a pile of ammunition boxes and food carriers on a platform made of empty boxes. Back of them came Grigsby, Putney, and the two Taiping that were still too weak to do any more than steady work pack their rifles and belts, but ready to spell any of the others. Alongside of the Yid stalked Red Dolan, waving a fan, made of several shirts, very solicitous of the Yid's comfort.

The first night out they dug a shallow trench, running at right angles, then back on a half curve. There was no attack or attempt at one. They could see the fires of the Afghans, way out in the desert, all around them. The second day and night passed, but no Afghan came within a half mile. The third day went by and now they could see the range from which they had come down in the desert.

They had refused horses offered, because of the carrying of the statue, the Bean stating that Afghana had rather be carried.

At halts the Yid would get down from the hammock and sit on a box or walk around, always inside the little circle formed around him. "Let them take a look-see," Jimmie said. "But not too close a one."

When they made camp that night Jimmie said, "Go out about two hundred yards, Bean, and wave in the old birds. Tell them that the time has come for Afghana to go back with them. That in the morning they are to come for him when they see him standing alone. That he commands that they no longer circle his friends and that they are to withdraw two miles in the rear. Say that Jeremiah, his father, comes tonight to take his friends further on their journey and that it won't be at all healthy for any of them to see the old man—chief it up better than that, but that's the idea. As soon as it gets good and dark, we'll stick the old boy up, the Yid can cover his slim, beautiful form with a few clothes, and we will do the snake wiggle for the hills."

"And right then," said Putney, "we will find out just how far we have pulled the cork of our boy friends!"

CHAPTER VII

"THE—HIS HAND TURNED!"

THE BEAN GOT back with the statement that Afghana would be obeyed to the word and after it became fairly dark they brought the statue out and as they got ready to set it up on the shallow trench top, Jimmie said, "For once in my life I can state truthfully that gold does not look near as good as it generally does to old man Cordie's son Jimmie. We've been in some tight—what the hell is the matter with you, you bean pole?" Jimmie finished, as the Bean staggered back against him. The Bean and the Yid had been fooling around the statue.

"His—*the hand turned!*" the Bean ejaculated. "It turned! Anyone would jump back. I took hold of it and—look! Something is sliding out!"

The hand of the statue had turned as the Bean said. He must have touched a hidden spring. It had turned and fallen back, hanging on a hinge from the forearm which was on a downward slant. For some little way up, the forearm must have been hollow, because as the Bean spoke a short, fat little roll slid down the arm and dropped to the ground almost at the feet of the Yid.

"A package wrapped mit gold!" he gasped, and picked it up. It was not more than six inches long and about four inches through at the thickest part. The gold of the thin plates that made the tight wrapping was not tarnished in any way and glistened in the light from the little "Indian fire" like a golden spider in the sun.

"Vat de hell can it be?" demanded the Yid holding it out at arm's length. "Maybeso it is poison, vat?"

"Open it up, Yid," suggested Jimmie. "If it's poison, only you will get it."

THE YID produced a sturdy pocket knife and began to charily pry open the bent over corners. "Writin' mit it," he said, as one came up. "Same as before, Hebrew—Vat de—oi, smell dat? Frankincense and myrhh—und—vat de hell is dot—aloes—calamus—camphor—my, vat a lofly—"

"All right, Yid," interrupted Jimmie. "Come back to earth. We haven't got such a heck of a lot of time, you know. We all know what the old timers used to make mummies with. Open her up!"

"Hold it," said Grigsby. "Read what's on the gold sheet first, Yid."

"Who me? In dis light? Vell, maybeso I can if one of you hold it a flash down low so de Afghans don't see it und vonder vot is doin'."

The Bean squatted down beside him and held his light.

"Vell, it says—*I am*—" and the Yid hastily put the package down. "You hold it, Jimmie."

"Are you wishing something on me?" demanded Jimmie, as he picked it up.

"No, but me, I don't—vell, it says—*I am de son of Jenghiz Khan—who is*—hold de light closer, Beaneater. It is hard for me to make it out—vait till I remember. Oi, now I am glad dat so many times you took it the slipper to me, popper—now I got it vonce more, wait till I can say it proper mit de right words —

"*I am Jagatai, the son of Jenghis Khan, Lord of the World, Leader of the Hordes. My name is Jagatai. I conquered the Kanklais—destroyed Otrar—Lahore—Herat. I, like my father, am the scourge of God. This is my heart—my fighting, pitiless heart that knew not fear. Read and obey—on my death which is soon, my heart is to be taken from my body and hidden in the forearm of the image of Afghana that I took from the hills and kept with me always. He was a fighting man, and his children's children are fighting men. None better could guard the heart of Jagatai. This—that my heart will remain in the hills that I love and my spirit will come here to be near it—this I have ordered as I lie in Samarkand on my deathbed. Woe be unto him that disobeys. I am Jagatai!*"

The Yid finished and looked up. The eyes of them all were on the package held in Jimmie Cordie's hand.

"My God," said Jimmie softly. "The fighting heart of Jagatai Khan!"

"Und vorth," said the Yid, once more back to his usual manner of speech, "all de money in de Metropolitan Museum or de London—"

"Is it now, Yid?" demanded Red. "Well, any wan of us can carry that."

"Sit down, you birds," said Grigsby. "Wrap that sheet around it again, Jimmie. Listen—it is probably just what the Yid said. Any museum in the world would pay thousands for it. But—did you get it—*'this—that my heart—will remain in the place I love.'* Do any one of you birds want to see the heart of a fighting man like Jagatai, who fought at the head of his hordes down through all the world that he knew, opened up in some damn museum and pawed over and looked at by men that would call a copper if a cripple threatened them? I say to put it back and turn the hand again—and let his heart stay where he wanted it. I don't often sound off about things, but I am sure doing it this time. We're fighting men—he was a fighting man—what the hell is money to us—we've all got plenty of it. I—"

"And even if we didn't have," interrupted Jimmie Cordie, "what difference would that make. Picture us going along, knowing that we sold the heart of Jagatai Khan. By gosh—let's admit that we got licked, for once—licked good and proper, and if it hadn't been for a damn lucky break we would all be pushing up whatever kind of flowers they've got in this man's country!"

"That's right, Jimmie," said Red firmly. "I know what ye mean, ye scut. Sure it would be like—like—wan of us sellin' out the rest. Put the damn thing back, Jimmie."

"What's all the blub-blub about anyway," asked Putney. "We better be on our way if we are going, instead of holding a sewing circle chat. George is right—even if he did put it as clear as mud. And so is Jimmie. We got our heads in the lion's jaw and if it hadn't been for Jagatai using that statue for his heart and having it buried under the floor, we would have gotten our heads bitten off. Put it back where it belongs and lets go!"

"How about you, Bean?" asked Jimmie. "You see the point, don't you?"

"Certainly," answered the Bean gravely, "several of them. Whoever is sat—"

"Vell," interrupted the Yid with a grin. "I don't—but vat is jake mit de rest, is jake mit me, always, ain't it, Jimmie?"

"Yeah, boy," answered Jimmie Cordie with a smile that told how much he really thought of the Yid, "All the time, Abie, old kid!"

"Put it back, Jimmie," said Grigsby. And the five hard-bitten soldiers of fortune watched him gently place the heart of Jagatai, once more wrapped in the golden plates, far up in the forearm of Afghana, and twist the hand back in place. After he had finished he turned with a grin. "Get His Royal Joblots up on the top side, and pray to Heaven there'll be no moon!"

"No will be," announced Wang Li, who had gravely watched and listened. "Much dark, very soon."

HIS PROPHECY was correct the darkness fell suddenly like a black blanket over the desert.

"All right," Grigsby announced finally.

"Let's go. Four pointed star, wounded in the middle—take the point, Red. Jimmie, take the rear. We'll darn soon find out about the cork-pulling stuff."

If the meeting of no Afghans or anyone else was proof, they had pulled the cork. When dawn came they were in the second range of hills beyond any pursuit, which did not come. They marched steadily on toward where Jimmie's friend was waiting for them.

The Fighting Yid stopped suddenly, an expression of deepest concern came over his still more or less blackened face, and he began to hunt frantically through all his pockets.

"What's the matter with you, you Yid ape?" demanded Jimmie Cordie, sitting down on a convenient rock, the rest following his example. The Yid paid no attention to them at first, then, "Oi, such a business! I know dat ven I strip in de hole to be—I put it oudt to remember it—und forgot it. Maybe I von't catch—"

"You forgot what?" demanded Red.

"My handkerchief," moaned the Yid, "und—"

"Holy cats," said Jimmie, beginning to laugh as they all did but the Yid, and Wang Li, who was regarding the Yid with astonishment.

"Your handkerchief," repeated Jimmie as soon as he could stop laughing. "Well, Abie, you have my royal permission to run back and get it. We'll wait for you."

"Better I should do it," answered the Yid still mournfully, "than catch the hell I will from my girl, ain't it? She gave it to me mit my initials on it und everything. Now she will think I giv it to some odder girl und—"

"What?" interrupted Red sternly. "Ye get in where the skin of ye ain't worth a bad cent—yet get out of it—ye have held the heart of a fighting lad in the hand of ye—on top of that, ye have been carried like a king for days, wid me fannin' ye an now ye stand raisin' hell about a nose-wiper! Double shame on ye for a—"

"Vot is all dot to vat I get ven I get back to Hong Kong from my girl?" demanded the Yid hotly. "You don't know my girl, Mister Viseguy Redhead!"

"The Yid's right," said Jimmie Cordie. "I wasn't quite sure before, but now I am. He's got the relative importance of things sized up correctly. *Allons, mes enfants!*"

THE JEWEL IS CONTENTMENT

W. WIRT HAS written us the lowdown on his latest yarn. In "The Jewel in the Lotus" he re-introduces those four fighting gun slingers, Dolan, Cordie, Grigsby and Putney. Mr. Wirt was for a long time a special agent for American, British and other interests in the Orient; and he gets his stories first hand. His dope is almost as good as the yarn itself, which you'll admit is going some. The story's almost word for word true, although, Mr. Wirt sheepishly admits, his colorful imagination has done just a little work here and there.

"These guys did ramble hither and yon through the Foreign Legion, the A.E.F. and under gents of various breeds who felt a need for mercenaries who could handle a machine gun or so, plus some Winchesters and Colts. For the most part though, the four were on their own bat. They had absolute confidence in their ability to go anywhere at any time, and the fact that they might get knocked off doing it didn't matter at all.

"First, I took the setting and the Chinese characters and the locale from a place I had been. The young war lord was there, also the High Priest. We had been hired by the Lord to come up and help him throw the High Priest out on his ear. The little girl, his daughter, at once adopted us as her war lords. We were not supposed to jump the High Priest and his gang until the young war lord had everything arranged. Well, it seems that the other lad had been doing some arranging himself and at one of the three hundred and sixty-four celebrations or feast days at the temple we were jumped good and proper and without a moment's warning.

"The little girl who is just exactly as I wrote her in the story came down the path and reached her father just before it started. He was stooping to pick her up in his arms when Red shouted and shot, all at the same time.

"**THEY** were ten to one and then some and they ran us back to the big idol platform. Then a case of Pow-Pow-Pow.

"The war lord pointed to the little pagoda up on the hill and we did alle same story. We did get down to the temple proper, that night, and the war lord did kill the High Priest.

"There was no king cobra in it really. I let the vivid imagination I have been accused of loose and put him in anyway.

"Now for the 'Jewel.' Not long ago I met an old playmate, Major Arthur Carnduff of the A.E.F. who was born in a dynamite factory and weaned on T.N.T.

"The Major, after a few personal remarks which are not printable, said to me, "Wirt last night I saw a little wooden statue. It was a figure of a fat old man sitting crossways on a block. It was almost a Buddha, but I classified it as a statuette of a Tibetan Lama or a crude concept of Buddha according to Lamaist Buddhism. It was evidently carved from Lotus wood and that is what made the inscription significant, '*Om mani padme hum*' is Sanscrit, and means 'Lo the Jewel in the Lotus.' What disgusted me was that the crowd with me were only interested in the possibility of a jewel; they did not realize that '*Om mmn padme hum*' is the most sacred of invocations to millions of human beings. The real jewel is peace and contentment, the lure of Nirvana.'

"Some bird in an off moment, basing his story on the jewel in the lotus made it a real jewel up in a real country, to make the story more interesting.

"Red Dolan heard of it and came back all het up. We were to go and get it and were to start from where we stood. Jimmie

Cordie told him what the real meaning was and that's all there was to it.

"*Adios Amigo, hasta mañana.*

W. WIRT."

ABOUT THE AUTHOR

ANOTHER WRITER WHO makes his bow to readers is W. Wirt—a man whose life has been packed with adventures. We asked Mr. Wirt to stand up and introduce himself so that we can all get some idea of what sort of hombre can spin a salty yarn such as this. Mr. Wirt has the floor:

Born—Boston, Massachusetts, 1876.

People on both sides hard-boiled Maine and Massachusetts Presbyterians of strictly English descent. All but one—but that one was a direct descendant of one of Sir Francis Drake's captains. The King of Spain had a standing offer of one thousand golden crowns to the hombre that would present him with "That pirate devil's head." Every once in a while one of the elect breaks out. The rest of the family at once put it down to the old pirate.

My late pa was one of them, all right. I think he had more than his share of the blood. He was a special agent and one of the very few Americans who served in the Secret Service of foreign countries. He went here and there, all over the world, in the oddest places, from northern China to the South Sea Islands, from there to Alaska and way points. Sometimes for Uncle Sam in the Post Office Department; other times for other people.

My education and experience? They are part and part. If there ever was a scrambled one I had it. When I wasn't much bigger

than knee-high to a grass-
hopper my pa began taking
me along with him, when-
ever he could do so safely. I
remember military, private,
public and every other kind
of school in a dim way. He'd
leave me in one somewhere,
go and attend to his knit-
ting, then come back and
get me, and away we'd go
again. But the constant
education I received from
him regarding the conduct
of "an officer and a gentleman" under any and all cir-
cumstance still remains

vivid in my mind. One month we'd be in England, evening
clothes after six as regular as clockwork, down at one of the big
estates for the week-ends, then, in a month or a darn sight less,
we'd be in some "flop house" as poor broken-down bums—I
acting the part of the devoted son who wouldn't leave his poor
old ex-con father, and so forth.

After I reached eighteen I worked with him for a good many
years, and when he was called to join his venerable ancestors I
carried on alone. No matter where I was, in the Orient or
anywhere else, I missed him—with his cool laugh in the face
of death and his never failing, slow, amused drawl. His favorite
weapon was a sawed-off shotgun carrying buckshot. This, of
course, was for use in the places where the little yellow and
black brothers congregate mostly. I miss him yet, and always
will—and that's that.

I have been behind a badge for Uncle Sam some little time
and at present am still special agenting, but on my own, seldom
going out of the States and not hunting for any trouble at all,
having more than my share already. I've had my gun in the ribs

and ears of a few jaspers and used to say "Put 'em up!" so darn often that my longhaired partner—now bobbed haired—every once in a while wakes me up with a demand to know if I have any good reason for poking my finger in her side and hollering at her in the middle of the night.

Then there have been many times when the reverse English was in force and I did the reaching for the blue sky, promptly and in haste. All in all, I lived and rambled when things were wide open, no blue laws or anything, just help yourself to the mustard if you wanted any. And I am darn glad I did. Man, howdy, you could go over the mountain, in "them" days and see things—and do 'em likewise, if you wanted to.

I and Schley whipped the Spanish fleet together, I as a volunteer and Schley as a regular. There were a few others present, but we did most of it. In the late argument I did some "hush, hush" stuff.

My present standing? Well, been married seventeen years; have two children, boy and girl. Have an old place in Maryland near Washington, a police dog, three or twenty-six kittens and cats, an old "colored lady" named Medora to make the corn bread, plenty good old corn lick—I mean corn licorice—to drink and am "out of commission."

A lot of my old buddies drift through, hang their hats up behind the door and drink my said good old yellow-with-age corn licorice, eat some fried chicken and curse me in all the living and dead languages because I won't let go all holds and go wild-catting over the hills once more. They don't get a rise out of me at all. I'm like the colored man who, when asked if he wanted to make a quarter, replied: "No, suh, I done got me a quarter." All I want is peace and quiet.

THE ARGOSY LIBRARY ™

SERIES 1 INCLUDES:

* DENT * KETCHUM * KLINE *
* MacISAAC * ROSCOE *
* ROUSSEAU *
* SELTZER *
* TUTTLE *
* WIRT *
WORTS

THE BEST FICTION
FROM THE FRANK
A. MUNSEY LINE

GENIUS JONES
BY THE CO-CREATOR OF DOC SAVAGE
LESTER DENT

WHEN TIGERS ARE HUNTING
THE COMPLETE ADVENTURES OF CORDIE, SOLDIER OF FORTUNE, VOLUME 1
W. WIRT

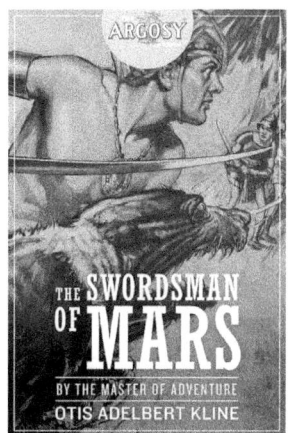

THE SWORDSMAN OF MARS
BY THE MASTER OF ADVENTURE
OTIS ADELBERT KLINE

THE SHERLOCK OF SAGELAND
THE COMPLETE TALES OF SHERIFF HENRY, VOLUME 1
W.C. TUTTLE

GONE NORTH
BY ARGOSY READERS' FAVORITE
CHARLES ALDEN SELTZER

THE MASKED MASTER MIND
BY THE AUTHOR OF PETER THE BRAZEN
GEORGE F. WORTS

BALATA
BY THE AUTHOR OF THE RAMBLER
FRED MacISAAC

BRET-WALDA
BY ARGOSY READERS' FAVORITE
PHILIP KETCHUM

DRAFT OF ETERNITY
BY THE CREATOR OF JIM ANTHONY
VICTOR ROUSSEAU

FOUR CORNERS
VOLUME 1 • BY ARGOSY LEGEND
THEODORE ROSCOE

SERIES 1 • AVAILABLE SPRING 2015

www.ingramcontent.com/pod-product-compliance
Lightning Source LLC
Chambersburg PA
CBHW071836020726
47502CB00004B/1381